THAT MOUTH

Those lips promised the most beautiful smile while whispering the dirtiest jokes. That mouth could give the most mind-blowing kiss without any effort.

It was every man's fantasy.

Fantasy? No. Jack took an instinctive step back, a flash of anxiety searing through his gut. Not his. He was not intrigued by a lady who didn't have a lick of common sense. He was *not* interested in this woman who was behind bars. At all.

He was the sheriff. Jack purposefully reclaimed the step he lost. He was a man of authority. Integrity. At least, he was trying to be.

Old Man Schneider's words mocked him.

Trouble's coming.

Yeah. She had arrived.

BOOK YOUR PLACE ON OUR WEBSITE AND MAKE THE READING CONNECTION!

We've created a customized website just for our very special readers, where you can get the inside scoop on everything that's going on with Zebra, Pinnacle and Kensington books.

When you come online, you'll have the exciting opportunity to:

- View covers of upcoming books
- Read sample chapters
- Learn about our future publishing schedule (listed by publication month *and author*)
- Find out when your favorite authors will be visiting a city near you
- Search for and order backlist books from our online catalog
- Check out author bios and background information
- Send e-mail to your favorite authors
- Meet the Kensington staff online
- Join us in weekly chats with authors, readers and other guests
- Get writing guidelines
- AND MUCH MORE!

**Visit our website at
http://www.kensingtonbooks.com**

Confessions
of a
"Wicked" Woman

Susanna Carr

KENSINGTON BOOKS
KENSINGTON PUBLISHING CORP.
http://www.kensingtonbooks.com

KENSINGTON BOOKS are published by

Kensington Publishing Corp.
850 Third Avenue
New York, NY 10022

All Kensington titles, imprints and distributed lines are available at special quantity discounts for bulk purchases for sales promotion, premiums, fund-raising, educational or institutional use.

Special book excerpts or customized printings can also be created to fit specific needs. For details, write or phone the office of the Kensington Special Sales Manager: Kensington Publishing Corp., 850 Third Avenue, New York, NY 10022. Attn. Special Sales Department. Phone: 1-800-221-2647.

ISBN 0-7582-1080-9

First Trade Paperback Printing: June 2005
First Mass Market Paperback Printing: May 2006
10 9 8 7 6 5 4 3 2 1

Printed in the United States of America

Chapter 1

Buck nekkid cannonball.

That's how Jack Logan and his friends would have greeted the swollen stream twenty years ago.

Hell, he would have done that ten years ago.

Jack studied the stream and knew that those carefree moments were long gone. Today he wore a crisp police uniform and stood a safe distance from the edge. It was quiet except for the sound of rushing water. Instead of a gangly bunch of kids, Jack was with Old Man Schneider, who always wore a bow tie and hat for every occasion.

Schneider took off the newsboy cap and rubbed his bald spot with a gnarled finger. "Doesn't look good."

"Nope."

The old man's nose twitched. "More rain is coming."

Jack looked up at the sky. The clouds appeared innocent, but he knew better. As much as he hated to admit it, Schneider was right. You didn't live round these parts for this long without being able to smell the rain coming.

He returned his attention to the river that flowed nearby and fed the stream. "Do you remember it ever being this high?" he asked the old man.

Schneider puckered his lips. "Nope."

"That's very reassuring," Jack said dryly.

"Ach, I'm wrong, Little Jack."

Jack clenched his jaw. Wasn't there a statute of limitations on childhood nicknames?

"How could I forget?" Schneider put his cap back on and readjusted the brim. "The flood of '70."

"Would that be 1870 or 1970?"

The old man's rheumy eyes twinkled. "1970."

Jack didn't recall his parents ever talking about it while he was growing up. Then again, he hadn't exactly been the most attentive kid. "It got this high?"

The old man gave a sharp, decisive nod. "Yep."

And the town survived. Good to know. Jack felt the weight slip off his chest and he breathed a little easier.

"Of course," Schneider continued, "it didn't rain after that."

Jack's shoulders sagged.

"It was like God wrung the clouds dry," the old man said, gearing up for a long story.

More rain was coming. Jack was certain of it. They were going to be dealing with a flood. People would be looking to him for answers.

And he had none.

Jack remained still until the sickening dread evaporated. Schneider's stirring rendition of the Flood of 1970 faded in and out. He hoped he wasn't going to be tested on it.

What he needed to remember was that he was trained as a police officer. He came from a family of them. He had the experience, even if he was new at being sheriff.

Fortunately, he didn't have to do it all. The impending flood wasn't solely his responsibility. He could work with the mayor, the city council, and the fire chief.

Aw, who was he kidding? The city council was a joke. It was every alderman for himself, making sure he got the one and only plow to shovel his street first thing in the morning after a snowfall.

At least the fire chief was experienced, responsible, and intelligent. But the guy had been fire chief since Jack was a kid and was desperate for retirement. Jack couldn't blame him and he had a feeling that would happen in a matter of weeks.

That left the mayor, and everyone knew that Dean was an idiot. The only reason he got the job was because his opponent died during the mayoral campaign. Rumor had it that Dean still managed to lose to a corpse in the election. Whether it was fact or fiction didn't really matter anymore. Dean had planted his butt in the mayor's office and showed no signs of leaving.

Jack knew he wasn't one to judge. His own election was a close call, and he couldn't shake off the feeling that he got the job because his dad, the late and great Big Jack, had been the best sheriff the town had ever seen.

Maybe the gossips were right, but it was too late

to do anything about it now. His detractors kept bringing up his misspent youth. Jack didn't feel that was an issue. The real issue he kept to himself.

He knew better than to let anyone know that he was in over his head. That there were times like today when he knew he wasn't ready for whatever lay ahead. How much faith could a town place on their sheriff if they knew he was scared? Not much.

Schneider looked up at the sky and sniffed. "Yep. Trouble's coming."

The old man's words disrupted Jack's train of thought. He reluctantly looked up and felt the first raindrop hit his cheek.

Stephanie Monroe stepped on the brakes and wiped the fog from the windshield with the side of her hand. "Venus Gold," she yelled into her cell phone, "you are supposed to be back at the office."

"Yeah, I know," her business partner replied, sounding somewhat apologetic. "But something came up."

"And you didn't want to give me any advance notice?" Stephanie asked in a growl. "Did you decide that I would eventually figure it out?"

"Basically."

Stephanie exhaled sharply. Why wasn't she surprised? This is what happens when you go into business with a stylist to the stars who was better known for her irreverent lifestyle than her avant-garde creations.

Stephanie could imagine Venus right now. She would be lounging sideways on a comfy chair—the woman could never sit properly—and probably painting her toenails in her favorite color of the month, wild cherry red. With glitter.

She, on the other hand, was freezing. Stephanie rubbed her bare arms, but the goose bumps didn't go away. She turned up the heater, but only tepid air streamed weakly through the vents.

Stephanie regretted not changing clothes before hopping onto the plane. The snug yellow halter top, low-slung periwinkle blue jeans, and dark blue platform sandals were perfect for the trendy L.A. scene. Wearing something head-turning was good for business, but today, it was only good for getting an upper respiratory infection.

Wasn't America's heartland supposed to be hot in the summer? She glared at the rain pinging against her SUV. Stephanie would have known about the chill had she gotten the chance to watch the Weather Channel like she did every day. But noooo, this is what she got for disrupting her daily schedule.

"You run Venus & Stephanie . . . fine without me," Venus said, the static intruding. "Anyway, I'm only . . . gone for a while."

"Yeah, I believe you said you were taking a weekend trip back home." Stephanie squinted through the streaked windshield. It was dark and there were no landmarks or signs to guide her. Unless she was supposed to follow the moon or watch which way the corn blew. If that was the case, she might as well declare herself lost right now. "That was two weeks ago."

"Really? Has it been that long?" Venus sounded genuinely surprised. "I'll be back . . . a week. Two, tops. I promise."

"Two weeks!" Stephanie's hands squeezed the steering wheel, her knuckles turning white. The situation was worse than she realized.

"It's no big—"

"Yes it is," Stephanie argued, the panic gurgling in her stomach. "*I* can't put together Jennifer's outfit for the awards ceremony."

Venus's pause clung and the static crackled. "Oh, yeah."

"Oh, yeah?" Stephanie repeated, incredulous. "That's all you have to say? You *forgot* that you're supposed to be creating an outfit that will get us international coverage?"

"I'll call Jennifer and talk to her," Venus said in the very breezy tone that always made Stephanie quake in her four-inch heels. "She'll understand."

"Why don't you tell her that face-to-face?" And she would sit in the meeting to make sure Venus didn't lose the commission.

"Jennifer . . . in Mayfield?" Venus snorted. "Not likely."

"No." Stephanie pressed her lips together and tried to count to ten to restrain her temper. She made it halfway. "You need to come back to L.A. and tell her." Stephanie wondered how she was supposed to be the makeup artist in the partnership but wound up adding babysitter to her job description.

The static garbled Venus's reply. "What?" Stephanie asked, wincing as she tried to make out the words. "There was interference."

"I said . . . get . . . as soon . . . . I can."

Oh, this phone connection was really annoying her. "That's going to be sooner than you think."

"I can't hear . . ."

"I'm coming to get you," Stephanie said, enunciating each word. If Venus knew what was good for her, she'd quietly return to L.A. Stephanie was aware that was wishful thinking on her part. "Quiet" wasn't in the wild woman's vocabulary.

Venus's laugh came through loud and clear. "This connection . . . bad. I thought you said . . . coming to get me."

"I am. I just reached Mayfield. I think." She grabbed the wrinkled map and glanced at it. She was stunned that travelers still used paper maps. Then again, she couldn't believe the rinky-dink car rental didn't have a GPS available.

"And . . . no way can you handle small town . . ." Venus continued, her voice wavering in and out. "Not even for five minutes."

"You'd be surprised," she muttered.

"Stephanie?" Venus called over the hissing static. "Stephanie, are you there?"

"Unfortunately." She reached for the phone as she drove through a puddle. A giant fan of water sprayed out and slapped the side of her vehicle.

Stephanie yelped as the tires lost traction. The SUV suddenly had a mind of its own. Her feet froze with indecision, her mind racing as she tried to remember what to do in case of hydroplane. Of course, she never encountered this problem before since she believed in preventative measures. She always had her tires checked.

"Stop it!" she said aloud, her voice thin and reedy. What did that TV news magazine say? Fragments of the intense, action-packed segment flickered in her mind, transposing art with reality, which wasn't what she needed at the moment. "Uh-uh . . . don't brake, don't accelerate. Got it."

"Check your rearview mirror." Her wild gaze flew to the mirror and she watched the road behind her drift to one side. Why was she doing this? There was no one else around. "Think of something useful!"

Shift to neutral? Sounded good, but for all she knew she was making it up as she went along. Stephanie shifted the handle to neutral with jerky moves.

The SUV fishtailed and Stephanie's moan dragged from her throat. She must be doing something wrong. Maybe she did all of this out of sequence. That sounded like her.

Whatever the problem was, the vehicle still wasn't responding. Then again, she hadn't crashed spectacularly. Ha! Venus had been wrong all these years; she *could* think positively. If she lived through this, Stephanie would be sure to tell her.

"There's something else. Something else . . ." Her fingertips tapped maniacally against the wheel. Steer? Probably. But was it where you want to go? Maybe it was where you don't want to go? Or was this all for when you hit an ice patch?

Knowing her luck, she was following the procedure for brake failure. Her arms locked as she slowly rode out the puddle, keeping her tires straight. The moment she was able to regain control of the SUV, Stephanie firmly pressed her foot down on the brake pedal.

She sighed with relief and rested her forehead against the wheel. She wanted to hurl. Her shoulders were tense and aching. Pain pricked at her neck, thanks to her awkward sitting position, but Stephanie couldn't quite release the steering wheel.

"Venus—" She stopped, turned her head, and listened, realizing they had lost the connection. Stephanie grabbed the phone, hung up, and redialed with shaky fingers. Nothing.

She was in a dead zone. In more ways than one, Stephanie decided, peering through the windshield. She tossed the phone onto the passenger seat with disgust.

It was so damn quiet. Silent, almost. All she heard was the rain, the wind, and the windshield wipers that managed to smudge the one spot on the glass that was at eye level. The rhythm of the wipers was getting on her nerves. It was like they were whispering *hurry . . . hurry . . . hurry*.

She *was* hurrying. It wasn't her fault that Venus decided to take a trip down memory lane at the most inconvenient time. It wasn't her fault that she had to come and get her. And it certainly wasn't her fault that Venus's hometown was three hours away from civilization.

Hurry . . . hurry . . . hurry. The windshield wipers obviously didn't play the blame game. They didn't care if she was stuck in the middle of nowhere, a place showing no signs of intelligent life. That she was surrounded by fields of something she couldn't even identify.

Stephanie quickly fiddled with the radio, trying to find a station. She might as well hear the monotone guy with the thickest Midwestern twang who discussed crop prices. She could listen to country music, even though she hated it with a passion. At this point she would take the static over the silence.

She'd accept anything but another cheerful weather report. After all, she *knew* it was raining. She knew they were experiencing a cold snap. She got that. She was living it.

Okay, so maybe she wasn't the best of travelers, Stephanie thought, as she tuned in to hear the riveting news about soybeans. She never performed well when she was hungry, cold, and tired. She preferred comfort over adventure. She got motion sickness easily and bugs from miles around would seek her out.

And since she didn't even want to take this trip, Stephanie felt she was entitled to be grumpy. It seemed that with each step she took getting closer to Venus, the need to turn back grew stronger. Like when she got on the rattling airplane and the flight attendant handed out earplugs. Right then and there, Stephanie had to fight the urge to bolt.

But instead, she had stayed in her seat on the airplane, legs crossed, elbows tucked in as the sweaty businessman took over the armrest. She knew she had to take the trip. There had been no other choice.

Sure, she had other things to do rather than chase after her business partner, Stephanie thought, as she slowly headed down the country road that stretched before her like a shiny black ribbon. She didn't even need to refer to her PDA to remember her to-do list.

Stephanie reached a fork in the road. Unable to recall seeing this on the map, she flicked on the interior light and studied the multicolored knot of lines. She might have gotten along just fine without a college degree, but why did she always feel incredibly stupid when reading a map?

She felt a spurt of satisfaction when she found the minuscule spot on the map. Flipping the light off, she made a left turn. Her car crept down the road for several miles, the rain starting to pour, before her headlights caught the sign partially hidden by an overgrown tree.

Welcome to Mayfield. Population 13,000.

She was here. Stephanie sat straighter in her seat and pressed her foot down on the gas pedal. She was almost at Venus's house. She was one step away from returning home. So close to making her dreams happen.

Her dreams were just an arm's length away. Stephanie could feel it. Venus & Stephanie was about to make it big, make some significant money, and make their mark.

And that was the only thing that had kept Stephanie from turning back on this Venus hunt. She had worked too hard and too long to lose the momentum now. And once she made her mark, no one would be able to erase it.

She drove the SUV down the hill and the road took a sharp, steep rise. Stephanie grimaced as she heard the metal scratch the pavement. She hoped the rental company didn't notice that.

The road took another dip. Stephanie frowned, wondering what happened to the myth that the Midwest was supposed to be flat. She saw the puddle at the bottom of the hill and decelerated.

The spray engulfing her car was larger and more powerful than the last one. The wheels trudged

through the water. Stephanie's hand hovered, ready
to shove the engine into neutral. She knew how to
handle puddles.

The vehicle stalled and sputtered to a stop.

This was no puddle.

Stephanie's eyes widened as the SUV started to
sink.

Chapter 2

Stephanie jerked her seat belt off and scrambled for the door. She punched down one lock with her fist while stretching her leg to the passenger side. After she kicked the other lock down with her heel, Stephanie curled into the corner of the driver's seat, tucking her knees under her chin.

Uh-oh, was that right? She wasn't so sure if she was following her self-preservation instincts or giving in to panic. Her gaze darted wildly around the car. *Am I supposed to stay inside, or get the hell out?*

Mashing the seat belt into her fists and hanging on for dear life, Stephanie slowly leaned over and looked out the window. The water swallowed the small SUV's wheels and splashed at the hood.

Stephanie bit her lower lip as her heart pounded against her chest. She couldn't remember any news show about this. Her jumbled mind flipped through her memory like a remote control. A reporter had to have covered this! Barbara Walters? Oprah? Geraldo?

She did remember that late-night movie where

Paul Newman and some woman got trapped in a room filled with water. She distinctly remembered Paul barely holding his face out of the water as they reached the ceiling. Those famous blue eyes were pressed against the solar window they had failed to break and escape from.

Stephanie glanced at the closed sunroof and shuddered. Yep, that was enough for her. She was so out of there.

She fiercely jiggled the window button, but it didn't slide down. "Oh, right," she muttered, her voice barely heard over the steady rain and her thumping heartbeat. Damn automation.

Flattening her hands against the driver's-side window, she pressed against the glass that began to fog. Stephanie squeezed her eyes shut and gritted her teeth as she pushed. "I. Really. Have." She grunted and gave one mighty shove after another. "No. Upper. Body. Strength."

She plopped down on the driver's seat, turned toward the passenger side, and planted her feet against the glass. If her weight didn't make the window shatter, her killer heels should at least make a hole. Stephanie groaned as she pushed hard.

Nothing happened.

She kicked and her heel skittered down. The window remained intact. Stephanie blew the hair from her eyes and glared at the unmarred glass.

She really needed to go to the gym more often.

Turning her attention to the driver's-side window, Stephanie wiped the condensation from the glass and analyzed the situation.

What did she have here? There was no phone connection. She hadn't passed another car for quite some time. No houses or buildings were along the country road. The water wasn't going anywhere. There was only one other thing she could do.

She had to get out and find Venus on foot, Stephanie decided reluctantly. *Oh, the fun never ends.* Her friend owed her big after this.

Stephanie took a deep breath to prepare herself. Her outfit was never going to be the same after this. It was "dry clean only." She mentally added the loss on the growing payback list she was going to give to Venus.

"Stop procrastinating," Stephanie whispered to herself. She closed her eyes and took another deep breath. With determined, brisk moves, she pulled the lock up and lifted the handle.

Stephanie pushed, but she could barely crack the door open. The force of the water slammed it back at her. She stared mutely at the quick stream that trickled inside.

"That's it. I'm hiring a personal trainer tomorrow," Stephanie vowed.

What was she saying? Why was she planning that as if she had a future? She was in trouble. Big trouble. She needed a plan to get out of this car if she wanted to survive. An escape route. Anything.

She held her hands up, halting her train of thought. Plan number one. Stephanie grabbed her cell phone. It didn't matter if she was in a dead zone. She would never leave that behind.

Stephanie stuffed the phone in her purse, another item she needed for survival. Hooking the purse strap over her shoulder, she looked around the car, wondering what else she needed to take with her. Her suitcase.

She looked over her shoulder and studied the bright red carry-on. Damn, that looked heavy. Those miniwheels at the bottom were not going to be useful today. Nothing she could do about it now. She'd haul it from the car when she got out.

Okay, she was ready. Stephanie rolled her shoulders and cricked her neck. Or, rather, ready as she would ever be. She grabbed the door handle. *One* . . . Her fingers flexed nervously. *Two* . . . She didn't want to do this. *Two and a half* . . . She really, really didn't want to do this. *Three!* She pushed the door open with all of her might.

"Whoa!" She fell forward and gasped as the cold water gushed over her. She squeezed her eyes shut, doing her best to keep her face above the water. Stephanie was stuck, sitting sideways, holding the door out as the water tried to push it forward.

She struggled to keep the door from slamming closed on her neck. The visual alone gave her a surge of strength. She pushed the door out and tumbled.

Stephanie splashed around as her knees hit the rocky ground. *Yep, that's going to leave a bruise.* She wrestled to a standing position. Digging her heels in the mud, she thrust out of the water, gasping for air as a wave crashed into her mouth.

"Pfft! Plah!" She spat the water and raked her teeth over her tongue. "Disgusting!"

She splayed her hands out and away from her sodden clothes. *You know what?* she asked herself. *Let's not dwell on the types of germs harboring in the water.*

Wow, the water was cold. Bitterly cold. It wasn't the kind of temperature that you would eventually get used to. Goose bumps were already dotting across her arms, chest, and back and her skin felt icy.

"Great," she muttered to herself, her teeth chattering. Trust her to go to the Midwest in the summer and find the only spot that would give her hypothermia.

Pulling the dripping wet ropes of hair from her face, she turned and immediately saw the mess inside her rental. Stephanie clapped her wet hand against her mouth, stifling her wail. She didn't want to dwell on that, either. All she wanted to do was get out of the water before the level went above her waist. Or before she turned into an ice cube. Whichever came first.

Stephanie did her best to ignore the interior of her car, but it was no use. The sight of the saturated floor made her stomach twist with dread. The water level climbed up the seats and sloshed against the dashboard.

The rental company was definitely going to notice this. There was no way she could explain it, either. Those guys wouldn't believe her anyway.

Stephanie leaned her head against the edge of the doorframe. She was up to her waist in water and the rain was coming down hard on her. Things couldn't get much worse. Well, actually, they could, Stephanie reminded herself, especially if she didn't start moving.

She slowly lifted her head. She knew this wasn't the time to consider the damage or the cost. One problem at a time. Her first priority was getting out of the water with her stuff intact.

She pushed at the driver's seat, but it wouldn't

go all the way down. Stephanie decided to blame it on the quantity of water filling the car rather than the quality of her muscles. She dragged the piece of luggage past the wedged seat, noticing the ominous squelching sounds from the bag.

The carry-on luggage was waterproof and has a lifetime guarantee, she assured herself. Anyway, so what if it got a little wet? The overnight bag held the basic necessities of life—her favorite pair of jeans, her birth control, and her makeup. She wasn't going to leave any of it behind.

She dragged it out of the car, the bag incredibly heavy. Her knees sagged and she felt the ground slip and shift underneath her.

Stephanie's eyes widened. Okay, that can't be good. She had to find higher ground, and fast.

She looked around but didn't see anything close, unless she counted the top of her car. Stephanie eyed the roof as the steady rain bounced off the metal. Good enough.

The water pushed and pulled at her as she hefted the bag up onto the roof. It hit the metal with a splat. She paused and stared at the carry-on. "Waterproof. Lifetime guarantee," she muttered under her breath.

Pulling her purse strap across her chest, Stephanie grasped the side of the SUV with cold, tight fingers. She slipped and slid as she crawled to the top of her vehicle. Her clothes now weighed a ton and drew tight against her legs. "Make that"—she groaned and shimmied up to the roof—"*two* personal trainers."

She lay spread-eagle across the roof, her cheek resting against the wet metal. The rain actually hurt when it hit her skin. *Keep moving.* She had to keep moving . . . Or was she supposed to stay awake?

No, that was for a blizzard. Okay, she obviously had been watching too many This Could Happen to You disaster segments on TV. All the advice was mixing her up.

She swung her legs around and draped them over the windshield. Her shoulders were hunched, warding off the rain. She was undoubtedly going to get a cold after all this. With her luck, it would develop into bronchitis.

Stephanie sneezed, her body jackknifing. The sound echoed far in the distance.

Make that double pneumonia.

Okay, what's her plan now? She couldn't just sit here until the mother of all puddles evaporated. She needed to get help.

Stephanie unzipped her purse and retrieved her phone. Her fingers shook as she tried to punch the keypad. It was no use. She was still in the dead zone.

She tossed the electronic back into her purse. What was she going to do? Stephanie rubbed her forehead with tense, pruney fingertips, trying to come up with a brilliant strategy. She froze when she felt the SUV shift underneath her.

Oh, sweet mother . . . She clamped her hands along the edge of the roof. No, it was just her imagination. Stephanie looked out of the corner of one eye and then the other. She must be disoriented. Obviously a symptom of impending hypothermia.

The car wouldn't turn over. Would it? She tried to block the image from her mind, but her brain was intent on mixing the consumer-reporting videos of flipping SUVs and scenes from The Road Runner cartoons. She was going to wind up flat as a pancake, just like Wile E. Coyote.

"That's not going to happen!" Stephanie reminded herself out loud, her voice echoing, reaching far into the distance. "Hello?" she called out. "Anyone out there?"

There was nothing around her. No people. No Lassie. Not a flicker of light, or even a tree. Nothing but rain. Constant, driving rain.

She felt the SUV shift underneath her again. Okay, it was official. The car was undoubtedly moving, and she was unquestionably getting off.

She hopped down onto the hood and immediately fell on her butt. She winced as her back collided against the windshield wiper. Stephanie glared at her Lucite heels and slipped them off. She unzipped her bag and stuffed them inside, along with her purse.

Hmm . . . the clothes inside her case seemed awfully damp. No, she wasn't going to think about it. She zipped up the bag and gingerly slid off the hood.

"Cold, c-cold, cold," Stephanie chanted, holding her bag above her head. Her arms trembled as they tried to support the weight. Maybe it wasn't a good idea to put in the shoes.

She wasn't going to repack now. Stephanie walked away from the car, hissing as the rock poked against her bare feet. "When I get my hands on Venus . . ." she swore under her breath.

The water was really pulling at her now. Almost as if it had a current, which was ridiculous. It wasn't like she was in a river or something. Stephanie stumbled, scratching her feet against the rocks.

She found her balance, but the water was strong

and tugging at her. The top of her head was holding her bag more than her arms were. It shouldn't take much longer to find higher ground. No way could the entire road be flooded out.

Something touched her arm. Stephanie yelped and reeled back, hoping it wasn't something with teeth. She squinted in the dark as she saw that it was a broken piece of wood and debris. Oh, that was just terrific. She was wading around in garbage.

She trudged forward, her clothes weighing her down, as she refused to think of what else could be floating around her. Mayfield better have a five-star hotel. With all the amenities. She gritted her chattering teeth as she stubbed her toe on a rock.

She took another step and fell into the water past her shoulders. Stephanie screamed, losing her grip on the bag. She spat out water and lunged for her suitcase as it dipped under the surface.

She recaptured the bag and held it close to her chest. Okay, it's deeper over there, Stephanie thought as she did her best impression of treading water. She's screwed. Big-time. She was not the best of swimmers. Her doggie paddle wasn't going to help her get across. She had to go back to the car.

Stephanie twisted around, stretching her legs until she could touch the rocks with her toes. She stared at her SUV and blinked. She rubbed the water from her eyes and looked again. That was weird. The car seemed even farther away.

Optical illusion. That was it. Or just plain tiredness. Stephanie took a step toward the car as the water swept the rocks away and she went under.

* * *

Jack took the call from the dispatcher since he was in the area. They'd just received reports that the small bridge had washed out. He wanted to check the area before he considered having some of the officers set up roadblocks.

He slowed down his car where the bridge should have started. Nothing remained of the historical landmark. He wasn't too surprised.

Despite the upgrades and reinforcements, the bridge was too small and narrow by today's standards. But no one wanted to hear a word about closing it. The people of Mayfield didn't embrace change very well.

Something reflected off of his headlights. Jack narrowed his eyes as he looked past the rain. Was that . . . a truck in the water?

What the hell? Jack shoved his car into Park, his body on full alert. He radioed in to the clerk, but didn't ask for assistance just yet. Jack left his car with urgent, efficient moves just as he saw someone splashing around.

Sudden adrenaline raced through his veins so fast it was almost painful. He headed toward the person. "I'm coming to help!" he called out.

In all the years he was a cop, he never had to save someone from drowning. Kind of strange since he was the sheriff of a river town. Bad time to think about that, Jack decided, as he ran into the cold water. He needed to act like he knew what he was doing.

All random thoughts disintegrated as his strokes sliced through the water. He swam in the direction of where he had last seen the person. Jack paused and started to tread, looking around.

Shit. Where did they go? It was too dark to see. The sounds of the water and rain made it difficult to locate. "Hey?" he yelled out, spitting out water as it slapped against him. "Where are you?"

"Here!" The voice was weak but nearby. "I'm . . . I'm over here!"

And the voice was definitely feminine. That was good, Jack thought, as he swam in the direction of the voice. She was probably shorter and lighter than he, which made her easier to carry.

He finally found her. It wasn't anyone he recognized. Probably some unlucky traveler who made a wrong turn. No one visited Mayfield on purpose.

She was treading, but her face was partially above water. Her dark, long hair was plastered against her face. From what he could tell, she was pale, probably in her late twenties, and freaking out.

"Oh, thank God." Her voice was hoarse with relief. The woman launched out of the water and lunged for him. Jack tried to hold her back, but it was too late. She slammed against him, throwing her arm around his shoulder. He braced himself as they both went under.

Jack couldn't see anything. He grabbed the woman by the waist and hoisted her up. He followed by using fierce scissor kicks.

When he broke the surface, Jack inhaled big gulps of air. "Lady," he called out. "Don't pull me under when I'm trying to save you."

"Sorry." She gurgled water as her hand bit into his forearm. He wasn't going to be able to hold her up like this for much longer.

"Is there anyone else with you?" he asked as the water pushed him against her.

"What?" Her eyes narrowed with incomprehension. "Oh, no. It's just me."

Something knocked against his side. It was heavy and solid. "What do you have with you?"

"My stuff."

Her stuff? What kind of stuff? He followed the length of her arm with his hand and found her holding the handle of a suitcase.

No wonder she was having so much trouble keeping her head up. Whatever she had in there was obviously important to her, but he couldn't risk the extra weight. "Let go of the bag."

Her eyes widened with disbelief. She shook her head violently and moved her arm out of his reach. "No way. It's—"

"Drop it."

"You don't understand." She swallowed water and started coughing. "It has all of my—"

"I don't care," he said in the harsh, authoritative tone that usually worked. "Now drop it."

"No, I can't."

"Fine. I'll do it for you." Jack moved his leg and gave a sharp kick. The bag shot out of her grasp.

"Oh, no!" She frantically looked around the dark, murky water. The woman took a deep breath and was about to dive for it when Jack grabbed her by the waist.

"Leave it," he ordered. Jack pressed her back snugly against his side. He stretched his arm across her right shoulder to her left hip. He made sure he had a good grip on her as she continued to flail around.

"Lady, do me a favor," Jack said, his patience

snapping when her heel kicked his leg again. "Shut up before I have to knock you unconscious."

The woman immediately went rigid. She didn't say a word. If it weren't for the rise and fall of her chest under his arm, he'd think she needed medical attention.

Who knew that threat would have worked? Jack thought as he continued swimming to land. He dragged her along with him, her arms and legs stiff and unyielding.

He might not be an expert in saving drowning victims, but he understood the startled, angry silence of a woman. He knew that once he stepped onto dry land, he'd better watch his back.

Chapter 3

Jack gave another suspicious glance at the woman seated next to him in his car. Other than a prissy thank-you for giving her a blanket, she hadn't said a word. Didn't even look at him.

He hid a smile and kept driving. If she wanted to give him the silent treatment, that suited him just fine. He was all for keeping the peace.

"Where are we?" she finally asked as he turned into the almost-empty parking lot.

"The police station."

He saw how her eyebrows rose. He knew what she was thinking. The small, decrepit brick building didn't inspire a lot of confidence.

There was nothing much he could do about that, Jack thought, as he escorted the woman from the car and up the stone steps. Even if he felt like it. It wasn't as modern or as well-equipped as other police stations in the area, but it suited them and filled their needs.

He held the door open for the woman, and she

gasped as she stepped into the air-conditioned entrance. She pulled the blanket tighter around her and huddled into its warmth. Her teeth started to chatter.

"Where are the bathrooms?" the woman asked softly.

"Downstairs. Here, I'll show you." He took a turn and guided her down the old steps to the dank, shadowy basement. "Right over there."

"Thanks." She hurried over to the door, the rough, gray blanket trailing behind her. The woman stopped and turned around. "Thanks for everything."

"Sure. I'll meet you upstairs and we'll deal with the incident report."

"Oh," she said, sounding surprised. She didn't quite meet his gaze. "Right. I forgot about that."

Jack watched her enter the bathroom and close the door behind her. The adrenaline was still pounding through him, but he felt oddly dissatisfied.

It didn't make sense, Jack thought, as he headed toward the locker rooms. The woman came out alive and so did he. Mission accomplished. A job well done.

By the time Jack changed into a dry uniform and was rubbing a brown paper towel against his soaking wet hair, he realized the source of the problem. Saving the woman from drowning was the most action he had had on the job since he became sheriff. It was probably the most excitement he had had on duty in a long time.

When was the last time he did something like that? When did he last feel the urgency? The risk? It had been too long if he couldn't remember.

Jack slammed his locker closed and headed back upstairs. Well, what did he expect? He knew that when he came back from the big city, life and police work would slow down. He made that decision with his eyes wide open.

And when he ran for sheriff, he knew there was going to be a lot of paperwork and managerial skills involved. Jack climbed up the stairs, shaking his head over his naïveté about the job.

Jack wasn't averse to the mountain of paperwork. It wasn't his favorite thing in the world, but he could handle it. His dissatisfaction stemmed from something else.

It was the politics. Town politics, people politics—hell, even office politics. The Mayfield police squad was a motley crew of misfits, each bringing their neuroses and antisocial behavior to the job. Dealing with clashing personalities among his officers was Jack's least favorite assignment as sheriff.

And he really didn't feel like facing it today. Jack swung the door open and strode in. If he kept his head down and didn't make eye contact, he could get to his office and close the door before anyone bugged him.

The front desk officer nodded at him as he took two bites from his sandwich, his jowls moving from the sharp move. The guy always reminded him of his neighbor's pug dog for some reason. Maybe it was the lines and wrinkles between his eyebrows.

"Hey, Jack."

"Mackey." He took the messages and kept walking. "Did you get a hold of disaster relief?"

From the corner of his eye he saw Mackey shake

his head. "They're busy with the floods up north," he replied, his words muffled.

That meant no guidance from disaster relief. Jack wanted to sit down and put his head in his hands. But he couldn't. He wouldn't. Instead he kept up his brisk stride to his office. "Okay, thanks."

"Jack!" he heard the deputy call out. "Jack!" The nasal voice sounded like he was right behind him.

He gritted his back teeth. Damn, he almost made it. Jack squelched the temptation to dive in and slam the door shut behind him. Deputy Wesley Cochran would only follow him in and Jack would have no means of escape.

This had better not be about the police blotter. Every week they had to have a meeting before they sent the information to the local newspaper. It was one of Jack's most hated tasks.

He would always feel the dread pushing against him every time Deputy Cochran came into his office with the clipboard. And, like their predecessors, the deputy would read out all of the incidents that were recorded for the week, and the sheriff tried not to fall asleep.

It was all Big Jack's fault, Jack decided. His father started the ritual. The sheriffs that held office between the first and second Sheriff Logan continued the tradition. Deputy Cochran seemed to enjoy the meeting. Jack privately found it a big waste of time.

But this was Wednesday. They didn't do the police blotter on Wednesday. Jack pivoted on his heel and almost collided into the shorter man. "Yeah, Cochran?"

"Didn't you notice that *Officer* Mackey," the two exchanged a glare, "is eating at his post?"

No, he didn't, nor did he care, but at least it wasn't about the police blotter. Only he couldn't give his response as Cochran recited the code of conduct.

Jack stood silently and rocked back on his heels. He remembered Cochran had been the school snitch at Mayfield High. One would think that the guy should have grown out of that by now.

"What do you want me to do about it?" Jack interrupted when Cochran drew another breath.

The deputy frowned at Jack's question. "I want you to reprimand him."

"Mackey." He spread his arms out and gave the officer a help-me-out-here look.

Mackey gave him a thumbs-up. "Gotcha," he said around his soda straw and slurped the cup dry.

Cochran let out something that was between a squeak and a squawk. "You consider that a reprimand?"

"Yeah," they said in unison. Jack turned on his heel, ready to escape before the deputy launched into the official description of a reprimand.

"Jack?" Mackey yelled, the urgency coming through loud and clear. "Just to let you know . . ."

"Yeah?" His hand clasped the doorknob to his office.

"Mrs. Keller is in there, waiting for you. She's, uh, been there for a while."

Jack closed his eyes. *The day just keeps getting better and better.* "Thanks."

He opened the door and stepped into his office.

Freda Keller was a vision of gray from her bouffant hair to her dull shirtwaist dress. She sat primly in the visitor chair, her spine ramrod straight. The matriarch of Mayfield didn't acknowledge his presence, but rather studied his framed diploma with open suspicion.

He closed the door with a sharp click, but she didn't turn. "Mrs. Keller," he greeted and shook her hand, her heavy, ornate rings poking into his palm. "What can I do for you?"

"Did you know," she asked in her distinctive raspy voice, "that the words on the movie theater marquee have been rearranged to say 'You Suck'?"

Jack paused. "Uh, no. I didn't know that."

"The movie theater is across the street from my husband's office."

"Did you let the manager know about the marquee? It sounds like the work of teenagers." He knew from personal experience that there wasn't much for kids to do around town other than cause mischief.

Her lips pinched tight, the lines around her mouth deepening. "I think not."

Great. Another conspiracy theory. He didn't have time for this. Jack kept his face expressionless as he sat down behind his desk.

Freda often felt that the townspeople coveted her status and money. He didn't know how true that was, but he also didn't know of anyone who wanted to take those things away from her. Lately her assumptions were coming fast and furious. Jack wished he could dismiss her claims, but as his dad once said, even paranoid people have enemies.

"As you know, Keller Brewery is celebrating its

jubilee this weekend. Mayfield is also honoring my husband with the Humanitarian Award."

Jack rested his elbows on his desk. "Yes, Mrs. Keller, I know." What he hadn't known until a few months ago was that the town *had* a Humanitarian Award. Either they didn't have a lot of good citizens in Mayfield, or the honor was a very recent brainchild of Freda's.

"I want your personal guarantee that there won't be any . . ." she looked directly at him ". . . unpleasantness."

It would be easy to say "Sure, no problem" and end the meeting, but he wasn't going to give her any false hopes. "I can't do that."

"I see." Her eyes narrowed with displeasure. "Your father could."

Jack's chest tightened like it always did when he was compared to Big Jack. He knew he always came up short. "I'm not my father."

"What a shame that is," Freda said as she reached for her black handbag. "Especially since your heritage won you the election."

Jack's nose flared, and he felt the anger washing over him, but he restrained himself from responding. He'd bet it was obvious how he felt, if Freda's smirk was anything to go by.

"Now," Freda continued in a conversational tone while retrieving a piece of paper from her purse, "about the security procedures for the jubilee . . ."

Stephanie leaned over the ancient sink and twisted her hair into a rope. She squeezed tightly as the water ran down the drain. When only droplets remained, she repeated the process.

She finally gave up and fluffed out her hair, which probably looked like a rat's nest. The hot-air dryer and paper towels did little to blot up the water from her skin and clothes. She stood on the scratchy blanket, keeping her bare feet warm. Miss America, she ain't.

She caught a glimpse of herself in the mirror and hurriedly glanced away. She couldn't look at her reflection. It had less to do with the tangled hair and ruined clothes, and more to do with her actions. She had never been so embarrassed in all her life.

What possessed her to behave like that when someone tried to save her? She'd like to blame it on stress. Panic. Pure fear.

But she knew that was only a part of the answer. For someone who created a successful business from scratch, she should have acted more reasonably. Instead, she held on to her suitcase for dear life and almost went after it at the risk of her own safety and that of the police officer.

She felt her face flush red. Stephanie busied herself by grabbing the blanket from the floor and folding it. What that cop must think of her. She cringed at the possibilities. Stephanie hoped he'd seen worse. This was one time when she didn't want to be memorable.

And now she had to face him again. Her face went hot. She would be happy if she never set eyes on him, but this would give her an opportunity to make things right. She didn't want him to think that she was unreasonable and ungrateful.

She didn't think she could excuse her behavior, but she might be able to explain it. But how could she? She didn't exactly understand it herself.

How much of a lunatic would she sound like if she explained that the items in her suitcase were more than just her livelihood? They represented the life she had struggled to achieve. Not only that, but they were the tools that transformed her. They reinvented the woman that she had always dreamed of becoming.

But the water washed it all away, and she couldn't shake off the feeling that they were gone for good. Now that she'd lost her things, she had to wonder what was going to happen. Was she still the Stephanie Monroe she wanted to be without the trappings?

"That's ridiculous," she whispered fiercely. "Of course you are." They were just things. Replaceable things that enhanced her image. She was going to be just fine without them.

Okay, she stayed in here long enough. Stephanie tilted her chin up. No amount of twisting, squeezing, or hot-air treatment was going to get her drier. She folded up the blanket and set it aside.

She marched out of the bathroom, determined to get the report filled out and find Venus. The sooner she focused, the sooner she would get out of this moldy building and the hell out of Dodge. Nothing was going to distract her, not even the thin layer of dirt coating the bottom of her bare feet. She wasn't going to think about it.

Well, at least the grungy feet completed the drowned-rat ensemble, Stephanie thought with a roll of her eyes. Her custom-fit jeans chafed her wet skin and the cotton halter barely concealed the dusky areolas of her nipples. She couldn't even get rid of the raccoon eyes without her makeup remover. What she wouldn't do for a spa treatment right about now.

Stephanie opened the double doors and strode into the main room of the police station. The officer at the desk looked up with a bouquet of French fries sticking out of his mouth. His eyes widened when he saw her.

Stephanie wondered if she could get her incident report done with him and not deal with the other police officer. It was a chicken move, especially after all that pep talk in the bathroom, but she wasn't above trying.

"Hi!" She flashed her most dazzling smile—the one she reserved for car valets, dry cleaners, and computer repairmen. Basically, anyone to whom she was handing her most valuable possessions.

He sucked in the fries. "Ma'am."

Stephanie watched his throat bulge when he swallowed. Okay, maybe the smile was too powerful on the unsuspecting. She lowered the wattage and leaned forward. "Can I use your phone, Officer"—she glanced at his badge—"Mackey?"

The man let out a powerful cough, his cheeks billowing. Stephanie took a prudent step back.

"I've got a bit of a problem," she continued sweetly, watching the policeman with extreme caution.

Officer Mackey let out a series of powerful coughs. Stephanie was surprised he didn't rupture something. She frowned with worry as he started to thump his chest with his fist.

"Are you okay?" Her eyes widened and she pointed

at him with both hands. "Do you need the Heimlich? I can so do that." However, she did find it was impossible to self-inflict. Not for lack of trying, though.

"He's fine."

Stephanie jumped at the unconcerned voice beside her. She whirled around and found another police officer standing at her shoulder. She cringed as the ends of her long, wet hair slapped the shorter guy on the forehead.

"Sorry," she muttered and hooked her hair behind her ears. Stephanie had a sense that anything she said or did would be held against her with this officer. Guilty before proven innocent. She needed to watch her step with this one if she wanted any assistance.

"Mackey, go get some water," the other policeman said impatiently from the side of his mouth. "I'm Deputy Cochran," he identified himself. "And you are?"

"Stephanie Monroe," she answered absently, watching Officer Mackey stumble into the next room.

He folded his arms and puffed out his chest. "Are you visiting or passing through Mayfield, Miss Monroe?"

"What?" She turned her attention to the deputy. "Oh, I'm . . . visiting my friend."

"And who would that be, ma'am?"

She tipped her head to the side. What was his problem? He acted like it was an exclusive gated community and she was trespassing. "Venus Gold," she answered.

The deputy became alert. He shifted his feet and braced his legs while placing his hands on his waist.

Stephanie knew that somehow she had given the wrong answer.

"You're going to need to change your clothes, ma'am," Deputy Cochran said in an officious tone.

"I'm aware of that, but I don't have any others," she said, her politeness wearing very thin and very fast. All she wanted to do was get back home. "What I could really use right now is a tow truck and the biggest squeegee I can find."

"Ma'am," he said loudly, his eyes focused on her midriff. "Are you aware that you're violating a city ordinance?"

"Say what?"

His gaze flickered up and down her cold, shivering body. "Your clothes."

"What about them?" she answered tightly. She felt like she was speaking a different language. "It's against the law to get wet?"

He pursed his lips. "It's against city ordinances to expose your breasts, have your waistband below your pelvic bone, or show . . . genitalia."

She hurriedly glanced down and behind her, wondering if she was inadvertently flashing the guy. Nope. The halter had shrunk a little, but she was in no way popping out of the low-cut neckline.

The jeans were skintight but didn't fail their purpose. The waistband was constructed to be low-slung, but it didn't reveal her thong. Not through sleet, or snow, or all that other stuff. "I don't understand." And maybe this guy needed to look up the definition of "genitalia."

"The intent of your outfit is to shock or harass." The police officer sniffed and rotated his shoulders back. "Which classifies this situation as a public disturbance." He reached for his belt. "I'm citing you for indecent exposure."

Stephanie's mouth dropped open. "You have *got* to be kidding me."

"No." Metal handcuffs dangled from the deputy's fingers. "You're under arrest."

Chapter 4

Stephanie stared out the window. The old-fashioned streetlights cast a warm glow on the steady rain. It would have been a beautiful scene had not the iron bars from her holding cell been in the way.

The jingle of jewelry penetrated her thoughts. She turned, her heart kicking up a beat. Only one person would wear that many bracelets and dangling earrings.

Venus Gold suddenly appeared next to her cell, all wild red hair, strong nose, and fiery green eyes. The familiar sight nearly undid Stephanie. Tears of relief pricked at her eyes, but she blinked them back as she studied her business partner's outfit.

The sheath dress looked like something Venus pulled off a shower rod, but Stephanie immediately recognized it from the hottest haute couturier's collection. The rubber duck pattern on the transparent vinyl was at odds with the sleek, tanned body it barely covered. Mingled with the gold bracelets and hoop earrings, Venus wore plastic shower curtain rings and hooks. Bright blue flip-flops that cost more than Stephanie made an hour completed the outfit.

"Hey! No fair!" Stephanie pushed off the wall and stomped across the cell, each angry step echoing. "Why are you walking around free and I'm stuck in here?" She knew Venus wore taupe biker shorts and a sports bra underneath, but the ensemble still made her do a double take. If that wasn't an outfit designed to shock, then nothing was!

Venus clucked her tongue with disappointment and sighed. "Stephanie, Stephanie, Stephanie."

"Not a word. Do you hear me?" She wrapped her fingers around the bars. "Not. One. Word."

"Whatever you say." She leaned her shoulder against the bars. "Jailbird."

"You're living dangerously." Stephanie glowered at her. She was never going to live this down.

Venus's eyes brightened. "The guys back at the office—"

Stephanie pressed her face between the bars. "*No one* in L.A. is going to hear about this."

"Aw, come on." Venus tilted her head to one side and batted her fake blue eyelashes.

"Venus," she said carefully, as if she were speaking to a child, "think of our competitors. What are they going to do when they hear how a cop mistook me for a hooker while I'm wearing an outfit you put together?"

"Oh, pshaw."

"P-what?" Where did Venus come up with *that* word?

"The Mayfield Police Department doesn't know much about haute couture. Have you seen what they're wearing?" She motioned at the door with her thumb.

"I'm not amused." And she was beginning to regret using her one phone call on Venus. "I want you to call my lawyer about a wrongful arrest."

"Stephanie, it's going to be okay."

"Easy for you to say. You're not the one behind bars, and I'm still trying to figure out how you managed that. Did you bribe them?"

"Breathe." Venus rotated her wrists, her bracelets jangling as she motioned to fill the lungs. "Do it with me. He, he, he."

"No, I'm too angry to breathe. Do you realize that I could have been injured and all this cop cared about was the state of my clothes?"

Venus flicked the concern away with the wave of her hand. "Cockroach has always been zealous—"

"Cockroach?"

"Sorry. *Deputy Cochran*," she said loftily before rolling her eyes. "The officer who booked you."

"I've been arrested by a guy named Cockroach?" Stephanie looked up at the cracked ceiling. "When will the humiliation end?"

"Names from the playground tend to stick."

"Yeah?" Stephanie met the other woman's gaze. "So do police records. Let's see how Venus & Stephanie, Inc.'s credit stands up when our vendors discover that they're dealing with an ex-con."

Venus's brow wrinkled as if she'd been thrown a trick question. "They'll think it's business as usual?"

Stephanie's composure snapped. She grabbed Venus's dress, the vinyl squeaking in her fist. "Get me out of here. Now!"

Jack looked at the time on his computer and leaned back in his chair. He rubbed his eyes with the heels of his hands, but they still felt tired and gritty.

His shift ended hours ago and he knew he should go home. But what would be the use? He hadn't been able to sleep since the river started to rise.

Maybe he needed to go to Croft's Tavern. It wouldn't cure his insomnia, but it had been a while since he'd seen his friends. If he could forget the job for an hour or two . . .

He looked at his desk. No, he was going to prove he was worthy of being sheriff. He might have won the position because of heritage, but he was going to keep it because of merit.

Deciding that was the plan, Jack rose from his chair and grabbed his empty, coffee-stained mug. When he opened his office door, he saw Mackey furtively ducking his head behind the front desk.

Okay, that was strange. "What's up, Mackey?" he asked as he walked over to the other officer. He set his mug on the scarred wood surface and peered over the high edge.

"I know my rights!" someone yelled in the distance.

Jack swiveled his head in the direction of the holding cells.

"I watch *Court TV!*"

He turned back to Mackey and saw the man munching ferociously on something. "What's going—?"

Mackey slid the file to him. "Indecent exposure."

Damn. It was the woman he pulled out of the water. He forgot to tell Mackey.

Jack set his mouth into a firm line and reluctantly took the folder that already sported greasy fingerprints. He didn't like the new ordinance Alderman Zimmer had pushed through. Probably because he knew it was inspired by the Zimmer girls, who tried to dress like their favorite pop stars.

He might not like the ordinance, but until it changed, he had to enforce it. Jack walked to where he heard the woman yelling about some plot point in a popular courtroom drama. He wondered if he could get to the bottom of this and find a solution that would satisfy everyone. He didn't think so.

Pushing the door and walking into the holding cell area, Jack's steps faltered the moment he saw the woman. She didn't look anything at all like she had when he saw her earlier.

The first thing he noticed was her shoulder-length brunette hair. No brush would survive those tangles. Streaks of blond zigzagged in the wild mass, indicating she lived where there was sunshine and lots of it.

Jack's gaze skipped down. Her lean body was almost all arms and legs. She wasn't wearing shoes.

The pale blue jeans were damp and stretched tight at her knees and thighs. The pants hung lower than any he had ever seen. He was sure more than one red-blooded male had stared at them, waiting with bated breath for the waistband to slide. The sequins winked back at him, as if letting him know it was going to be a long wait.

Jack's fingers tingled when he gazed at her bare stomach. She didn't have rock-hard muscle, but her flat abdomen had a touch of curve to cushion the palm of his hand. He wanted to reach out and touch the pale, smooth skin that promised to be warm, soft, and silky.

What was he thinking? Bad idea. Jack shook that wayward thought away, but it held firm. His hands felt heavy as he imagined how it would feel to dip his fingers into her navel. Followed by the tip of his tongue.

Jack swallowed roughly, his throat tight. She really needed to cover that belly button up. Like with a diamond.

No, that would be worse. Jack squeezed his eyes shut, but the vision remained, taunting him. Much, much worse.

He forced his eyes open and fixated his attention on her halter. Her tight nipples pushed against the sodden fabric that stretched across her small breasts. It was as if everything she wore was one size too small.

The woman jutted her hip to one side, her fist resting on the other. Her shoulders were angled, ready to deflect any challenge that came her way. She tossed her head back, her angry gaze colliding with his silently assessing eyes.

Jack felt the energy whoosh through him, his blood crackling in the aftermath. His skin felt tight, his body heavy as he met the big brown eyes head-on.

The flaked mascara didn't diminish the raw power of her uncompromising gaze. There was no other trace of makeup on her lean, angular cheeks or her wide mouth.

That mouth. His cock stirred with interest.

Those lips promised the most beautiful smile while whispering the dirtiest jokes. That mouth could give perfect, deep-throated head or the most mind-blowing kiss without any effort.

It was every man's fantasy.

Fantasy? No. Jack took an instinctive step back, a flash of anxiety searing through his gut. Not his. He was not intrigued by a lady who didn't have a lick of common sense. He was *not* interested in this woman who was behind bars. At all.

He was the sheriff. Jack purposefully reclaimed the step he lost. He was a man of authority. Integrity. At least, he was trying to be.

Old Man Schneider's words mocked him.

Trouble's coming.

Yeah. She had arrived.

The woman's glittering eyes narrowed and she shifted her stance. "What are you looking at?" she barked out.

He wasn't sure, but he was going to guess his most difficult challenge. Wrapped up in the most tempting package. He wondered if this was how Samson felt right before Delilah whacked off his hair along with his strength.

Jack flinched as the door behind him banged open.

"Quit hollering," he heard Venus Gold order the other woman. "Here's something dry for you to wear. I even remembered the shoes."

The brunette didn't look grateful.

"Oh, hey, Jack." Venus appeared next to him. "Didn't see you there."

"Venus," he said hoarsely and cleared his tight throat. He gave a cursory glance at his former classmate. "Nice rain gear."

She smiled prettily. "Thank you."

"Wait a second!" The other woman said in a huff. "She's wearing something see-through and it's *nice*?"

"In case you haven't noticed," Venus replied, walking to the cell, "my dress covers me from my shoulders to mid-thigh. Just as the law requires. It never indicated that the material had to be . . . what's the word? Opaque."

Jack felt his mouth twitch in a smile. He could always count on Venus Gold to tease the law.

"Don't worry." Venus looked over her shoulder at him. "No nail files in these clothes."

"Imagine my relief," he muttered. Now if only his body weren't on high alert. Jack unclenched his fingers from the folder and opened it.

"Who *are* you?" the brunette asked, her question brimming with attitude.

He kept his attention on the paper in front of him. "I'm Jack Logan. The sheriff." And she was Stephanie Monroe, according to the file. Somehow the name fit. "What's going on here?"

"False arrest, according to Stephanie," Venus answered as she wiggled a shoe between the bars.

"What happened?"

"What happened?" Stephanie asked, the shoe clattering onto the ground. "I'll tell you what happened. You forgot that I was supposed to file an incident report—"

"I'm sorry about that. Something came up." It wasn't a very good excuse, but he didn't think she would be impressed with the fact that he was overworked and disorganized these days. He glanced up and saw Stephanie squatting to grab the shoe from the floor. To his disappointment, the jeans didn't dip at all.

"Can you believe this? The guy saves me from drowning and doesn't remember I'm around five minutes later."

"So like a man," Venus replied.

He flipped the paper over and looked at the next form. "This still doesn't explain how you managed to get arrested within five minutes after I left you."

"I'm gifted that way."

Jack raised his eyebrow at Stephanie, who glared back at him. He slid a look at Venus, who was snorting with laughter.

"You know, I felt bad about the way I acted over my suitcase. I feel stupid about it, actually."

"Good to know," Jack murmured.

"I was going to apologize, but what happens? You stuck me with some whacko who doesn't understand the definition of genitalia."

"Deputy Cochran is not a whacko," Jack felt obligated to point out as Venus's snorts grew louder. "He is a conscientious officer of the law."

"Who needs a refresher course in vocabulary," Stephanie announced. "And maybe cognitive thinking, while we're at it. He books me for indecent exposure. You know, when it rains, there's a good chance my clothes will get wet with a possibility of becoming transparent."

Jack's shaky restraint and wild imagination could have done without that forecast.

"But when that happens, it would be accidental and not"—she cast a withering glare at Venus—"intentional."

"Try not to get me arrested," Venus suggested as she shoved the last of the clothing between the bars. "Or there'll be no one to bail you out."

Jack snapped the file shut. "Even if your clothes were dry, they wouldn't meet the legal requirements." She needed to know that if she planned on staying a while.

Stephanie scoffed. "What kind of place expects a dress code?"

"A nice one."

Jack immediately regretted his quick reply. He was fully aware that his hometown wasn't paradise and he was often the first and most vocal to point out the problems. But like most natives, he didn't like it when outsiders complained about Mayfield.

He didn't mean anything about Stephanie, or how she wasn't suitable to visit a nice small town. But Jack knew she took it that way and took it to heart. He saw how she flinched. She pressed her lips tightly together and turned her back sharply. Stephanie focused on her task of spreading her clothes onto the thin cot of her cell.

Venus's lips drew into an "O" as the tense silence stretched. "You know, I think I'm going to see how Mackey is doing on releasing you. I'll be right back."

Jack watched her scurry for the door. He scrunched his eyes for a second and resolutely turned back to Stephanie. Whatever he had to say disappeared in his throat as Stephanie pulled the string from her halter top and let it fall.

Chapter 5

Stephanie's finger stiffened with shock as the strings fell from her grasp. She had been so angry that she hadn't paid attention to what she was doing. So of course she had to whip her shirt off while the authorities watched. How else was she going to complete the worst day of her life?

She felt her halter slip, and she instinctively arched her back to keep the damp fabric from falling to the floor. It was too bad her breasts didn't offer much of a plateau.

Stephanie reluctantly caught the halter with her forearms and held it tightly against her breasts. She wanted to clunk her head against the bars and knock some sense into her. Instead she kept her gaze fixed on the wall in front of her and exhaled slowly.

Oh, this is going to keep me locked away for life. Especially since Sheriff Jack Logan already made up his mind that she wasn't fit to be seen in this town.

Her mouth went dry as the meager options spun around her mind. She could oh-so-casually bring up the fact that she was raised in a house filled with sisters. They never had enough money—or enough space—so there had been no such thing as privacy.

It was one hundred percent true, and her lack of modesty over her body was probably because of that fact. But even if she threw in the bit of trivia of having to share one bathroom as well, Stephanie didn't think the sheriff would care.

Act natural, she silently ordered herself as she tossed the crumpled halter onto the cot. The movement revealed the underside of her breast.

The tension arced between them and boomeranged in the small room. Stephanie wondered if she gave him a glimpse more than she first thought. *Don't make a big deal out of changing your clothes and then he won't call you on it.*

Her exposed skin tingled under his stare. Awareness flared deep inside her as his gaze traveled down her spine. She wished she had the nerve to raise her arms above her head and stretch slowly, rolling her hips and pushing at the heaviness that settled low in her pelvis.

Instead she reached for the button of her jeans. A slight tremor swept through her fingers as she wrestled with the stiff denim. She knew she should be reaching for the blouse Venus loaned her. But the naughty thrill coursing through her veins was infinitely more appealing than the safe path she usually followed.

As much as Stephanie strove to be noticed, she never thought she had a streak of sexual exhibition in her. But the idea of giving Jack a private peep show made her pulse go wild.

Having the iron bars between them made her feel bold and daring, Stephanie realized as she drew down her zipper. He could look, but not touch. Or maybe because she knew she was never going to come across Jack Logan again. There was something to be said about no consequences.

Stephanie gripped her waistband in her hands, but hesitated. She couldn't hear him. What was he doing? What was he thinking? Was he as affected as she was? Or was she the only one getting excited while he was concentrating on her file?

Don't think about that. Keep the conversation going. Her eyebrows dipped in a frown. Had there been a conversation? She couldn't remember.

"Is there anything else?" she called out to Jack, the stark room amplifying her wavering voice. She looked down at her sequined jeans and slowly shucked them off.

She felt jittery, almost light-headed as the denim slid past her hips. Parting her legs, she bent at the waist and guided the periwinkle denim down her thighs. The ivory thong left her buttocks exposed.

When she heard Jack's breath hitch in his throat, she kicked the jeans from her bare feet. She stood before him with her back turned. She wore nothing but a scrap of cotton, but she felt incredibly powerful.

Nervousness and wild lust swirled inside her, creating a potent magic. She wanted to tease him. Tantalize. Stephanie wanted him to reach for her, but at the same time, keep the cell firmly locked between them.

"Sheriff?" She looked over her shoulder, her tousled brown hair falling in her eyes.

Jack Logan's harsh face showed no expression, but she saw the desire glittering in his dark eyes. The ruddy color slashed across his cheeks, his skin pulled tight against his skull. His chest rose and fell with every shallow breath.

She darted her tongue across her parched lips. "Was there anything else?" she repeated the question.

"No," he answered, his voice low and husky. "I think that covers it." He reached for the door as if it was his lifeline and left without looking back.

An hour later, Stephanie stood in front of another brick building. This one was not as well-kept as the police station—which wasn't saying much. The bricks were chipped and pink with age. Neon lights flickered in the pitted glass windows. What she had originally thought was faded graffiti turned out to be the establishment's sign: Croft's Tavern.

She squinted at Venus, ignoring the rain that pelted at her head. The black asymmetrical kimono tunic she borrowed wasn't going to last long in the deluge. The blouse's raw edges and fragile ties were made for the music videos and hip-hop concerts, not for Mother Nature. The frayed denim skirt that *just* hit mid-thigh might hold up better, but Stephanie wasn't going to bet on it.

Still, she wasn't ready to go in. Ever.

"Venus, what do you mean?" she yelled, trying to be heard over the live country band playing inside. "Of course you're going back to L.A. with me. Immediately!"

Venus shook her head, raindrops spraying from her vivid red hair. "Can't."

Stephanie stared open-mouthed at her business partner, who turned and skipped up the slanted concrete steps, splashing in the shallow puddles before heading inside.

"That's it?" Stephanie called after her. "That's all you have to say? 'Can't'?"

Venus showed no signs of hearing her and disappeared into the crowded bar. Stephanie put her hands on her hips. "Venus Gold, I'm talking to you! Get back here right now."

Oh, great. Now she was sounding like her mother. The day couldn't get much worse.

Thunder rumbled in the distance. Stephanie froze at the menacing sound. *Then again, maybe it could* . . .

She hunched her shoulders and slanted a quick look up. Rain splattered against her cheeks. She couldn't remember hearing thunder like that before. Stephanie quickly followed Venus inside.

The bar was hot and steamy. She wrinkled her nose at the stench of cigarette smoke and yeasty beer. Squinting in the dark, she caught sight of Venus.

The lighting was horrible, Stephanie decided, navigating the maze of people, tables, and chairs. The only lightbulbs that seemed to work were at the band stage and dance floor. Of course, those would be located at the other end of the narrow building.

She reached her redheaded friend and was tempted to drag her back outside. She had a feeling the fine people of Mayfield might take offense at a stranger manhandling one of their own. Her ignorance of this town's etiquette was the only thing that stopped her.

"Need I remind you," Stephanie called over Venus's shoulder, "that we have a business that is in need of constant attention?"

"We're doing okay," Venus said, skirting around a hodgepodge of tables.

"Not if we neglect it," Stephanie answered, her spine growing hot under the stares. Some of the gazes were curious, others were hostile. She wished she had the nerve to stare right back.

"Taking a break isn't going to kill us."

"Yeah, it is. There's this thing called momentum."

"I'm all for momentum," Venus replied and sat at an empty table, brushing off the peanut shells with the sweep of her hand. "But you're getting frantic about it."

Stephanie gingerly perched on a rickety chair. "You haven't dealt with the financial aspect of Venus & Stephanie."

"True," Venus agreed and sighed. "You can still do business from here."

"Oh, yeah. That'll hold me for a day." Stephanie made a face as the waitress sidled up next to her.

Venus held two fingers up. "Two beers, please."

"What are you doing?" Stephanie asked. "You know I hate drinking beer."

"Then you're going to go thirsty," Venus predicted and leaned back on her chair. "That's pretty much all they serve."

Mayfield was more backward than Stephanie first realized. "How long do you think we're stuck here?"

She lifted a shoulder. "Hard to say."

Stephanie's jaw tightened with impatience. "Do you want to tell me *why* you're here?"

"I'm dealing with some old business." Venus turned to watch the dancing couples circle the small floor.

"Can't it wait?" Stephanie asked, studying her friend's profile.

"No."

Stephanie saw the rare lines bracketing her friend's mouth and frowned with concern. "You want to tell me what it's about? Maybe I can help."

Venus didn't hear her offer as a group of three women walked by the table. They were dressed similarly from their lacquered, feathered bangs to the outdated cut of their blue jeans.

Stephanie had those women pegged at first glance. They hadn't changed their style, or even their hair products, since they were teenagers. And why would they want to? Ten, fifteen years ago, judging from the thickness of those shoulder pads on the dishwater blonde, they probably ruled the fashion world in Mayfield.

While the other women moved on, their hair growing shorter as their list of family responsibilities grew longer, these three women were holding on to those moments of glory. It was kind of sad in a way, Stephanie thought, but then, she never really had a glorious moment.

"Hey, Missy," Venus called out. The blondest of the women paused. She coldly stared at Venus and Stephanie before walking away. The other two followed her without saying a word.

Stephanie watched the trio's retreat. "Small-town hospitality isn't at all like what they show on TV."

"And you're seeing them on their best behavior," Venus shouted over the drum solo. Her sly smile was the only indication that she had achieved whatever obscure mission she had set out to do. "With you being a stranger and all."

"I'm touched."

The waitress returned with two amber bottles. "Here, I'll get that," Venus said, reaching for her purse and flashing a wad of bills.

Stephanie's hand flew out over the table as she seized Venus's wrist. "What are you doing?" she hissed and gave a furtive glance around the bar. "Are you planning on getting mugged?"

Venus rolled her eyes and extracted her hand. "We're not in L.A. anymore," she reminded Stephanie as she paid the waitress.

"Thanks for the update. I would never have figured that one out." Stephanie took a swig of the beer and gagged. She glanced at the label and discovered it was made from Mayfield's own brewery. No wonder it tasted like swamp sludge. "Mayfield better take credit cards or—" Her eyes widened with horror. "Oh, no."

"What?" Venus looked behind her. "What is it?"

"My SUV. Give me your phone." She motioned frantically with her fingers. "I need to call the tow truck."

Venus winced. "Yeah, about that. Stephanie, there's no easy way to tell you this, but it's gone."

"Gone?" She gasped as realization hit hard. "My SUV? What do you mean, *it's gone?*"

"As in *floated away.*"

Stephanie stared at her with incomprehension.

"As in *submerged,*" Venus continued. "As in *never to return.*"

"Submerged?" Stephanie repeated slowly. "That's impossible! It was stuck in a puddle."

"A puddle?" Venus stifled a chuckle and took a quick sip of beer. "Well, that puddle has a name."

Stephanie drew back and scrunched her nose. "You name puddles around here?"

Venus's jaw slid to one side. "No. Your puddle is called Schwartztrauber Creek."

"Wow, that's a mouthful," she muttered and then blinked. "Creek?"

"Yeah, creek. How could you not have seen that? Didn't you have your headlights on?"

Stephanie leaned back in her chair and splayed her arms out wide. "Why would this armpit of civilization make a road in the middle of some creek?"

Venus closed her eyes and visibly held onto her patience. "Mayfield didn't. They built a cute little bridge over it."

"Wanna bet?" She took another gulp of the beer and winced, but the flavor wasn't a shock to the system. Obviously the first sip was supposed to cauterize the taste buds.

"The bridge washed away earlier today." Venus shrugged. "Like your SUV."

She flopped her arms on the table and laid her head down. Her transportation, her way out of town, and her unblemished driving record were all gone. She knew she should have paid extra for travel insurance. That expert on *Good Morning, America* said so.

"It's going to be okay," Venus said.

"My overnight bag. My limited edition Coach purse." She bolted out of her chair. "Oh, my God, my organizer!"

"Okay, breathe, Stephanie."

"Enough with the breathing! That's not going to fix anything. What am I going to do?" Her legs began to shake and give out. She slowly drifted back into her seat.

"You can stay with me at my mom's place."

Stephanie felt herself nodding like a bobblehead. "Uh-huh, okay." That took care of a problem she hadn't even considered.

"You can borrow my clothes."

"Unh-unh." She didn't look good in vinyl, not to mention the fact that Venus was *much* smaller. Stephanie might as well skip a step in the legal process and take up residence in the holding cell.

"We'll figure out the rest as we go along."

Stephanie felt her scheduled life just crack and splinter. She didn't know how she was going to repair her meticulous calendar. She laid her head back down as her world went spinning out of control.

"You're buying me another drink," she informed Venus. "A real one, this time."

"You can have anything you want." Venus patted her on the head. "As long as it's beer."

* * *

Jack watched Stephanie from the far edge of the bar. He knew the minute she walked into the building and he hadn't been able to keep his eyes off of her. There was something about the woman that made him a mess inside.

His instincts urged him to swoop down and claim her, but at the same time he nestled into the shadows, determined to keep his distance. Jack wanted to look away and ignore her, but he couldn't wait to see what she was going to do next. His tired mind begged for indifference, but the fire Stephanie ignited inside him was addictive.

Jack stretched and shifted, almost as if he was uncomfortable in the gray T-shirt and jeans he changed into. As if he was uneasy in his own skin.

He forced himself to remain still, but his hands refused to listen. He watched his thumb rub circles against the dewy beer bottle in his hand. "Something's wrong with me, Croft."

"No shit." His friend didn't look up as he dried a glass with a towel.

Jack saw Stephanie wince after a drink of beer. He felt the smile tug at his mouth, remembering his reaction when he first sampled the dark brew. He had blamed it on his underdeveloped and underaged sensibilities. "How do you think I've handled being the prodigal son?"

Croft paused from his task. "You've paid your dues," he answered solemnly.

Jack thought about that, vaguely hearing the music, or the thunder, rolling over the tavern. People still remembered all the stupid stuff when he was a kid, and they don't want to forget. John Croft was his associate in every crime and caper, and sometimes the mastermind, but that didn't matter. You'd expect that from a Croft.

"Have I been on the straight and narrow since?" he asked, propping his head up with his hand. "The bad boy gone good?"

"Yeah, and it's been hell. Mayfield hasn't been the same since." Croft scrubbed with enough force that Jack was surprised he didn't put a hole in the beer glass. "What about it?"

"I thought I'd been good long enough that all my impulses, all my reactions would be . . ." He trailed off and shrugged, almost embarrassed. "Virtuous."

The glass slipped and Croft caught it before it hit the floor. "Yeah?" He shelved the glass and slapped the towel over his shoulder. "Where'd you get a stupid idea like that?"

"It *was* stupid." He gave a heavy sigh. "I didn't know that until I met Venus's friend."

"The hot brunette?"

There was something more to her than that label, but he hadn't figured it out yet. "Her name is Stephanie Monroe. The moment I saw her, it hit me."

"It?" Croft rested his elbows on the bar.

"The wildness. That white heat, that energy that wants to burst out of your skin." He sensed his friend's nod of understanding. "I haven't felt that way in a long time and today it hit me. Hard and fast."

"Finally!" He slapped his hand on the wood surface. "It's about damn time."

"No, Croft." He glanced at his friend from the

corner of his eye. "This isn't something to celebrate."

"Yeah, it is."

Jack pulled his gaze away from Stephanie. "This is bad timing. Bad luck."

"You've handled that before."

He shook his head. "Not like this." He had to deal with the Keller Jubilee, the possibility of a flood, and his detractors were popping out of the woodwork like spiders before a cold spell.

He couldn't forget to include the overwhelming duties he dealt with on a daily basis. Everything was coming at him from all directions. The last thing he needed was Stephanie distracting him.

"You know what you need?" Croft asked. "A woman."

A vision of Stephanie popped in his head. She would be sprawled naked on his bed, ready to accept him. Her long brown hair would flow like waves against his pillow.

"Croft, haven't you been listening?" He pushed the beer bottle away, wishing he could dispose of the fantasy with as much ease. "My problem *is* a woman."

"No." His friend snatched the bottle before it skidded across the counter. "You're problem is that you haven't *been* with a woman since you've become sheriff."

"Don't tell me," Jack said, tiredly rubbing his face. "There's a lottery going on about it."

Jack felt Croft's hesitation. He leaned back and pinned the bartender with a glare. "And you're holding it, aren't you?"

His friend held his palms up. "I stand to make a lot of money."

"Glad to hear it," Jack replied dryly. "But that's why I shouldn't listen to your advice. It would fix the lottery in your favor."

"I wouldn't stoop that low."

Jack leveled him with a look of disbelief.

"But if you're thinking about it," Croft added in a low, confidential tone, "Danielle is the woman for you."

"I'll keep that in mind." His friend was right about one thing. Danielle would be the ideal girlfriend for the sheriff. But that didn't necessarily mean she would be perfect for him.

A customer motioned for Croft. "Be right back."

"Yeah, sure." What was he thinking? He *was* the job. It wasn't something he could put aside off-hours when he took off his badge.

If he was truly a bad boy turned good, he would consider someone like Danielle. The woman wasn't squeaky clean, but she didn't have any gossip clinging to her. She was well-mannered and well-liked.

Danielle was as far away as you could get from a woman like Stephanie Monroe.

Or was she? Jack allowed his gaze to settle on Stephanie. There had been something about her eyes that set his preconceived notions into a tailspin. A wild innocence shone beneath the veneer of sarcasm and experience. Stephanie Monroe might look like a fallen angel, but she wasn't ready to dance with a devil like him.

Jack liked that theory, but that could be pride talking. After all, it sounded more noble that he held back to protect her rather than keeping his distance out of self-preservation.

There was only one way to test out his theory. Jack stood up, his heart pounding, accepting the call of the hunt. He made his way to where Stephanie sat, each step ringing with determination.

He stood at her side and she immediately glanced up, sensing his presence. Her lips parted as a blush crept up her pale skin.

"Dance?" he asked in a low, gruff tone.

Stephanie jolted out of a daze, her eyes widening with surprise. "Um, no, thank you." The table bucked and she winced as Venus gave a not-too-subtle kick to the shin.

"I insist." He extended his hand. The anticipation of her touch gave him a buzz.

"Or what? She ducked her hands under the table and looked at him suspiciously, as if she was ready for him to pull out the cuffs. "You'll haul me to the station for resisting?"

Jack raised his eyebrows. "Now *there's* an idea."

Chapter 6

Stephanie reached for the sheriff's hand, *really, really* wishing she hadn't flashed him earlier that evening.

She guessed it was like mooning a passing car. You accepted the dare and felt deliciously naughty and cool doing it at the time. You thought you had gotten away with it until you see the guy you mooned at the next gas station.

And, of course, the guy somehow recognizes you. You hope it's the car that stirred his memory, because if there's a resemblance between your face and your butt, you might as well go play in heavy traffic. But it's too late to run in the middle of the street because the guy you mooned is approaching you, ready to deal with you on that one time you threw caution to the wind.

And she could tell from the glint in the sheriff's eyes that he was going to torment her about the impromptu performance. Well, Stephanie decided as she reluctantly reached for his hand, as long as he didn't critique her routine, then they'd both survive the next five minutes.

She took his hand and her stomach twitched. Her mouth suddenly went dry. Adrenaline, raw and powerful, slammed through Stephanie as her skin glided over his.

Oh, this can't be good, she thought frantically as the noise faded and her surroundings blurred. Her gaze darted around and connected with his dark brown eyes. And her world tilted.

Because he felt it, too.

Now she really wanted to snatch her hand back. But Jack Logan wouldn't let her. His long fingers wrapped around her knuckles, and guided her from her seat. He wasn't going to let go until he was ready.

This had better not be a slow, seductive song, Stephanie hoped, her skin flushing hot at the thought. Each breath she took became more difficult. It was like her ribs had shrunk and pressed against her lungs.

Although, Stephanie thought, her mind fluttering wildly like a butterfly caught in a net, considering how her luck had been going, the band would immediately become Pink Floyd wannabes the minute she got on the dance floor. They'd play something that Just. Won't. Ever. End.

Jack led her to the dance floor. His long, ground-eating strides made her quick steps seem girly. She didn't like the way her control of the situation was seeping away. Stephanie especially didn't like the way his possessive hold made her want to curl into his side. If anything, his silent claim should make her keep her distance.

The other bar patrons made way for him as he

cut through the crowd to the dance floor. Stephanie vaguely wondered how Sheriff Logan did that. He didn't even have to shoulder anyone out of the way.

And the sheriff had strong, sleek shoulders. Stephanie's eyes locked onto the bold, sculpted lines that his gray T-shirt couldn't soften. Those shoulders were the kind you could lean on, the kind that would shelter you until the storm passed.

Her attention drifted down to the worn jeans. The faded denim clung to his lean hips and compact, hard muscles. Her pulse quickened. The sheriff had the kind of butt you wanted to grab and hold onto while he was driving deep inside you. She could imagine her fingertips digging into his flesh, the hard muscles clenching and resisting, mirroring her own.

He turned, their eyes clashing, and she quickly diverted her attention, knowing her defensive move came too late. He probably knew she had been checking him out the whole time.

The band on stage started to play a song she didn't recognize. It wasn't a seductive tune that would make her melt, but it wasn't a raucous "Twist and Shout," either. The music was created for an excuse to hold someone close and sway to the beat.

Wrapping his sinewy arm around her waist, the sheriff drew her against his rock-solid chest. Her breath hitched in her throat and she inhaled his scent. It triggered something deep inside her.

Her pulse went haywire as his right hand spanned her back. His left hand cupped her right one and held it against his chest, directly above his heart. Stephanie rested her other hand on the edge of his shoulder. She stared at a fixed point on his shirt, hating every shy bone in her body.

It was just a dance, Stephanie fiercely reminded herself. It wasn't a prelude to sex, no matter how her body was responding. She could do this. After all, what was she worried about? Jack Logan was a hick policeman.

Stephanie cast a look at his face from underneath her lashes. Her heart skipped a beat as she took in the stubborn jaw, the sexy mouth, and the glimmer in his gorgeous brown eyes.

The very eyes that were staring right back at her like she was the only person in the room.

Alrighty, Stephanie thought as she looked away. Her heart pounded harder, making up for the lost beat. Maybe not a hick policeman. But he was a policeman from a hick town. She'd dealt with plenty of those, played their game and wrapped them around her finger. That's all she needed to remember.

She could still feel his intense gaze and it unnerved her. Her clothes scratched against her hot skin, her breasts felt heavy and tight. She needed to distract the sheriff until the song was over, and then she could leave.

Stephanie cleared her throat. "By the way, thanks," she said to his shoulder.

"For what?" His mouth was at her ear. She shivered as his warm breath fanned the wisps of her dark hair.

"For letting me off with a warning." He gave her a document to sign about the wrongful arrest and she was set free, for which she was eternally grateful. She didn't think she could have handled going before a judge tomorrow morning. She would have been the first textbook case for dying of embarrassment.

"I didn't do you a favor. I'm keeping the holding cells empty for the real criminals."

"Oh. Okay." She didn't know what else to say and fell into an uncomfortable silence. A white-hot tension stretched across her. She felt hot, flushed, and exposed under his unwavering stare.

Jack Logan's need strained under his skin. He held her firmly, his heat rolling off of him and billowing against her. She could sense the desire ready to burst from him.

"You know," she said, her voice tinged with exasperation, "you already have a mug shot. You don't need to memorize my face."

"I'm not." She heard the smile in his voice. "I just noticed something about you."

Typical. He had saved her life and forgot about her minutes later. She had let her temper loose and told him off. She had whipped her clothes off in front of him, and he just now noticed her? That was her life in a nutshell.

"What?"

He paused. "You're not really a troublemaker."

Stephanie felt the jolt go through her, from her scalp to the tips of her toes. *Yes, I am!* She wanted to argue. *I worked hard at being one, too. I could be trouble with a capital T when I put my mind to it.* "What makes you say that?" she asked calmly.

"Instinct."

"Is that right?" The same way her instinct was

screaming that this guy was major trouble. She would bet her plasma TV that the sheriff was a natural-born troublemaker.

But then why did she hear relief in his husky voice? Did he think that because he was designed for trouble, no one else could give him any? Was he under the misconception that he could handle her?

Then the sheriff was in for a shock, Stephanie decided as her eyes narrowed with intent. It was the methodical troublemakers who didn't always call attention to themselves that were the ones to watch out for. He'd find that out soon enough.

"I'm disappointed in you, Sheriff Logan. You should never underestimate the power of a wicked woman."

She felt his chuckle rumble in his chest. "You're not wicked."

Stephanie bristled. "And when did you figure this out? When you first saw me behind bars?"

"I know a good girl when I see one," he said softly against her ear. "It doesn't matter where she is or what she wears."

She arched an eyebrow with disbelief. "Oh, really?" Bull. Because if he hadn't seen her behind bars, she would have been invisible to him. "You've had a lot of experience with good girls?"

"Well . . ."

She turned and met his gaze head-on. "You wouldn't know a good girl even if she came up and bit you."

"Now, there you're wrong." The corner of his mouth tilted into a slow smile, revealing the edge of his teeth. "Good girls don't bite."

"They do if they want to kiss it better."

His attention zeroed in on her mouth. Her lips felt heavy and she parted them. She forgot to breathe as the energy shimmered between them.

The song ended with a flourish. Stephanie pulled away as the last note hung, but his fingers tightened. She waited without looking at him, without fighting for her release, until he set her free.

"Good night, Sheriff." Whirling around with a backward glance, Stephanie marched to where Venus sat. Her mouth still tingled as if she had already been kissed.

She kept her eyes fixed on her destination. She didn't need to turn back to see if the sheriff was still watching her. She knew he was. She could feel it.

Worse, she liked it. Stephanie was tempted to turn around and give her best come-hither look just to see how he would respond. And that's what scared her, because she never made a move unless she could predict the outcome.

"We need to leave," she informed her friend, trying to mask the urgency coursing through her. Stephanie had a feeling she failed miserably.

"Sounds good to me, jailbird." Venus rose from her seat. "But I need to make one more stop before calling it a night."

Stephanie found herself lurking around in the shadows of the minuscule downtown park, standing guard. "We're going to get caught," she declared in a whisper.

"No, we're not," Venus said as she wrapped her

legs around the copper statue of a man and crawled up.

"Shh!" she hissed, looking around. As far as she could tell, all the good citizens of Mayfield were tucked in bed, but she couldn't be sure. Stephanie glanced suspiciously at the cluster of trees on the other side of the park.

It was too quiet. Too dark. The rain had let up, leaving the scent of wet grass. She tensed when she heard a car splashing through puddles in the distance. "I hear something. Let's go."

"Not yet."

Stephanie wiggled her nose, warding off a sneeze. She wanted to go to bed, but no, first she had to test her newfound freedom. Why Venus had to dress a statue with a costume, she had no idea. It must be one of those peculiar ancient customs small towns seem to like.

Knowing her luck, only virgins could participate. Or natives. Outsiders wouldn't get legal immunity. She could see Venus getting off scot-free while she got arrested for vandalism.

And even though she wasn't technically taking part in the vandalism, Stephanie could imagine "aiding and abetting" on her police record. She should have stayed in the car. What was the fine for loitering in a car?

Stephanie wondered about that, shifting nervously from one foot to the other. She wasn't sure, but she knew once she got caught, Sheriff Jack Logan was going to throw away the key.

And she would be under his watchful eye. Those dark chocolate eyes that already saw her nearly naked. That saw things she hid from everyone else.

Those same gorgeous eyes that could see right through her.

She shook the idea away and turned back to the statue, hoping Venus made progress. Stephanie winced as she saw her friend's legs wrapped intimately around the statue's waist, crushing the white pleated dress they threw on the statue minutes before.

Forget vandalism, Stephanie decided. They'd get hauled into jail for lewd conduct.

"Are we done yet?" Stephanie whispered fiercely.

"Almost," Venus said with a grunt as she secured the blond Marilyn Monroe wig on the statue's head.

"Do you realize how completely juvenile this is?" Stephanie asked, keeping her voice low.

"Yes." Venus's smile was bright in the shadows. "What's your point? Hand me the boa."

"Marilyn didn't have a boa," Stephanie muttered as she rifled through the duffel bag.

"I'm using some artistic license." Venus uncurled her legs from the statue and hopped down.

"Who is this guy, anyway?" Stephanie pulled the purple feather monstrosity from the bag.

"Ronald Keller."

"Ah." Like that was supposed to explain everything. "And why are we doing this?"

Venus shrugged and took the boa. "Because it's here?"

"Good enough for me," Stephanie said, watching impatiently as Venus draped the feathers on the outstretched arms.

"There." She fluffed up the feathers. "I think Mr. Keller is ready for the induction ceremony tomorrow."

"Come on, come on," Stephanie urged as she hurried over to the white tarp crumpled on the wet sidewalk. "We don't have time to admire your handiwork. Help me cover this guy up before someone sees us."

Replacing the damp cover was a struggle. Stephanie had to admit that jumping at every sound didn't help. She grabbed the duffel bag as Venus smoothed the tarp down.

"Hurry," Stephanie ordered and grasped her friend's arm. Their footsteps echoed in her ears. She paused as she heard a sound. It was getting closer.

Stephanie hesitantly looked over her shoulder. Her eyes widened as she saw a black-and-white car turn on Main Street.

"Duck!" She pushed Venus into the nearby bushes. She threw the incriminating duffel bag next to her friend before diving after her. Stephanie muffled her grunt as her stomach hit the wet mud.

The tires rolling through the puddles grated on Stephanie's frayed nerves. She had to see where the car was. Crawling on her elbows through the squelching mud, Stephanie pulled back the foliage and peered through.

A cold chill swept through Stephanie as she saw Deputy Cochran behind the wheel of the police car as he drove by. She heard Venus moan. Stephanie risked a quick glance at her friend, who stared at the night sky with a dazed expression. "Are you okay?"

"I'm flat on my back in the bushes with Cockroach snooping around." Venus shook her head. "Talk about high-school flashback."

"I don't want to know. Save it for your scrapbook."

Stephanie continued watching the squad car slowly circle around the park. Her throat ached as she held her breath. She went weak with relief as the police car turned and went down the next street.

"That was too close for comfort." Her arms and legs felt shaky as she sat up. "I can't handle the idea of dealing with the cops again."

"Speaking of cops," Venus said as she brushed the mud off her bare arms. "There's one that's available."

"Cockroach?" Stephanie wrinkled her nose in disgust. "Ew! That's disgusting."

Venus made a face. "No, I'm talking about Jack Logan." She stood up and swatted at the mud on her vinyl dress. "You know, the sheriff."

"Why are you telling me this?" she asked nonchalantly.

"So you can go after him. Duh." Venus scooped up the duffel bag and gingerly stepped out of the bushes.

Bad idea. If she even tried that, Jack would turn the hunt around so fast her head would spin. She would lose all control as he pursued her. The thought alone had Stephanie shooting out of the bushes.

A thorn caught her thin kimono shirt as she jerked back. "Why would I want to waste my time and do that?" Stephanie asked, her head bent as she disentangled herself.

"Because it would be so much fun once you caught him." Venus said. "Have a one-night stand with Jack. Better yet, a wild weekend."

Stephanie couldn't believe that the wildest woman she knew was suggesting that. Maybe Venus hit her head when she pushed her into the bushes. "You want me to do a *sheriff*?"

"Yeah." Her mouth curled in a naughty smile.

"The guy who agreed that I was guilty of indecent exposure? Oh, yeah." Stephanie scoffed at the idea while her heart knocked against her ribs at the possibility. "That should be really fun. He'll probably expect me to keep all my clothes on. Give new meaning to safe sex."

"Come on, Stephanie. Just because he cited you for a public disturbance doesn't mean he feels that way." She pointed her key ring to her car and unlocked it. "He's just doing his job."

Stephanie shrugged. She knew what Venus said was true. She just didn't want to give Jack Logan any points in his favor.

"And Jack hasn't always been Mr. Serve-and-Protect."

Stephanie had figured that out the moment she looked into his eyes. He might wear the uniform and be in absolute control of himself, but she saw the ferocity lurking underneath. She felt the challenge to break that iron control and see him untamed.

And then he could focus all his pent-up desire on her. Live out every decadent fantasy with her in the starring role. Stephanie forgot to breathe as her body tightened. Her thighs clenched and locked.

"I can't afford any distractions," Stephanie finally said in a husky voice. "Anyway, I don't have time for a fling or even a one-night stand." She paused, ran her hand through her hair and extracted a twig.

"Yeah, you do."

"No, I really don't." She flicked the twig out the window with fumbling fingers, vaguely wondering what the law was for littering around Mayfield. "I'm too busy getting you back to L.A."

Venus ignored the pointed jab and started the car. "And that's a full-time job?"

Stephanie quickly buckled her seat belt. "Believe me, it's becoming one."

Chapter 7

Jack lay in bed, stripped down to his boxers, and listened to the thunder rumble in the distance. He bent one arm behind his head and closed his eyes, desperate for some sleep. For oblivion.

Stephanie Monroe ruined any chance of that. He shifted against the cool bedsheets at the thought of the sexy brunette. What was it about her? What was it that drove him to the brink of all reason?

The striptease definitely had something to do with it, Jack wryly admitted as he burrowed his head deeper into his pillow. It fulfilled fantasies he didn't even know he had, while creating a few more he knew he would never satisfy.

The woman really was trouble.

His cock still twitched at the memory of Stephanie removing her halter. Jack had wanted to press her spine against his chest and cup her breasts. He had wanted to feel her nipples bead and tighten against his palms before he squeezed them between his fingers.

It was only through sheer luck that he'd had enough restraint to remain silent. To stay still. And he believed he would have acted the same way if the holding cell had been unlocked.

But had he been in the locked cell with her . . . Had she wanted his touch . . . Well, that was a no-brainer.

He would have grabbed her hips and pulled her against him. Jack closed his eyes as he imagined it. Tear the thong off her sleek hips. Rub and dip his fingers into her until she begged for more. And then he would slide deep into her, again and again, until she came.

Or, he could have taken her on the cot. No, that wouldn't have quenched the primitive hunger he felt clawing in his chest. The iron bars would. Maybe she would have taken him against the bars. He could see it now . . .

The cold iron bit into his back as Stephanie pressed her naked breasts against him. He was determined to taste her, feel her silky skin against his tongue. Stephanie wrapped her fingers around his wrists, equally determined to tease him.

As he dipped his head, he saw a glint of silver in the corner of his eye. It should have been his first warning, but he ignored it. All he cared about was suckling her taut nipple into his mouth.

And then he heard the click. The fine hairs on his neck prickled in alarm. He straightened to his full height and was yanked off balance, his back slamming against the wall of iron bars.

He tried to look behind him, but it was impossible. Glancing up, he saw that both hands were above his head, caught in his handcuffs. He pulled, the sound of metal grazing metal echoing in the cell, but he couldn't break free.

The cool air wafted against his chest. He looked down and saw the devilish glint in Stephanie's eyes as she unbuttoned his shirt. She slowly pulled back the dark blue cotton, pausing to press her lips against his collarbone and swirl her tongue against his hot skin.

He swallowed back the moans that rumbled deep in his chest. Jack refused to surrender to his feral side. No woman had unleashed it before—though they might have seen a glimpse before he pulled back.

Stephanie knelt before him on the icy cement floor. He tensed and reared back as she grabbed his buckle. He wanted her mouth on him, more than anything else. He had to stop her, but instead he watched her drag his belt free and toss it on the floor.

As she unzipped his trousers, Jack bucked forward, his cuffs clinking against the bars. The control he held over himself was slipping and there was nothing he could do about it.

Stephanie withdrew his cock from his boxers, holding him with a reverence that made him clench his teeth. She cupped his balls with one hand while grasping the base of his cock with the other. She pursed her luscious mouth against his wet tip, and Jack knew he was in for a special brand of torment.

His knees crumpled from her soft caresses. His skin crackled as the blood rushed through his body. The thunderstorm crashed like cymbals. The buzzing in his ear grew louder. She caressed him with her fingers before brushing against the tip of his cock.

Jack's fingers ached to bunch into her hair. He wanted to grab the back of her head and thrust into her welcoming mouth. And Stephanie knew that, but wouldn't let him have it.

She slowly, almost with exact precision, kissed every inch of his cock as he fought against the metal chaining him. She fondled his balls, the sensations driving him to the brink of reason. Just when he thought he couldn't take any more, her hand squeezed hard.

Jack's groan rang harshly in the cell as she stroked him with bold, fast moves. His body went hot, his skin flushed red, sweat trickling down his back, as she took him deep into her mouth.

His arms tingled, his hands clenching and un-clenching. Jack was desperate to grab hold of Stephanie and never let go. He yanked at his cuffs, but he wasn't strong enough.

Stephanie took all of him, her nose nestled in the wiry hair at the base. His cock throbbed and twitched in the moist, tight channel. He couldn't take it anymore. He had to come. He had to—

A ragged cry burst from Jack's throat as Stephanie abruptly withdrew. He would have fallen to his knees had not the chains held him up. His cock was erect and stiff, smacking angrily at his belly.

She rose from the floor, her eyes challenging him. Jack stared at her with disbelief as she turned around and strutted to the other wall of bars. How could she do this to him? He needed her. He needed to claim Stephanie as his.

He watched as she unsnapped her jeans, his chest rising and falling rapidly. She bent from the waist to slide the stardust denim down her legs, and the wild beast inside him broke free.

The cuffs shattered and broke away from the bars. Jack charged after Stephanie, the sirens wailing in the distance. Flashing lights danced across the bare walls. He ignored them all. The only thing that mattered was getting Stephanie.

She kicked the jeans away as he grabbed her by the waist. Stephanie gasped and looked over her shoulder. The wavy brown hair fell in her eyes and she smiled.

That knowing, wicked smile that shattered his golden-boy façade.

Stephanie grasped the bars in front of her as his rough hands roamed the contours of her naked body. He ripped the thong from her curves before plunging into her wet core. Jack stopped as the sensations stampeded through him, leaving him shaken.

He held onto her hips and thrust. Stephanie dipped her back and moaned. The sound ignited a jagged fork of lightning at the small of his back. He felt that familiar kick in his bloodstream and knew he was going to come.

The siren shrill invaded his head. It was as insistent as it was distracting. But first he had to come inside her. He had to claim Stephanie.

Lightning split through the night sky, awakening Jack. The thunder boomed above him, shuddering through his home. He bolted out of bed, wide awake, his heart in his throat.

He flinched as the phone rang next to his hand. Jack snatched the phone, his hands trembling, his cock throbbing and wet. "This is Sheriff Logan," he said tersely, sucking in air as if his lungs were starving.

"Hey, Jack," Mackey greeted him. "I've been trying to call you."

"Sorry. What's going on?" He looked at his alarm clock. Had he gotten any sleep?

"The thunderstorms have caused major damage," Mackey informed him before taking a slurp of something. "Possible flash floods in the eastern part of the county."

"I'll be right in." Jack hung up the phone and stared at the bed. The sheets were wrinkled, and the pillow was balled up against the headboard.

He absently rubbed his wrists, although there were no marks around them. The dream bothered him. He wasn't into handcuffs. He wasn't into losing control.

But in the dream, he liked it too much. He wanted to lose control with Stephanie. Let his impulses run free and show his wild side. The dream made his body crackle with a fire he thought he'd snuffed out years ago.

He had been wrong.

That wild streak was running strong inside him, and he wasn't going to let it break free. No matter what.

Why did it have to show up now? Jack wondered as he wearily headed for the bathroom and hit the lights. Why did it have to show up at all?

He had been wrong about a lot of things, Jack realized as he turned on the shower. He was talking big while he danced with her. He had been trying to convince himself rather than stating a fact.

But now he knew the truth. That woman was more trouble than he could handle. He had to stay away from Stephanie Monroe.

It's going to be one of those days, Stephanie decided, ending her phone call. She was still recovering from a bad plane ride, a near-death experience, jail time, and a late night. To top it off, it was bright and early Thursday morning, and Venus was already in her face. Literally.

She cast a sideways glance at Venus. The bright orange bucket hat clashed with the red hair. The zebra print bustier and sleek black rhinestone jeans would have been perfect for the red carpet of an indie movie. It was downright painful first thing in the morning.

Venus bounced up and down on the balls of her bare feet. Stephanie was surprised the cozy trailer home they were staying in didn't pitch to one side. Where did the woman get the energy?

"Was she always like this, Mrs. Gold?" Stephanie asked as she hung up the telephone.

"No," Venus's mother replied as she rinsed her hands at the kitchen sink. "She's calmed down considerably."

Scary thought. Stephanie walked back to the table and sat down. The home-cooked breakfast beckoned, but she firmly concentrated on her long to-do list that sat next to the frosty glass of orange juice.

Stephanie inhaled the scent of cinnamon and melting butter as she crossed out several items on her list. Mary Gold was nothing like she expected. She wasn't quite sure what she thought Venus's mom would be like, but definitely not this serene lady. The older woman had a calming influence, even though her hands were always busy.

Venus's late father must have handed down the spirited personality. Unless it was one of those genetic things of two laid-back people creating a hyper child. The only things Venus seemed to have inherited from her mother was the green eyes and bright red hair.

"Come on, Stephanie! Let's go to town." Venus clasped her hands together. "Please? Pretty please?"

"No way." She wasn't stepping outside the trailer unless it was to take the long ride back to the airport.

Anyway, she wasn't dressed for being seen. The simple white T-shirt was about two sizes too small. It strained against her breasts and rode up her stomach. The ruched effect around the sides and armpits was not intentional.

She had paired it with a brown aboriginal print sarong. While it brushed past her knees, it was too gauzy to wear in full sunlight. After all, it was supposed to go with Venus's swimsuit, but was practically brand new since her business partner didn't believe in the term "cover up."

"Venus, leave the poor girl alone." Mary Gold briskly toweled her hands dry. "She hasn't even eaten."

"She never eats breakfast," Venus informed her mother, never taking her eyes off of Stephanie. "She functions on pure anxiety."

"I do not." She wasn't an anxious person. She was a businesswoman with a gift for anticipation. That was a much cooler description.

"And I really, really, really"—Venus stomped her foot a la Marisa Tomei in *My Cousin Vinnie*—"want to see and hear how our little surprise went over."

Mrs. Gold paused while folding the red-checked kitchen towel. "Surprise?"

Dread twisted Stephanie's stomach. She didn't need a gift for anticipation to see trouble coming with *that* plan. "Forget it."

"Come on . . ."

"Venus," the older woman said in a tone only a mother could use effectively, "have you been up to no good?"

"It's what I do best, Mom." Venus flashed a big, toothy grin.

Her mother groaned. "I don't know what you girls have done, but I don't want to hear about it."

Venus pulled a chair from the kitchen table, whirled it around, and straddled it. "You'll know about it soon enough," she said unrepentantly.

Mary held her hands to her ears. "Then let me act genuinely surprised when I hear the gossip." She headed out of the kitchen.

"Fine," Venus replied with a touch of exasperation. She waited until her mother left the room before confiding to Stephanie, "It's for everyone's good. Mom is the worst actress."

"Why do you want to go into town?" Stephanie asked, resting her elbows on the table. "The criminal always returns to the scene of the crime. Don't you know that? Isn't that common knowledge?"

"Which is why we should go," Venus said with absolute certainty before filching a piece of toast from Stephanie's plate. "They'll know that we know. They'll expect us to stay away, so we have to go and make an appearance."

"Oh, that makes perfect sense." Stephanie's tone dripped with sarcasm. "And they would never suspect you in the first place, of course. I'm sure half of the town owns purple feather boas."

Venus wagged her eyebrows and Stephanie knew she didn't want to know what went on behind closed doors in Mayfield. "If we stay away," Venus said with her mouth full of pancake, "people might think we're feeling guilty."

"And they would be right."

Venus pouted her bottom lip. Her eyes widened and she began blinking rapidly.

"Not the puppy-dog eyes," Stephanie said. "No, don't give me the puppy-dog eyes. I mean it." She motioned at her list. "I've got too much work to do."

"I can help."

"By hopping on a plane right now?" Stephanie asked wistfully.

"No can do," Venus replied. "I have some old scores to settle before I can go."

Stephanie leaned back in her chair. "And these 'scores' involve dressing statues?"

"More or less. But I promise"—Venus drew an "X" over her heart—"we won't do anything remotely illegal if you come with me now."

The offer was tempting. Stephanie was already

getting claustrophobic, and she would have liked to step outside without worrying.

But she only had so many hours in the day. She had been up since the crack of dawn dealing with the loss of her rental car and her purse. "How about after I return my business calls?" she bargained as she rose from the table and walked back to the phone.

Venus's eyes lit up with pleasure. "It's a deal."

"But if anyone suspects a thing, I'm not bailing you out," Stephanie warned Venus, pointing a finger at her. "It'll be an I-know-nothing, I-see-nothing case. I'll be like Schultz."

"Who?" Her eyebrows dipped into a "V."

"Schultz," Stephanie repeated as she punched the numbers on the phone. "From *Hogan's Heroes*. You know, the old TV show."

Venus shook her head, her red hair shimmering in the bright sunlight. "Never saw it."

Stephanie rolled her eyes and glared at the ceiling. "I'm surrounded by the uncultured masses!"

Chapter 8

"Where did you get this outfit?" Stephanie asked over the roof of the car. "Tell me which designer gave these to you right now so I can remove him from our Rolodex."

"You don't like it?" Venus locked the car. "What's not to like?"

"The T-shirt is fine. Great, actually." Stephanie smoothed the hem of her turquoise shirt. It was form-fitting, but there were no peekaboo cuts or suggestive pictures. The neckline didn't even hint at her cleavage.

Even Venus dressed down for the promenade around town. The heels were exactly what one of their clients had worn on a magazine cover earlier this year. Her jeans were skintight, but Venus's polka-dot shirt was almost charming. The crystalline beading in the center of the shirt was a bit weird, but she wasn't going to complain.

And neither could Deputy Cockroach—no, what was his name again? Stephanie sped through her memory bank. Cochran. That was it. Deputy Cochran. She needed to think of him as that or she might slip up.

"What's wrong with your leggings?" Venus asked as she gingerly stepped onto the sidewalk.

Stephanie raised her legs and pointed at the black shiny fabric. "They're latex."

"So?"

"I'm a walking condom," she announced. Stephanie winced as an elderly gentleman walked by. She had to be more careful. In L.A., she could practically say anything and no one would notice.

"Ladies," the man greeted, tipping his fedora. Stephanie hoped he was hard of hearing.

"Morning, Mr. Schneider," Venus said with a smile. She waited until he walked out of hearing distance. "Then your outfit is perfect. Mayfield is going to freak."

"No, they're going to think that *I'm* a freak."

Venus rolled her eyes. "What are you complaining about? You look hot."

"I *am* hot. As in roasting," Stephanie clarified. "How much do you want to bet that I'm allergic?" The thought made her suddenly itch.

"You're not. I promise," Venus said, preoccupied with the inside of her shirt. She stuck her tongue to one side as she reached to the side, like she was dealing with a scratchy tag. "You know what would go great with the outfit?"

"Baby powder?"

"I was thinking more of this very cute jacket that I saw on—what?"

Stephanie's voice squeaked out of her mouth as the crystalline beads on Venus's shirt lit up. And flickered like a neon sign. The little lights were arranged into three little words: I Did It.

Stephanie closed her eyes, her bottom jaw thrusting out. "I hate you, Venus," she said in a growl.

"Aw." She tilted her head and smiled radiantly. "You're just saying that."

"No, I'm not." She should have known the deal Venus made was too good to be true. The woman wanted to get caught. She wanted people to admire her little deed.

Stephanie turned toward the car and pulled the handle. It was locked. Of course.

"I'm so fed up with you right now, Venus," she said, her voice shaking with anger. "I've had it. I want to go back to L.A."

"Then go," Venus's voice rose. "Leave. Vamoose. No one is stopping you."

Stephanie clenched her teeth. "I have no car, no money, nothing." She once swore that would never happen to her again. She had done everything to prevent it. Lots of good that did her.

"That's never stopped you before," Venus threw back at her. "Go, already."

"And I also need you in California," she reminded Venus, her hands clenched on the door handle. "I'm a makeup artist, not a stylist."

"I'm not going back. Not yet, but soon, I promise. Come on, Stephanie," she pleaded. "I haven't seen some old friends yet."

Those friends were probably the judge, the jury, and the executioner. Not to mention the entire police squad. And probably the statue's sculptor, who would take great offense at their "improvements." "I'll stay here."

"No, you're not."

"Yes, I am." She turned and leaned her back against the car. Stephanie rested her heels against the edge of the sidewalk before folding her arms across her chest.

"Stephanie, you can't. Read the sign." Venus gestured to a street sign a few feet away.

No Loitering.

"You're coming with me," Venus said, grasping Stephanie's elbow and pulling her back onto the sidewalk. "And you can meet some of my old acquaintances."

"Oh, joy." Stephanie reluctantly followed, doing her best to ignore Venus's shirt. "How long will that take?"

"Not long. Hi, Mrs. Lang," Venus called out to a woman wearing a denim dress and wide hat. Mrs. Lang looked to be around Mrs. Gold's age. "How are you this fine day?"

"Can you be any more over the top?" Stephanie muttered under her breath. She gave Mrs. Lang a polite smile, but the woman glared back, pursed her lips, and walked past them.

Stephanie silently watched her go, the woman's hips jiggling from side to side as if she couldn't get away fast enough. "Are we contagious or something?"

Venus prodded Stephanie to keep walking. "I'm not exactly popular around here."

No kidding. Stephanie wanted to make a wisecrack about it, but she heard the catch in Venus's voice. Venus could talk lightly about it, but it was a burr in her side.

"So why did you come back?" Stephanie asked.

"To show off, of course." Venus raised her chin and smiled. There was a spring in her step. "I want them to know that I'm bigger and better than their wildest dreams."

Stephanie scanned Main Street. The storekeepers and customers stared at them, but not in awe. Foreheads crinkled, eyebrows beetled, and frown lines deepened.

"Hi, Mr. Newton," Venus said to a gray-haired man and waved. The shoulder-shoulder-elbow-elbow-wrist-wrist move almost made Stephanie wonder if Venus had been a Miss Mayfield in her past.

The man didn't wave back. "They're not kowtowing," Stephanie said from the side of her mouth.

"They're running scared." Venus's chin took a defiant tilt. "And they should."

"Just for the record, when you scare a town, they become a mob. I'm not suggesting anything!" Stephanie held her hand up. "I'm just saying." She didn't understand the ins and outs of small-town living, but she knew a few things. "If you want their admiration, I think we can officially say it backfired."

The radiance in Venus's face took a harsh edge. "Their admiration means squat to me."

"I'm glad to hear it," Stephanie forced a bright tone into her voice. "And I think you've done all that you've wanted to accomplish. It's time to head back to L.A."

"Oh, I'm not finished," Venus responded, her tone flat. "Not by a long shot."

The familiar sense of dread gripped her stomach. Stephanie usually ran for cover when Venus had a plan. "What are you going to do?"

Venus's shoulders straightened. "Do what I do

best. Cause trouble." She gave Stephanie an exaggerated wink. "And you're going to help."

Stephanie shuddered at the thought. "Think again." She looked down the street and saw a corner store that seemed to specialize in selling the odd combination of milk and cigarettes. "Hey, does that place sell other stuff?"

Venus drew her attention away from a side street. "Huh? Yeah, Mr. Knox sells everything. The milk and cigarettes are the only things not overpriced."

"Can you loan me some money?" Stephanie already had her hand out. "I need to get some bottled water."

"What's wrong with the tap water around here?" Venus's voice rose with indignation.

Stephanie wasn't going to insult the pipes in her friend's home or hometown, but water wasn't supposed to have a tangy flavor. "Travelers have to be careful about their water source."

"If you're visiting a third world country," Venus added, giving Stephanie a strange look.

"Not necessarily," Stephanie argued. "Didn't you see that Hepatitis A segment on *60 Minutes*? I told you to watch it."

"Here, take this money." She slapped some crumpled bills in Stephanie's palm. "Go buy your water. I'll wait for you."

Jack saw Stephanie standing outside of Mr. Knox's store with a bulging plastic bag, glancing up at the sky as it began to rain again. He skidded to a stop when he saw her outfit. Those shiny pants were something else. Tight and sleek.

He shouldn't think about the slippery feel of her clothes. Or how Stephanie's T-shirt clung to her breasts. In fact, the only thing he should think about was turning the corner and avoiding her altogether.

She turned, as if she felt his eyes on her. Their gazes connected. Held. What was it about her brown eyes that gave him a buzz?

Well, he couldn't turn back now, Jack decided as he walked toward Stephanie. He should be neighborly. Friendly. Strong. It was his duty, he reminded himself. It had nothing to do with the energy pulsing inside him after one look from Stephanie.

"Morning, Ms. Monroe." The formal title felt weird against his tongue.

Her eyes flickered up and down his dark blue uniform. "Please call me Stephanie."

He was more than willing to do so. Addressing her as Ms. Monroe gave his dream an added dimension he didn't want to think about. "Only if you call me Jack."

"Sure." She smiled her agreement and looked around, squinting through the rain. "I can't find Venus. Have you seen her? She said she would be right here."

He looked in the direction of the downtown park, where he had been heading. "She's probably playing dress-up with another statue."

Stephanie stiffened. "What makes you think—" She took a deep breath and tried again. "What are you talking about?"

"Everyone knows that Venus did it." He wasn't sure if he could explain something that just was. "Around here people know each other so well that we can almost guess what's going to happen before it does." If only he could have the accuracy as well as the anticipation. Then he wouldn't have had to suffer through the unveiling of the statue and Mrs. Keller's wrath.

Stephanie made a face. "Oh, that's a bunch of bull." She pivoted on her heels, raindrops splattering, and started walking toward the park.

Yep, it was hard to explain it, but Jack found himself following Stephanie, ready to give it a try. Why he was going to waste his breath doing it, he couldn't say. It might have something to do with the fact that he wanted her company, and that possibility didn't sit well with him.

"It's like this," Jack said as he fell into step with Stephanie. "I can tell you right now that Freda Keller, who is married to Ronald Keller—"

Stephanie stopped abruptly. "She's married to the statue?" She bit her bottom lip. "I didn't know he was still alive."

"Oh, yeah." Jack placed his hand at the small of her back. The simple gesture was supposed to keep her walking, but it weakened his defenses. "Ronald Keller is alive and kicking and turning eighty years old this month. Unfortunately, Mrs. Keller was not happy to see her husband as a cross-dresser."

Stephanie stumbled and Jack's hand tightened against her back. "At the unveiling ceremony?" she asked with a guilty wince.

Jack nodded, trying really hard not to notice that his fingers brushed against the edge of her shirt. It was hard to concentrate on what he was saying. "The costume is gone now, but don't worry.

You'll get to see it tomorrow. The local newspaper photographer was there at the ceremony and managed to get a picture."

"Terrific." The single word was drawn out.

"Yeah, it was a memorable moment." Jack made an effort to drop his hand from Stephanie. "And Mrs. Keller isn't thrilled with Venus right now."

"What makes her think Venus did it? There's no reason to think so. For all you know, I could have done it," she suggested, thumping her chest with her hand, her plastic bag bumping against her hip.

"You could have,"—Jack looked both ways of the empty street before they crossed—"but it fits Venus's M.O."

"Now, you see?" Stephanie raised her hand in the air and slapped it against her leg. "This is what I hate about small towns. If they don't judge you by your relatives, they judge you by something you did years ago. They won't even let you be the person who you are now."

Wow, Jack thought as they crossed the street. If that wasn't describing his life . . .

Stephanie's pace quickened with anger. "It's like if your older sister has a brush with the law— one lousy brush—then whenever something is missing, one of the Monroe girls must have taken it."

"Now, Stephanie," he said in a teasing tone. "You wouldn't by any chance be from a small town, would you?"

Her lower jaw shifted to one side. "It's possible. But you don't know that." She pointed her finger at him. "Got it? No one knows that."

"It's not something to be ashamed of." Unless

she was from the next county that kept annihilating their high school football team. "Well, wait a minute. I take that back. Where are you from?"

"Nowhere in particular," she practically mumbled. "My relatives were migrant farmers." Stephanie eyes widened. "But you—"

Jack held his hands up in surrender. "Don't know that," he finished for her. What was up with her and her secrets? He didn't understand it, but he'd keep her secrets safe just the same.

"I mean it," she said, urgency thickening her voice. She looked around in case anyone was listening. "Even Venus doesn't know."

"I got it. I got it." And he wondered why she told him. Didn't anyone ask her before?

They stood at the edge of the park, which was now bustling with activity. People were staking down small white tents and wooden booths, gearing up for the festival tomorrow celebrating Keller's Jubilee.

"I don't see Venus."

"She might be on the other side." He should go down and check on the preparations at the festival. But he had plenty of time to do that. How many chances would he get to be alone with Stephanie?

"So how did you get to L.A.?" he asked as they walked along the sidewalk that bordered the park. Los Angeles was about as far as you could get from a small, rural community.

Stephanie's face lit up with pleasure and the sight made Jack's heart squeeze. "I always dreamed of going to California and working in the TV industry."

"Not the movies?"

She shook her head. "I didn't go see the movies

a lot when I was growing up. But I did watch a lot of TV. And I spent any money I had on makeup and tried to look like my favorite stars."

That explained a lot. "Do you like L.A.?" He'd never been there, and from what he'd heard about it, it was not his kind of town.

"I haven't seen as much as I would like to. I've been working a lot."

"Don't you ever get homesick for any of those small towns?"

"Not at all." Her expression made it clear that she would never miss the towns she grew up in. "I never felt any connection there. L.A. is my home. Oh!" she exclaimed as it started to rain harder.

"Come with me," Jack hunched his shoulders and grabbed her wrist before guiding her into an empty, shabby gazebo.

"Jack! This isn't the best place to run for cover during a thunderstorm," she said as she sluiced the water off her bare arms. "You know all about the crouching so you don't get electrocuted, right? I saw it on the news a while back."

He didn't know how to explain that this kind of rain only lasted about five minutes before the sun came out to make everything hot and sticky. "I promise if there's a hint of lightning, I'll drag you inside the nearest building."

"Okay, I'll hold you to that," Stephanie said, leaning against the white post. She watched some of the festival's setup committee run under their tents while others didn't let the downpour interrupt their work. "Don't you ever think about leaving Mayfield?"

"Leave Mayfield?" The question took him by

surprise. He placed his hand against the wall above Stephanie's head. "I haven't really thought about it."

"I guess you wouldn't. You were born and bred here. Probably get buried here, too."

"Probably." Everyone else in his family followed the same path. The family plot in the cemetery was getting crowded because of it.

"Have a son and name him Jack Logan Jr.," she continued, as if his life was already mapped out.

"No, he'd be the third. I'm Little Jack."

"Little Jack?" She pressed her lips together, trying to laugh. "Everyone here calls you Little Jack?"

Jack's fingers pressed into the wood. He shouldn't have said anything. "Only the ones that can get away with it."

She dipped her head to the side. Jack could have sworn he heard a muffled chuckle. He rolled his eyes. "I was an infant at the time," he explained.

She nodded. "Of course you were." She glanced down at his belt. "All babies have small parts."

Jack crooked his finger under Stephanie's jaw and tilted her chin up. The pad of his thumb rested underneath her sassy mouth.

"And it has nothing to do with that," he informed her softly. His thumb brushed against the silky bow of her bottom lip.

"Are you sure?" she asked, her eyes twinkling. "But then, I guess you can't call that part of you Little Jack. What *do* you call it?"

"Yours," he decided as he bent down to kiss her.

Chapter 9

The beat of her heart staggered, overwhelmed with anticipation. Stephanie watched in a trance as Jack advanced. The plastic bag in her hand slid to the warped wooden floor. Her eyelids fluttered shut as his mouth captured hers.

The touch pierced the haze and struck her to her core. His mouth was firm and demanding. He didn't want a taste, or even surrender. He wanted a response. He wanted her to give back as good as she got.

And didn't she want to do just that? The backs of her knees were ready to give out. Her blood slammed inside her veins. She clumsily grappled for his solid shoulders.

But this was a bad idea. The taste of him was too addictive. She hated to admit it, but they were the best damn kisses she had ever experienced. Where did these farm boys learn how to kiss this good?

An electrifying sense of power swept through her until Jack leaned into her. He surrounded and

pressed his hard body against her, making her feel
small and delicate, but his kisses made her feel
brazen and wild.

She wanted more. Would do anything for another kiss. Deeper kisses. And a lot more than kisses.
Everywhere.

Alarm scraped her befuddled senses. No. No.
Bad train of thought. She had to stop. Had to get
away. Just say no. Jack was not the gentleman he
pretended to be, but she knew he would drag himself away with that one word.

And she'd say it, but after one more kiss.

He surged his tongue into her mouth. Stephanie
greedily accepted and drew him in. She didn't
understand what was coming over her. She was
blown away by a wild hunger. She needed to de-
vour him and sate her ravenous appetite.

Jack's hands snagged her latex-covered thighs
before clutching her bottom. He roughly pulled
her against him. Violent tremors attacked her
body as she rubbed against his erection, needing
to get closer. Needing to surround him the way he
enveloped her.

She curled a shaky leg around his lean hip, but
it wasn't enough. She needed him in her. She was
desperate for his slick skin to mesh with hers.

Stephanie's fingers clawed at his shirt, her knuckles grazing at his metal badge. She burrowed her
hands inside. His heat sizzled up her arms and she
held back a shudder. Her nails scraped his hard
nipples and he hissed.

His control teetered at the edge. A purely feminine power welled inside her. Stephanie knew she
had the opportunity to take charge. She could take

him any way she wanted. Right here, right now. Right in this gazebo.

Gazebo? The word ricocheted in her mind. In public? In broad daylight? She pulled her mouth away from his. "Stop," she whispered.

Jack reared back as if he'd been struck. They stared at each other, their mouths barely touching. Jack's eyes widened as it dawned on him where they were.

"I'm sorry," he said, his voice slurred with desire. "I didn't—" He didn't finish, but disentangled himself from her, each movement thick with regret. His fingertips shook as they trailed the latex leggings.

The steamy air whispered across her hot skin. Her heart skipped a beat. She experimentally swept her tongue across her swollen, bruised lips.

Jack breathed deeply and he stepped back. His eyes didn't meet hers. "I'll see you around, Stephanie." And then he was gone, disappearing behind the curtain of rain.

Once the rain let up to a fine mist, Stephanie went searching for Venus. She found her business partner with a few women back at the car. The confessional T-shirt was still blinking. Stephanie didn't know how she missed it. Or how Venus hadn't suffered from electrocution.

And she couldn't miss how the three women had Venus cornered against the car. They weren't touching her—yet—but they were about ready to unsheath their claws.

"Venus! There you are!" She walked into the circle, acting oblivious to the malevolent atmosphere. After working with a few not-worth-the-effort divas, Stephanie had learned the art of when to act tough and when to act clueless.

"Hey, Stephanie." Venus stood a little straighter and Stephanie noticed the sparkle of relief in her eyes.

"Excuse me, thank you," Stephanie said to the tallest of the women. At the glimpse of the lacquered hair, she remembered she had seen them before. "Sorry to interrupt, but I have been looking all over for you."

"Gotta go, guys. Another time."

The women backed off with great reluctance. Stephanie flashed her smile as if it was a shield, but her cheeks were beginning to hurt.

"See you at the jubilee, Missy," Venus said with a crocodile smile to the blondest woman.

"Not if I see you first." The woman glared. Stephanie noticed she was pretty, in a trashy sort of way. Missy would fit in perfectly with those glamourous nighttime soaps she used to watch as a kid.

" 'Bye, y'all," Stephanie called out.

"Wrong dialect," Venus said from the corner of her mouth. "We are not in the South."

"Sorry." She hooked her damp hair behind her ears and watched the trio swagger down the sidewalk. "These are your friends?"

Venus pushed the button on her key chain to unlock her car. "Acquaintances."

"Is that what you call them around here? Back home, we'd call them the enemy." She got in the car. "Missy's makeup was so '80s. She needs a refresher course on eyeliner."

"Among other things." Venus didn't look at Stephanie as she sat in the driver's seat and started the car.

"What was all that about?" Stephanie asked as she put her seat belt on.

"Nothing much," she replied, being unusually tight-lipped. "Those guys used to give me such a hard time in high school."

Stephanie turned and stared at Venus. "Excuse me? We are mildewing in the Midwest because of some women who were mean to you when they were *teenagers?*"

"Partly." Venus looked in the rearview mirror and pulled out.

Stephanie refrained from reminding Venus to look in her blind spot. She knew she was a back-seat driver. And she wanted to know why these women had it in for Venus. "It's about a guy, isn't it?"

Venus grimaced. "Kind of."

The guy probably wasn't even worth it. Not then, not now. He probably didn't even know these two women were still fighting over him. "This part of your life should be gone, buried."

"You wouldn't understand." Venus stomped on the brakes at the red light and studied Stephanie.

"Can you turn on the windshield wipers?" Stephanie couldn't stand it anymore. "Please?"

"Why? It's barely raining," Venus pointed out. "What were you in high school?"

"Huh? Does it matter?" Stephanie asked as she stared at the water accumulating on the glass. She survived and got the diploma. That's all that was important.

"Around here it does. Student body president?" She gave a quick glance at Stephanie. "Nah, scratch that. Student body secretary."

Stephanie chuckled at the thought. "Not even."

"Tell me you weren't a cheerleader."

"Rest easy. I wasn't."

Venus considered the other possibilities. "The brain?"

"No, I didn't have the grades to get me into college. Or the money," she answered quietly and hesitated. "But I will one day."

Venus hit the gas as the light turned green. "You're going back to school?"

"No." She had no time to go back to school, and she didn't think she ever would. "I meant that one day I'm going to have enough money."

"Now who's the dreamer? Stephanie, you know there's no such thing as enough money."

"Sure, there is." She grabbed the dashboard as Venus took a wide turn, the wheels screeching against the slick pavement. "It's when you are never held back from getting what you want."

"I'm all for that." She glanced at Stephanie. "You're not going to tell me, are you? Is it some sort of secret?"

"About what?" Stephanie looked out the window.

"What were you in high school?" Venus repeated. The town was a blur as they sped by. "Invisible."

"Lucky you."

Jack strode into Croft's Tavern, his steps ringing against the hard floor. There were only a few patrons around this time of day, and the old-timers didn't glance in his direction, lost in their own world.

Croft met him at the bar. His friend silently filled a glass with soda and pushed it at him. Jack picked up the drink and drank a big gulp, barely registering the sweet taste. He slapped the glass onto the bar, drops spraying over the rim.

Jack stared at the cup. "I messed up." He raked his wet hair with his fingers. "I—Stephanie—"

"Okay," Croft said as he rested his elbows against the bar counter. "I'm guessing this is about you and Stephanie sucking face in the downtown park."

Every muscle froze in Jack's body. He just kissed Stephanie late this morning and the news had already hit town? "How do you—"

"Come on. This is Mayfield."

Jack placed his fists on the counter and slowly unfurled his fingers. "Who—"

Croft shook his head and started to wipe the counter with a towel. "I can't reveal my sources."

His fingers started to bunch again. He didn't feel like playing games. "Croft."

"But I will tell you who my source got it from," his friend said, never looking up from his task. "It was one of your coworkers who saw you."

It didn't take three guesses which police officer. "Cochran." Jack's lips twisted in anger. He clenched the glass in his hand and took another gulp of the sugary drink. It tasted bitter in his mouth.

"Yeah." Croft's eyes narrowed at the name. "Watch your back with that one. Sounds like the Cockroach is pissed off at you. I don't know why. All I get is something about indecent exposure and Stephanie's name." He darted a look at him for verification.

Jack kept his expression blank, his eyes focused on the glass in his hand. It was almost impossible as he remembered how hot Stephanie looked as she undressed. He would not discuss what happened to her, and he would make sure Cochran did the same. He'd deal with the deputy when his temper simmered down.

"What am I going to do?" Jack asked instead.

"There are plenty of things you could do," Croft said, his eyes lighting up. "The first thing you can do is punch Cockroach's face in."

He would like to. Really, he would. "It's not allowed."

"Some sort of police brotherhood thing?" Croft asked. "That sucks. Okay, fine. The second thing you should do is stay away from this Stephanie Monroe."

"Done," he answered tightly. After all, where was his discipline? He should have stayed away from Stephanie, like he swore he would. He knew better. She was trouble. Not to Mayfield. Only to him. Why was that?

Croft grabbed Jack's empty glass and quickly refilled it. "Second, find a nice girl. Immediately."

Jack gritted his teeth. Stephanie *was* a nice girl, but no one wanted to look past the sexy clothes or the wild friend. Of course, he wasn't one to talk since he didn't seem to notice her *until* he saw her wild image. But the townspeople took first impressions to heart. They were beginning to call her This Stephanie Monroe or That Woman.

"There are nice girls in Mayfield," his friend continued. "Take Danielle, for instance."

Here we go again. Jack closed his eyes wearily. "Knock it off, Croft."

"Danielle is going to be here with a few of her friends," the bartender confided. "One of the Gideon twins is having a bachelorette party or something."

Jack raised his eyebrow. "Why are you telling me this?"

Croft shrugged. "Just thought you should know," he replied, and whistling tunelessly, he wandered off to the other side of the bar.

Stephanie stepped into Croft's Tavern late Thursday night. She looked around and noticed that nothing had changed. The same people were there from the night before, even sitting at the same tables and booths. It was like they had frozen in time the moment she left only to come to life when she returned.

The only thing that seemed to have changed was her outfit. When she stood in front of the bathroom mirror earlier in the evening, the yellow tank dress had appeared sedate. Even boring. But now, surrounded by the faded jeans and dull T-shirts, Stephanie felt like she was an extra from *Star Trek* wandering into an old *Gunsmoke* episode.

She hurriedly followed Venus, who was hard to miss. The redhead wore a metallic dress that looked like beer caps held together by peel-off tabs. That had to be some pretty strong aluminum.

Stephanie wondered which haute couture designer created the monstrosity, wincing as the caps reflected the weak light. She couldn't tell if Venus was wearing a nude leotard underneath. Stephanie didn't want to find out one way or the other through any wardrobe malfunction.

"So let me see if I get this straight," she yelled into Venus's ear as they made their way into the darkness. "You come to the same bar? Every night?"

"Yeah."

"And you talk to the same people, do the same thing?" She paused as she looked at the band on stage. "Listen to the same songs?"

"Yep." Venus slid into a tiny booth. "Night after night."

Stephanie wanted to bang her head against the table. Instead she slid in on the other side of the booth. "What would happen if you, say, skip a night? Would the world end as we know it?"

"No, but you don't want to skip a night." She looked for the waitress. "You might miss something."

"I can't imagine what," Stephanie muttered.

"Hey, there's Jack Logan at the bar."

Stephanie felt her heart give a kick against her ribs. She did her best not to whirl around and stare. She didn't want to give Venus any ideas. She knew how that woman's mind worked, and it was a scary thing. If Venus knew Stephanie had already kissed the sheriff, she wouldn't leave Mayfield until Stephanie was celebrating her diamond anniversary with Jack.

Venus tapped her finger thoughtfully against her chin. "That's interesting."

"Hmm? What is?" She arched her eyebrows as if she could care less while her mind screamed, *What? What? Tell me now!*

"This is the most I've seen him out on the town the whole time I've been here."

Stephanie stared blankly at her friend. That's it? That was her interesting tidbit of news? "So?"

"And it's also the most I've seen him out of uniform," Venus said and turned back to look at Jack. "For a while there I was beginning to think he slept in that thing."

Stephanie finally allowed herself to turn and look at Jack. He didn't see her, and she missed feeling the heat from his gaze.

Reluctance and eagerness swirled around Stephanie's tight chest. She cautiously allowed herself to search for him. Her heart gave a funny jump when she saw Jack Logan standing by the bar just as Venus had said.

Her gaze traveled up the black linen trousers. The charcoal gray dress shirt stretched against his muscular chest. His sleeves were folded up at the elbow, revealing bronze, sinewy arms.

The pulse in her neck jumped wildly as she dragged her eyes past his solid shoulders and to his lean face. Her fingers tingled, wanting to caress his luxuriant black hair and harsh features. He looked good, Stephanie thought. Downright yummy, in fact.

Stephanie felt Venus's eyes on her. She schooled her expression and turned to her friend. "What is his uniform, or rather his lack of uniform, supposed to mean?" Stephanie asked.

"It means he's looking to get caught," Venus said in a singsong tone.

Stephanie made a face. "I'm not going to go after him."

"What?" Venus's mouth dropped open in surprise. "Why not? He's interested."

"So therefore I should go after him?" Stephanie

shook her head with distaste. "You know I don't work that way."

Venus spluttered. "But, but . . ."

"In fact, *you* are the only one interested," Stephanie lied.

"Now, wait just a second here." Venus held her hand up. "Is that the problem? Let me just say right here and now that I never have and I never will want Jack."

"No," Stephanie said with a trace of annoyance. But, come to think of it, Venus had better *not* want the sheriff. "You want me to have a thing for Jack Logan so I'll have sex on the brain and won't be focused on getting you back to L.A."

"Okay, that's true," Venus said with a smile. "You got me."

A chuckle escaped from Stephanie's lips. "You are so transparent."

Venus motioned for two beers as the waitress came around. "But I think you and Jack would make a great couple," Venus added. "That's just my opinion. Take it or leave it."

"I don't have room in my life for a guy." And if she kept saying that aloud, she might actually incorporate that in her routine and stop getting distracted.

"Oh, damn," Venus muttered as she looked in Jack's direction.

"What?" Stephanie turned and saw a petite blonde chatting up Jack. The woman wore skintight jeans and a snug T-shirt. Her hair was pulled back into a pert ponytail. Tiny diamond studs twinkled from her ears.

She had her elbows resting against the bar, her

denim-clad legs next to Jack's. The stance wasn't ladylike. It was more of a casual, one-of-the-guys attitude.

But the position required the woman to thrust out her breasts, so Jack was probably all too aware that he was talking to a woman. Stephanie narrowed her eyes, and started adding up everything from the partial highlight to her French manicure. Mmhmm. Stephanie knew it. While the blonde's image discreetly suggested that she was low-maintenance, she could tell that it was false advertising.

"What is Danielle doing sniffing around Jack?" Venus asked, her voice rising with each syllable.

"She's not sniffing." Although from Jack's body language, he was open to whatever the blonde had in mind.

"Oh, believe me. That is what Danielle does. All these guys think she's such a sweet thing. I think it has something to do with her button nose. You can't be vampy and have a button nose. It just doesn't work."

"I guess the button nose helps for the sniffing." Why wasn't Jack fending her off? And why did she care? Okay, yes, he kissed her and kissed her good. That wasn't exactly a commitment.

"But," Venus continued, her tone brighter, "like you said, you'll never have an affair."

Stephanie frowned. "I didn't say that."

"Well, it doesn't matter now."

No, it didn't. So why did she want to march over to the bar, grab Danielle by her cute button nose, and haul her far away from Jack? "One of these days I plan to have a whirlwind affair."

"Plan to?" Venus clucked her tongue. "Yeah, that

sounds like you. When is this cataclysmic event supposed to happen?"

"In three years after I launch our cosmetic line."
By then she could afford a distraction and would
be ready for a break.

"Oh, Stephanie. It's time to speed up your calendar."

"Uh-uh." Stephanie shook her head. "I set it up
very carefully. Nothing is going to get in my way."

"Yeah?" Venus looked over at the bar. "How's it
working for you now?"

Chapter 10

"I love this song!" Venus announced, hours later.

Stephanie fixed a smile on her face. "I can tell!" she called over the music booming against the walls of the tavern. She kept her smile up as her friend sashayed past, dragging a guy behind her.

Stephanie wondered why the men looked alike in Mayfield. Were they all related? Each guy had a part down the middle of his short hair. It was like they went to the same barber. They wore the same T-shirts, the same jeans, even the same shoes. She couldn't tell them apart.

Except for Jack. Stephanie closed her eyes and breathed deeply. No, she wasn't going to think about him. Or that cute little blonde who was all over him. The one Jack wasn't pushing away the last time she looked.

A crack of lightning ripped through the sky. Stephanie flinched, the beer sloshing from the bottle in her hand. Her heart banged against her chest as she glanced out of the warped windowpane.

She winced at the roll of thunder and scooted away from the window when the glass began to rattle. What the hell was with these thunderstorms? Shouldn't they be taking cover? Head for the basement or something?

Stephanie frowned as she watched the people milling about. They paused only for a second at the clash of thunder before continuing to laugh and chat as if they didn't have a care in the world. No one else seemed concerned, so she might as well relax. Although, considering whose lead she was following, Stephanie wasn't sure if that was the smartest course to take.

She gave a deep sigh and took a cautious sip from the amber bottle. Stephanie realized she was developing a palate for the swamp-sludge beer. That had to be a sign for her to head back to Los Angeles.

She shouldn't be here, anyway. Stephanie leaned back against the booth, rubbed her bare arms with her cold hands, and watched the couples dance. She had too much to do to just sit around. Unlike some people who could pursue two women in one day.

Stephanie narrowed her eyes at the thought. Nope, she wasn't going to look. She wasn't even going to think about it again. She didn't have time for him, anyway.

And if Jack slipped by her because she couldn't stop and enjoy a stolen moment or two, well . . . Regret hit her hard enough that she flinched. How much was she missing out by her single-minded focus?

Stephanie closed her eyes, not liking the answer.

She didn't want to think about that. Not right now. She chose a path and she was going to follow it.

She felt a shadow over her. Jack? Her breath caught in her chest and she looked up. She struggled not to show the disappointment when she saw that it was one of the local men at her side.

The guy wore a wrinkled T-shirt, faded jeans, and a wide smile. He looked harmless, but he hadn't been able to disguise his blatant interest in her. "Dance?" He held out his hand.

She hesitated for a second. She really didn't want to dance, but didn't have a good reason why not. "Sure."

She set down her beer bottle and took his hand. Stephanie didn't feel the trip of her heartbeat as he took her in his arms or feel a shiver of recognition when her bare skin touched his. She felt nothing.

The dance was mercifully short. When the song ended, Stephanie pulled away from her dance partner as the music turned into an upbeat, classic tune that even she recognized. The guy motioned for her to move to the rock beat, and she tried, but she couldn't find the powerful rhythm inside her.

The other dancers bumped against Stephanie as she drifted into the center of the dance floor. She was out of sync with her surroundings and once again, she felt like an outsider. No matter how much she tried, how much she pretended, she didn't belong. These past few days, the only time she felt comfortable, the only time she felt like she belonged, was when she was at Jack's side.

"Come on and dance!" The guy punched his arms wildly in the air.

Okay, whatever. Might as well. And what was she

getting all worked up about, anyway? So she kissed Jack and he didn't want to have anything to do with her. Fine. No big deal.

Stephanie jutted her chin out and took a half-hearted step forward. Her arms undulated to the beat. She exaggerated the sway of her hips, wishing she could pierce the numbness that took over her body. The pull of her muscles wasn't what she was striving for, but it was respite from the emptiness.

Stephanie pushed her body to the limit as she thought of Jack. She arched and dipped her spine. She shook and twitched her hips, matching the feverish pace of the music. Harder. Faster. Stephanie didn't notice the male attention she gained until she flipped her hair out of her face and saw the circle of cheering men surrounding her.

A flicker of black caught her eye. The color seemed shocking against the white T-shirts and faded blue jeans. She turned her head and the world drifted into slow motion.

Jack. Her arms fell to her sides and her feet missed a step when she thought she saw the familiar, proud figure. She blinked, but the apparition was gone as quickly as it appeared.

Disappointment crashed against her. She staggered from the weight of it. He wasn't going to seek her out. He probably didn't even know she was there. *Move on*, she reminded herself and moved to the music with reckless abandon.

Jack stared at the vision before him, the contradictory emotions beating against him in waves.

Danielle gave up on him earlier in the evening, and Jack was glad. He had a feeling he sabotaged the setup, and he'd have to make up for it. Once he had Stephanie Monroe out of his system.

Stephanie. It had only been a couple of hours since he'd seen her. It felt longer. He should now be controlling his life with an iron fist. Instead he was thrown into a dark whirlpool.

Unlike Stephanie. He looked around the dance floor with resentment. The noise burst and floated around him like confetti.

His gut tightened when he looked at Stephanie again. Her hair blew around her face like a flirty veil. She wasn't smiling, but the intense expression made her beauty mysterious.

But that was the only mystery she offered, Jack decided as he glared at the skimpy tank dress. His nostrils flared at the way the pale yellow couldn't conceal the outline of her tight nipples. The scrap of fabric clung to the peaks of her breasts like a second skin.

His gaze traveled down her trim, athletic body. The short skirt did something to him. The glimpses of her bare legs singed his blood. He clenched his teeth harder at each deep roll of her hips.

The circle of men moved in closer on Stephanie. She continued to dance, her sensuality exuding with every sinuous move. Either she didn't notice or care that the men drooled over her and eyed her curves.

He battled the urge to roar and violently stake his territory. That would get the town talking. Jack could do without that. He sliced through the crowd, intent on stealing her away.

When he reached Stephanie, her head was turned, the wild waves of her hair covering her profile. Jack grasped her wrist, drawing in a shallow breath at the electric touch.

"Hey, Stephanie," he said as thunder rolled above them.

He twirled her around and flushed her back to his front. His other arm wrapped possessively around her waist, her body fitting perfectly against his.

"Hey, Jack," she said in a low, husky voice. Jack noticed how she greeted him in true Mayfield form. He liked how it sounded coming from her. He liked it a lot.

Jack spun her out, keeping her hand captive. He didn't realize he was holding his breath until he saw her smile. The sight scalded his dark mood away.

She made a hesitant step toward him, jumping back as lightning ripped a jagged line through the sky. The people around them gasped as the old building shook.

Jack drew her close, the colors blurring around him like a kaleidoscope as he only had eyes for Stephanie. He was too impatient to feel her mouth on his. He needed Stephanie more than his next breath.

Jack needed to find somewhere private. Somewhere no one would bother them. "Come with me."

He pulled her through the crowded dance floor and spotted the door that was marked "Staff Only." Disregarding the sign, Jack entered with Stephanie. He guided her through the long hallway jammed with boxes until he found the exit. He shoved it open with his shoulder.

He held the door for her and helped her step down onto the slippery porch. The back door to the tavern was sheltered with a few plywood boards and a leaky roof, giving the skimpiest amount of privacy and protection they needed.

Rain speckled their clothes as he cornered Stephanie. "Kiss me," he ordered and roughly claimed her lips with his, caught in the storm that swept between them.

Stephanie's mouth clashed with his. Jack's whiskers chafed her skin as his vehement kisses attacked her lips. Her senses, numbed and hibernating, suddenly erupted to life.

Her mind clamored louder than the bellow of thunder. *Take him now. You might not get another chance.* Ferocious emotions hit and swirled around her like a cyclone.

Stephanie dragged her swollen lips away from him. She gulped the humid air, the scent of rain overwhelming her. Rain pelted her bare flesh and streamed down her hair.

She wasn't even going to look for nearby telephone lines or metal pipes that could conduct electricity. She wanted to search Jack's face as the water rolled down the stark lines and angles. The savage passion smoldering in his eyes slammed against her. Stephanie jumped as a bolt of lightning tore across the dark sky. She took an instinctive step back and her sandals slid against the slick cement.

Grasping at his shoulders, her fingers dug into his drenched shirt. Jack cupped her thighs and shoved her skirt up her trembling legs. Her hair flapped against the howling wind.

She burrowed her head against the crook of his shoulders. For protection from the storm crashing around them and for the one swarming inside her. She had craved Jack, had wanted his touch, yet she had never before felt passion. It scared her, twisting inside her chest until it clanged against her ribs.

But the heat flooding her body was too strong to ignore. With her heart thudding in her ears, Stephanie slicked her lips down his throat. She nipped and bit, scoring his skin as the fire inside her roared to an intense power that it almost pained her.

Jack shoved her tank down her shoulders and the peaks of her breasts. He arched her over his arm before bombarding her nipples with his fierce, greedy mouth. Stephanie clung to him as her senses battled the whirlwind inside her. She lost the fight and sank to her knees.

Jack followed her, his knees hitting the hard cement. Stephanie gasped as he pulled her panties down her hips. Her gasp transformed into a low, guttural moan as his fingers sought the heat between her legs.

Lightning dashed across her eyes as her muscles convulsed around him. Stephanie squeezed her eyes shut, panting for air as raindrops hit her face. The scent of wet foliage filled her nostrils as the rain ravaged her flushed skin.

He surged his finger deep inside her, stealing her breath. Stephanie's eyelids drifted down as a climax promised to fork through her. Her heartbeat faltered as the lights around them flickered before plunging them into darkness.

It took a second for her to realize the power went out. Her muscles tensed. "What—?"

"Ignore it," Jack urged her. She gasped as his fingertips moved inside her.

Her eyes were wide, her legs weak as she clung onto Jack. She couldn't see anything. No shadows, nothing. It should have spooked her, but instead she felt a secret thrill tripping along her veins. She felt safe and protected. Wild and free.

Stephanie could feel Jack's solid body against her and the heat of his skin. She inhaled his scent, now mixed with the tang of rain and wild nature. She could hear . . . his beeper.

The high electronic pitch was jarring. She heard Jack's harsh cuss over the wind. Stephanie gripped his wrist when he pulled back. Sensations rushed to her skin, desperate to burst. Sensations she hadn't experienced for a long time. A long, *long* time.

"Don't answer it," she whispered in his ear, uncaring of how desperate she sounded. She *was* desperate, damn it. She wanted the fury to break free inside her. "Don't leave me like this."

"I . . ." She sensed his shoulders sagging with disappointment. "I have to." Jack withdrew from her, each movement heavy with reluctance. "Next time," he promised and kissed her stunned, open mouth hard. "Next time will be better."

Oh, ya think? How could it possibly get much worse? Stephanie thought as Jack tugged down her skirt. Her skin ached. Her pulse pounded in her ears. Parts of her body throbbed.

Jack was going to have to make up for this big-time, she decided as he guided her to the door. She wasn't leaving town until he gave her the one-night stand that would last her forever.

The Golds' trailer shook violently as the storm raged on late into the night. The power hadn't come back on and Stephanie found herself getting ready for bed in the dark. Okay, not a bed, she admitted. Rather, a floor, thanks to a coin-toss that she suspected Venus rigged.

But she wasn't going to complain. She would sleep on the very small, very hard floor. Not to mention cramped. She had to sleep with her knees slightly bent because there was no room to stretch out. She hoped she didn't get an embolism from it.

Not that she was complaining. Much. It was better than no floor at all.

"When was the last time you had sex?" Venus suddenly asked Stephanie.

What? Stephanie whirled to face Venus, the bright beam from her flashlight spinning wildly across the dark room. *What do you know?* She suddenly felt exposed, even though she wore a stretched-out tank top and undies.

"Hey!" Venus held her hand in front of her face, warding off the blinding light. The sequins from her hot-pink nightie sparkled under the high beam. "Watch how you point that thing."

"Sorry." She angled the flashlight down. What was she worrying about? No one knew about what she did with Jack earlier tonight. And if the lights hadn't gone out, who knows what else she would have done?

That was one of the disadvantages of doing a cop. You won't get hauled in for having sex outdoors, but it didn't matter because the guy was always on call. You'd be lucky to get any sex.

Venus didn't know a thing about her rendezvous with Jack. The question was just coincidental, Stephanie decided as she cautiously tiptoed across to her sleeping bag. Venus usually did have sex on the brain.

Anyway, Venus believed her story about getting caught in the rain. Stephanie vaguely remembered saying something about making a wrong turn to the women's restroom and getting locked out back of Croft's Tavern. That she was soaking wet because she had to walk around the building to get back inside.

Stephanie didn't know if she was really good at telling a lie, or if Venus didn't have high expectations regarding her brain capacity.

"Now that I think of it," Venus said to the sound of the sofa dipping. Stephanie imagined she dug her elbow in the cushion and was propping her head up with her hand. "When was the last time you had a boyfriend?"

"I don't have time for one," Stephanie declared. Which is probably why she threw caution to the wind. Which is why her moments with Jack held more meaning than they should. "I'm married to the company. We are so close to breaking out and making it big, but—"

"Yeah, yeah, yeah." Venus interrupted the usual

spiel. "When was the last time you went out and had fun?"

"I go out all the time." And thank God for TiVo, Stephanie thought as she unrolled her sleeping bag and tossed down her pillow.

"You're missing my point." Venus's voice almost drowned out the thunder.

"What *is* your point?" She tried to open her sleeping bag, but it wouldn't cooperate. Oh, wrong end. She hated not having electricity. It made everything more difficult.

"When was the last time you went out that wasn't business-related?" Venus asked.

Stephanie shrugged at the odd question. "Why would I want to waste my time?" she asked as she flipped her bedding around.

"Ugh!" She heard Venus flop back on the bed. "You're worse than I thought."

"Venus & Stephanie is the most important thing to me," Stephanie said as she scooted into the sleeping bag, the nylon slippery against her bare legs. She seriously hoped she wasn't going to discover a creepy-crawly surprise. "Every year we get closer to hitting it big-time."

"And after every year it's harder to walk away because of the time invested."

Stephanie sat up straight, her heart pounding in her ears. "Are you saying you want to walk?"

"No way!" Venus exclaimed in surprise. "I'm just saying. Sheesh."

Stephanie breathed a little easier. "I want our company to make it so big that we are in every discount store, but our name is considered as chic as Coco Chanel. It's going to happen if we just focus."

"Focus. Right," Venus said with a snort. "Just remember that Coco had a sex life."

Stephanie punched her pillow and laid her head down. She listened to the rain pinging against the flat metal roof as she drifted to sleep with a smile. *So do I.*

Chapter 11

Stephanie slammed the phone down early Friday morning and stomped around the kitchen of the Golds' trailer in her bare feet. She exhaled sharply but she could barely let out a string of puffs, thanks to the straight-off-the-runway-model velour shorts and extra-small tube top.

She couldn't believe it. Stephanie puffed again. Tears pricked at the back of her eyes. This was not happening. She wouldn't let it happen.

Stephanie stopped in the middle of the kitchen, balled her hands into fists, and looked up at the ceiling. "Venus!" she yelled, the muscles in her neck straining.

She heard Venus moving around in the other room and she eventually shuffled into the kitchen. Venus scratched her red hair that was sticking out in all directions. Creases from the couch lined her cheek. "What is it now?" she asked and yawned.

Stephanie halted and glared at her business

partner, who was still in her hot-pink nightie. For some reason, that irked her even more.

"Do you remember," she said, each word carrying a bite, "that you were supposed to talk to Jennifer about the awards ceremony?"

Venus's eyes slowly widened. "Uh-oh."

"Yeah. Uh-oh," Stephanie mimicked. "Guess what? Her people called our office. They were furious, and they have every right to be. They are never going to use us again."

Venus leaned heavily against the table. "No way."

Stephanie started pacing the floor again. "Once word gets around about how unreliable we are, I'm sure Jennifer's friends won't, either."

"Stephanie, I'm really sorry."

"This was our big chance." She covered her face with her hands. She wasn't going to cry. Not now, and not in front of Venus. She wished she had a room to herself so she could be alone.

Why hadn't she followed up? She always kept meticulous records. This had been their biggest job. This had been why she came down here to bring Venus back.

"I'll call Jennifer," Venus offered, heading for the phone on the wall.

"It's too late."

Venus's shoulders sagged in defeat. "I'm really sorry."

Stephanie dropped her hands. "It's my fault, too." She should not have negotiated with Venus and instead yanked her back to L.A. She shouldn't have allowed herself to get distracted by Jack Logan.

"What are we going to do?"

"Well, there's no rush now, is there?" Stephanie sat down at the table. She wanted to lay her head down. "We don't have to be back until next week. Unless our other clients cancel when they hear about this."

"They won't." Venus jumped as the phone rang next to her shoulder.

"Don't be too sure."

"I'll just get this." She snatched the phone. "Hello?" she answered cautiously and gave a worried glance at Stephanie. "Uh-huh?"

Stephanie didn't think she wanted to know who was on the other end of that conversation. She was about to walk out of the room when Mary Gold came in from the back.

"Morning, everyone!" Venus's mother said with a bright, cheerful smile.

Stephanie's smile was wan and tired in comparison. As much as she liked Mrs. Gold, she wasn't all that fond of morning people. Being that happy in the morning was, in Stephanie's humble opinion, a character flaw.

"Someone called for you while you were in the shower." The older woman said as she hung up her keys by the door. "Let me go find that note. I think it was your insurance company."

Stephanie winced. She was already having a bad day. Did she really need to be reminded about her premiums skyrocketing?

"Here it is." Mary Gold tilted her head to look through her bifocals. "You need to go to the police station to fill out some more paperwork about your missing SUV."

"Thanks, Mrs. Gold. My day is now complete."

* * *

When Stephanie discovered Jack wasn't at the station, she felt her shoulders droop. She told herself that it was for the best. Although she wouldn't have minded a distraction as she endured the forms and the deputy's critical stare.

"Do you approve of the outfit, Coc—Deputy?" Stephanie quickly covered her slipup. "Does it pass your ordinance?" she asked as she returned the pen to the front desk officer she hadn't met before.

"Barely," he said in a grumble.

"Deputy Cochran!" An elderly woman's voice rang out from the entrance.

Stephanie slowly released her breath. For a moment there, she thought Cockroach was going to take out a ruler and measure her hemline. She shouldn't have said anything to the man. Her luck had already run out.

But she had thought she was safe in the outfit she chose to wear, with the hopes that she might see Jack. The neon-orange sundress was presentable, and she liked its flirty, feminine attitude.

Okay, the dress *was* iffy because it did hit her mid-thigh, but it covered all the essentials. Stephanie was quite surprised to find it among Venus's things. She suspected Mrs. Gold must have planted it.

"Did you see what Venus has done? She dressed the statue *again* last night!" the older woman continued. Stephanie's spine went rigid and she cast a quick look out of the corner of her eye.

The gray-haired woman, who had to be at least in her seventies, strode toward them with a regal air. Her companion scurried behind her just as a lady-in-waiting should. "My husband is dressed like a pimp!"

Stephanie's eyes widened as the word crossed the woman's mouth. Ah, that must be Mrs. Freda Keller. Pimp? She had to go check that out. She wondered where Venus had found the outfit—and when did she dress the statue?

"Mrs. Keller," Cockroach said, practically groveling at the woman's feet. Why doesn't he kiss her ring while he was at it? "You know how Venus is and—"

Stephanie gasped at Cockroach's ready acceptance of Venus's guilt. The two women halted at the sound and turned. Their eyebrows lifted as they studied her. Stephanie shifted under their direct gazes.

"Who are you?" Mrs. Keller asked sharply.

Okay, she'd play nice. Stephanie offered her hand. "I'm Stephanie Monroe." *Otherwise known as Venus's partner-in-crime.*

The women stared at her hand as if it was poisonous. *What? Did I say all of that out loud?* Stephanie dropped her arms when it became apparent the women weren't going to accept her polite overture.

"Fine," she muttered and walked to the exit. She didn't need this.

"I'm appalled at what women are wearing these days," Mrs. Keller stated, her voice loud and clear. "Aren't you, Martha?"

"Look, Freda," her friend said in a scandalized whisper that could be heard across the room, "that floozy isn't wearing pantyhose."

Floozy? Who uses that word anymore? Stephanie

looked over her shoulder. "I'm not wearing panties, either," she announced and walked out the door.

She paused outside. *Ohmigod.* A queasy feeling swirled in her stomach. What had she been thinking? She couldn't believe she said that.

No, she had nothing to feel guilty about. Those witches should feel guilty. Right. Like that was ever going to happen.

Stephanie stomped down the stone steps of the station, her heart racing with anger. She was surprised the light rain hadn't hissed and spat against her.

How dare they say anything about her appearance? Did they look in a mirror today? Who the hell did they think they were? Stephanie looked over her shoulder with a glare. Mr. Blackwell?

Stephanie's pace lagged when she turned the corner. She admitted that Freda Keller wasn't the reason why she was furious. Well, not the whole reason. She was mostly angry at herself.

She had liked her dress until Freda's first cold stare. Stephanie looked down at the dress, which would wake up anyone this morning. But after one disparaging comment, Stephanie found herself cringing and ready to change.

It was the damn "good girl" inside her. Keep your head down, her mom always said. Don't bring attention to yourself. Act like a lady.

Look at what being a lady had brought her. Nothing. Absolutely nothing. The good girl inside her was always worried about what people were going to think.

Stephanie slowed down and stopped in the middle of the sidewalk. She didn't want to be a lady. A lady had no power other than other people's opinion of her. She didn't want to be a good girl. What was the fun in that?

What was she thinking? Stephanie rubbed her forehead as her chaotic thoughts swirled around. She had her fun this week and she was already suffering the consequences. All that hard work and she had nothing to show for it because she didn't keep her head down.

But when was she ever going to lift her head and see all that she had accomplished. She had been working for ten years just to get to where she was. It would be another three to achieve her first major goal—that is, if she didn't suffer any setbacks.

Just once she didn't want to keep her head down. She would like to walk into a room and have everyone notice she was there. She wanted to make her mark, somewhere, somehow. Was that too much to ask?

But when was she going to get that chance? She wasn't, unless she made it for herself. What better time than now? If she couldn't make waves in Mayfield, she couldn't make them anywhere.

Stephanie looked around the quiet street, tension building up inside her. She'd do it. She would act like a wild and wicked woman. No calendar, no forecast chart, nothing. Stephanie took a deep breath to steady her nerves. With Venus at her side, she'd do just fine.

Stephanie tilted her head up and moved her shoulders back. It was time to cause a public disturbance or two. She'd have to look up what constitutes a public disturbance—or maybe not, Stephanie quickly corrected herself. She was an impulsive creature while in Mayfield. Wild women don't do research.

What do wild women do? They strut, for one thing. Stephanie loosened up her hips as she walked down the sidewalk. Okay, that might take some getting used to.

What else? They smile wide and laugh loud. They don't tuck their elbows in, they don't keep their opinions to themselves, and they always make eye contact.

They may even seduce a sheriff. Stephanie bit her lower lip as anticipation surged through her. Oh, yeah. It was time for the good girl inside her to take a vacation.

Ready or not, Mayfield. Here I come.

"Are you sure no one is going to miss us at the tavern?" Stephanie asked as she pulled on the black latex leggings. She couldn't believe she was wearing them again. Well, there were sacrifices a woman had to make to get a job done. "It might look weird if we skip a night."

"We'll go after this mission." Venus zipped her thigh-high black boots. "That way people will remember that we were there."

Stephanie stared at Venus's feet. How did the woman expect to run in those? Did she really think people dressed like Wonder Woman when they were righting the wrongs of the world?

"Did you call this a mission?" Stephanie asked. "It's a prank."

"Take it from me, pranks are not this planned out." Venus grabbed the torn-out notebook pages. "You made diagrams for it."

"Hey," Stephanie pointed at Venus. "Remember to destroy those papers. They can be very incriminating."

"Yeah, yeah, yeah." Venus folded the papers and stuffed them in her black tank top. "By the way, thanks for helping me out."

"Well," Stephanie said as she slid her feet into flip-flops, the only flat shoes Venus seemed to own. "It's not like I have anything to do since we lost the ceremony gig for Jennifer."

Venus rearranged the paper in her bra. "How many times are you going to bring that up?"

"Oh, I'm just getting started."

"Come on, Stephanie." Venus tossed her hands in the air. "There's only so many ways I can say I'm sorry."

"And there will be so many ways you will make up for it." She had already jotted down a few ideas and the list just seemed to get bigger and bigger.

"But I'm glad you're with me."

"No problem." Stephanie stood up and headed for the door. "But who is going to bail us out?"

"We aren't going to get caught." Venus clucked her tongue. "You are such a negative thinker. We need to work on that."

"No, we need to work out a contingency plan. Who do you think will bail us out?"

Venus's eyes drifted up as she considered the problem. "My mom?"

Stephanie shrugged and nodded. "Works for

me. Leave the bail money next to the phone and let's do this."

Jack stood before the main building at the Keller Brewery. The night shadows engulfed him as the rain bounced off his shoulders. He tottered on his feet, wanting to close his eyes and not wake up until morning.

It had been a long day. The power was still out in some areas, the river was higher than Old Man Schneider ever remembered, and there were worries that the levee up north of the river was going to break.

But what was he doing? Jack glared at the brewery with resentment. He was standing in a deserted parking lot at midnight with the idiot mayor, admiring how someone had mummified the building with toilet paper.

The culprits didn't have enough rolls to cover the building to the roof. Jack sensed that had not been their intention, anyway. After all, that kind of job would have required cumbersome ladders, making the getaway much more difficult.

The toilet paper was stretched tight against the corners of the first floor, concealing the windows and doors. There were layers upon layers. The pristine rows were in contrast to the streams of white toilet paper caught in the trees.

The timing was also interesting. He couldn't figure out why they would do it when no one would see it until Monday morning. Unless they had someone specific in mind.

No one would be around Friday night to disrupt the work of temporary art. And it was temporary, Jack thought as he squinted through the rain. The wrappings were going to be a disgusting mess in about an hour.

"That has Venus written all over it," Dean Vicks declared.

Huh. Jack cast a silent look at the mayor. Even an idiot could figure out who did this.

Jack didn't feel like pointing out that it had taken at least two people to do the job. It may have been Venus's idea, but the execution was pure Stephanie Monroe.

He was surprised by Stephanie's involvement. The good girl wanted to be mischievous. Jack would rather she saved up all her naughty impulses for him.

"Well," Dean's voice disrupted Jack's train of thought, "what are we going to do about her?"

"Do?" And what was this "we" business. This was the first time he'd seen Dean get out of his executive chair all month. Sure enough, the mayor moved on a situation that should be the very last priority.

"Yeah, we have to do something." Dean flicked the rain from his blond hair and sighed. "There's no talking to Venus. And her mom has always let her run wild."

"A bit of an exaggeration." There was no telling how wild Venus would have turned out had Mrs. Gold not shown the patience of a saint.

"Maybe the friend?" Dean asked, scratching his chin that didn't even show stubble this late at night. "What's her name?"

"Stephanie Monroe." The name tripped over

his tongue. He didn't know why. He'd been thinking about her all day, at the most inopportune moments.

"Yeah, that's right. She's the one who's supposed to be dragging Venus out of here." His pale blue eyes lit up with an idea. "Let's help her."

Jack's jaw shifted to one side. "What do you suggest? A police escort?"

"Only if she needs one," the other man said, the sarcasm escaping him completely. "Talk to her and find out what she needs."

"You talk to her." Jack turned and glared at Dean. He was not going to waste his time. "I'm busy."

The mayor scowled, the expression looking out of place with his boyish looks. "Do I need to remind you that Keller specifically—"

"No, you don't." Jack took a step and went toe-to-toe with the other man. "Need I remind *you* that this town is dealing with a flood, a jubilee, and everyday life?"

"Do it, Jack," Dean said as he retreated to his car. "Otherwise there'll be hell to pay."

Chapter 12

"This is never going to work," Stephanie decided early Saturday morning. "Where are we going to get a truck full of horse manure?"

Venus leaned her hip against the kitchen sink and looked out the window, her bright red terry cloth shorts hitching up her leg. "Lots of places," she answered, taking a sip from her coffee cup.

She cast a quick glance at Venus. Was she joking? From the way her friend was staring off into space, Stephanie was going to assume she wasn't. Mayfield was becoming one surprise after another.

"Okay—besides that," Stephanie continued, "the logistics are impossible." She motioned to the notes spread across the kitchen table. "There's no way we can pull a prank of this magnitude tonight."

"Do you have any better ideas?" Venus asked against the rim of the ceramic mug.

"Me? You're the one with the ideas." After seeing how Venus's mind worked, Stephanie knew she didn't want to make enemies with the woman. "How many more pranks are left in you?"

"This one will be my grand finale," Venus announced. "I'm ready to leave."

"You are?" Stephanie's head swerved so fast her neck popped. "Are we leaving tonight?"

Venus tossed the contents from her mug into the sink. "More like tomorrow night."

Stephanie looked up to the ceiling and pumped her fists into the air. "Yes!"

A slight smile appeared on Venus's mouth as she rinsed her cup. "Better get busy."

Stephanie splayed her hands in the air and looked around. "With what? My luggage is gone—along with my perfect credit rating, I might add."

"I'm talking about Jack."

Stephanie tensed as a secret thrill swept through her. For crying out loud, she had it bad if she reacted this way over his name. "What about him?"

Venus turned and faced her directly. She settled back against the sink, hooking one ankle over the other. "One more day and you'll never see the sheriff again."

Never again. She didn't like the sound of that. The relief she had just felt vanished into thin air. She couldn't wait to leave Mayfield, but she wasn't quite ready to give up Jack.

Venus folded her arms across her chest, the move straining the red sports bra she wore as a shirt. "Now's the time to take a chance."

A naughty smile danced across her mouth as she remembered the last time she had taken a chance. The pleasure nestled low in her stomach. She had

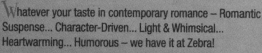

PLACE
STAMP
HERE

I||...Ill...Ill.Il.I.I.I.I.II.I.Il.Il.Il..Ill..I

Zebra Contemporary Romance Book Club
Zebra Home Subscription Service, Inc.
P.O. Box 5214
Clifton NJ 07015-5214

to move fast if she wanted to live out a fantasy or two.

The sharp knock on the door startled Stephanie out of her erotic daydreams. She looked away from Venus's watchful gaze. She felt the burn in her cheeks and willed it to fade as she listened to Mary Gold answer the door.

"Jack!" the older woman exclaimed with delight. "Girls, it's Jack Logan."

Jack! Stephanie turned sharply, her gaze locking with Venus's. The gleam in her friend's green eyes practically danced with amusement. The woman saw Jack coming and didn't warn her? Stephanie scowled. Oh, she was going to pay for that.

"Morning, Mrs. Gold," Jack said in a low, rich voice.

Stephanie's hands flew to her stomach, trying to calm the sudden flurries of butterflies.

"It's such a pleasure to see you," Mary said over the creak of the screen door. "Come in, come in."

Stephanie glanced down at the table, staring in horror at the notes and lists. She jumped from her seat, the chair legs dragging against the floor, and grabbed the carefully laid out paperwork. Venus calmly walked past, and Stephanie hoped her friend planned to block the door.

"Please sit down," Mary invited him. "Would you like some coffee?"

You're killing me here, Mary, Stephanie thought as she scooped up the pile and looked frantically for a place to hide her plans. *Don't come into the kitchen! Do not come into the kitchen!*

"No, but thanks," she heard him say and she sagged with relief. "I'm here to speak to Stephanie."

Me? Stephanie dropped the stack of papers and bolted for the doorway. Were they going to blame her for being the sole mastermind of the pranks? Stephanie hadn't considered that possibility. That would be so unfair.

She skittered to a stop at the edge of the kitchen, her gaze slamming into Jack. She gripped the doorframe tightly as wild, hot emotions fought inside her, struggling to surface.

Oh, no, I am not, she thought, staring at him as panic pushed to the forefront, squeezing her lungs. *I am not falling in love with Jack Logan. I simply refuse!*

She was just attracted to him. Yes, that was it. Okay, sure, she hadn't reacted this way to the other guys she had dated and thought she loved, but this was different. She'd never had a wild weekend.

Of course, she picked the sexiest guy in town to have a fling with. But who could blame her? She couldn't have chosen anyone else once she saw the sheriff. Everything about Jack seemed to command attention, from his luxuriant black hair to his sharp and lean bone structure. His enigmatic dark eyes made her want to unlock his secrets.

Jack's charisma and strength rippled off of him like waves, yet it was the sense of underlying steel of restraint that made him infinitely fascinating. But his discipline couldn't hide his primitive nature. Stephanie was constantly aware of his sexual aura, whether he wore casual clothes or his uniform. It was probably a good thing Stephanie had never seen him naked, or she would be completely at his mercy.

She, on the other hand, felt exposed under his mysterious gaze. Her breasts felt heavy under the tight tank top. Her bare legs tingled and she wished she hadn't worn the Daisy Duke shorts. They barely covered her bottom.

Stephanie nervously tugged at the frayed edge of her shorts when she realized everyone was watching her. Had she missed a crucial piece of the conversation? She'd thought her ears would have perked up had she been told that she was under arrest.

She took a deep breath and decided to play dumb. "Is this about my rental?" she asked. She wanted to cringe at the way her voice squeaked.

"No." He tilted his head toward the front door. "May we speak privately?"

His formality sent off warning bells in her head. "Sure," she answered cautiously. She cast a helpless glance at her friend, who responded with a silent shrug.

Big help there, Stephanie thought as she locked her jaw. *Thanks so much, Venus. Be sure to visit when they send me up the river.*

Jack held the screen door open for her and she silently walked out of the trailer. She felt the tension as she passed him. It didn't look good for her, whatever the problem could be.

The wet lawn was cold against her bare feet. Stephanie scrunched her toes as she waited for Jack. "What's up?" she asked when he stood beside her.

"Mayfield is going through a flood warning." Jack pulled his sunglasses from his front pocket. "If you want to get back to L.A., you need to do so immediately."

She exhaled slowly. She wasn't in trouble. Or

was she? Stephanie frowned, trying to make sense of it all. Was he giving her a get-out-of-jail pass, or was there something else? "What if I can't leave right now?"

"Then it might be impossible to leave when you're ready," Jack said as he put his sunglasses on.

Stephanie found herself looking at her reflection. "O . . . kay." She glanced up at the overcast sky. Something wasn't right. There was more to this offer.

She felt the need to move. She had to keep moving. She strolled toward the driveway where the police car was parked. "I have no car," she reminded him. "Nothing."

Jack followed her. "I can help you."

His flat tone made her stop walking. Oh, she got it now. He wanted her to leave. He couldn't *wait* for her to cross the city limit.

Was she the wrong kind of woman for him? He should have thought of that before. What was the problem? Too mouthy? Not enough pantyhose?

And why couldn't he just dump her, like an ordinary guy? Did he have to use his badge to bring the message home? She was so surprised, so disappointed that Jack would act like that. She thought he was different.

But apparently Jack thought the same of her. He must think she's going to cause trouble for him. Or it could simply be that he didn't think she was worth the trouble.

That was much more likely. Stephanie looked down at her feet. They looked pale and dirty against the muddy grass. She wished her toenails were painted wild cherry red. With glitter.

She wished she could stomp her foot and make a scene. Stephanie wondered where her wicked attitude was when she needed it most. The pranks and clothing didn't get her what she wanted.

"Why do you want to help me?" she asked, her throat feeling tight.

"I'm trying to get all travelers out of town." Jack braced his legs and rocked back on his heels. "Standard procedure."

"Uh-huh."

He didn't respond to her open suspicion. Jack stood still, waiting. Watching. She didn't like it.

"I can't leave without Venus," Stephanie finally said as the silence stretched between them. She motioned to the trailer home behind her. "And she won't leave knowing her mom may get flooded out of her home."

"I'll look after her mom," he promised.

She knew he would. He might be acting like a jerk right this very minute, but he had a code of honor. If he gave his word, he was bound by it.

"You know," Stephanie said as she put her hands on her hips, "I can't shake the feeling that I'm being run out of town."

Jack's flinch was slight, but Stephanie saw it. The disillusionment was so fierce, she felt like she was drowning in it.

"I thought you wanted to leave." Jack walked to the driver's side of his car and opened the door.

"I did," she called out to him. "I mean, I do."

"I'm doing what I can to help you," he explained as he got in. "You need to convince Venus to leave."

"Fine. Venus and I will leave tomorrow morning." Stephanie pivoted on her heel and walked away. "And not a minute before."

Croft's Tavern was quieter than usual when Jack stormed in minutes later. The place always looked different in the day. The sun struggled to shine through the old glass windows, dusty streams of light creating small spotlights in the large, dingy room.

He saw Croft behind the bar, stocking up. Jack made a straight line for him, the noisy game on TV masking his loud steps.

Croft glanced up. "Hey, what's your problem?" his friend asked as he tossed an empty carton onto the floor.

He tossed his glasses on the counter. "I fucked up."

Croft pressed his mouth together and looked at his friend cautiously. "Now what did you do?"

Jack shoved his hands into his hair and glared at the back wall of the bar. He could have done without seeing his reflection. "I told Stephanie that she had to leave and she had to take Venus with her."

Croft paused in the act of getting a tall glass. "What did you do that for?"

"I was doing my job." That's what he kept telling himself on the drive over here. It was the truth, so why did he feel dishonest?

"Okay," the bartender said as he scooped some ice. "Did you tell them why they had to leave?"

"Because of the flood," Jack explained.

"And what's the real reason?" Croft asked as he filled the glass with soda and handed it to Jack.

"That *is* the real reason!" It was a legitimate procedure. Why did no one believe him?

"No, seriously. Come on."

Jack paused and took a drink of his soda. He needed to tell someone. He wished he could have told Stephanie. But that didn't make any sense, did it? "I'm getting pressured," he admitted in a low voice.

Croft grabbed the remote control and turned the volume down on the television. "From who?"

Jack hesitated. He had a feeling he'd already told too much. But Croft knew when to keep quiet.

"The Kellers, by any chance?" his friend guessed.

Jack hunched his shoulders. No need to be discreet. That family was the obvious choice. "Yeah."

"Wow, Jack." Croft drew back and studied his friend. "I never thought you would cave."

Cave? Jack straightened his shoulders as his spine grew rigid. "I didn't."

"Yeah, you did."

Jack formed a fist as he reined in his temper. "You don't know what crap I'm dealing with. This stupid jubilee and this flood and now—"

"It doesn't matter what you're dealing with," Croft said as he grabbed a white towel. "The only thing that matters is *how* you deal with it."

Damn Croft for throwing back the very thing Big Jack used to say. Jack sat back and glared at his friend. Why did he come to this tavern and pour out his troubles? The soda was often flat, the advice not helpful, and he was beginning to dislike the company he kept.

Croft focused on cleaning a glass that didn't

show a smudge or speck as far as Jack could tell. "You eventually told Stephanie the truth, right?"

"Hell, no."

"Are you crazy?" Croft asked, setting down the glass.

"What would be crazy is telling her that she hit her mark. Do you think that's going to stop them? Think again! It's only going to make them more determined."

"Which is why you don't tell *Venus*. Did you say anything else to Stephanie?"

Jack squirmed under his friend's questioning. He should have handled the situation better. He could have confided in Stephanie, but he didn't. "I offered her assistance."

Croft's bottom jaw shifted to the side. "Huh."

Jack winced. "That offer sounded better when I first said it."

"Sure about that?" Croft's eyebrow lifted. "Sounds to me like you don't want her around."

Jack set his drink down with slow precision and kept his eyes on the half-empty glass. He knew better than to get defensive, so why was his temper rising? "It doesn't have anything to do with me."

"Yeah, it does. I saw you take her out back. And now you're dumping her."

"I'm not," Jack said through clenched teeth.

"Hey, don't get mad at *me*. I didn't even want you and Stephanie to hook up. Danielle was my pick, remember? I'm just pointing out that what you did—"

"God damn it!" Jack smacked his fist on the counter, looked up, and glared at the bartender. "All I'm trying to do is keep the peace."

"Start with yourself," Croft suggested. "Tell Stephanie the truth."

Jack recoiled. "No way. It makes me look worse."

"If you're just doing your job . . ."

"Okay, okay." Jack held his hands up in surrender. "I wasn't. Are you happy now? Running her out of town isn't in my job description."

He was following the unwritten rules without even noticing. He had been playing the game because it was easier than changing the rules. It was like he had been programmed. Jack didn't like what he saw. Worse, he knew Stephanie saw the same thing.

"She's leaving, anyway," Jack muttered, staring in his glass. "Tomorrow morning."

"So why are you mad?"

Jack swallowed down the rest of his drink. "Because I did cave, and I don't want her to know."

"Oh, that makes sense," Croft said dryly as he started going through another box. "You'd rather be seen as an insensitive jerk."

The choice was grim, Jack realized as he pulled out his wallet. He had to decide which image he would regret most. Either way, Stephanie wasn't going to remember him with fondness. It shouldn't matter so much, but he wanted her good opinion.

Hell, he wanted more than that, but he'd take what he could get. And he had less than twenty-four hours to make it happen. Jack let out a deep sigh and pushed away from the counter.

"Where are you going?"

Jack tossed his money onto the bar. "I have to apologize to Stephanie."

Static crackled from his radio. *"Adam Twelve, are you code seven?"*

"I'll have to do it after work." Jack hoped it wouldn't be too late. He grabbed his radio. "Twelve, en route to code thirteen, go ahead."

Chapter 13

"Whose bright idea was it to have a festival during a monsoon?" Stephanie asked with a grumble as she grabbed Venus's bright red umbrella from the cluttered glove compartment.

"It's not a monsoon, but a rain shower," Venus corrected, turning off the ignition. "And it's not a festival. It's a jubilee."

"Whatever." Stephanie stepped out of the car and straightened the handkerchief-style skirt of her black dress. "Are you sure this hemline is legal?"

"Yeah, pretty much." Venus grabbed her purse and hat before locking the car.

"You know, you've been holding out on me," Stephanie accused her. "I've been wearing latex and all this time you had this dress. Why didn't you tell me?"

"It's boring, it's black, and the designer and I had a falling-out years ago."

"Then why was it in your suitcase?" Stephanie

pointed out as they walked toward the downtown park.

"I had planned to put it on the statue."

Terrific. She thought Venus picked it out because the color would stick out among the partygoers. But no, it turned out she was wearing a dress fit for outdoor sculptures. Stephanie hoped she looked better than Ronald Keller would have. "Well, I like the dress."

"The boots make the outfit." Venus looked down at the thigh-high black shiny boots. "You look good."

"So do . . . you." Stephanie's compliment trailed off as Venus placed an oversized lampshade on her vivid red hair. The bright blue fringe that hung in her eyes matched her blue flapper dress.

Venus swiveled her head and her hips, the fringe swinging madly. "I'll be the belle of the ball," she announced, brushing the lamp's pull string from her eyes. She paused and turned sharply. "Did you just call me a dingbell?"

"Who, me? Nah." But she was definitely going to delete a certain experimental fashion designer from her database, Stephanie decided as she walked down the sidewalk. They stopped at the corner and looked at the downtown park, transformed into a glittering party.

Tiny white lights hung from the trees and along the booths and tents. Couples and young families strolled from one carnival game to the next, unconcerned by the mist of rain. Stephanie's stomach growled as the scent of fried bread and spicy barbecue wafted to where she stood.

She saw a pack of preteen girls wandering around the festival. From where she stood, Stephanie could see the streaks of blusher on their full cheeks. One girl's eye shadow was bright and glittery.

Those girls reminded her of herself at that age. She was always trying to add a hint of sophistication to her appearance. Unfortunately, she was often ordered to wash off the carefully applied makeup before she left the house.

But those hours in front of the bathroom mirror had been fun. She could add a little glitz to her otherwise boring life filled with chores and homework. She could become invisible at a new school by applying her eye shadow just like everyone else, or she could become someone totally different for her own enjoyment.

Sometimes she missed those moments of trying out something new, Stephanie realized as she watched the girls disappear behind the bratwurst stand. Those were the moments when she wasn't the least bit worried, when she didn't have a plan of attack, because she could always wash it off and try again.

"So what's the plan for tonight?" Stephanie called over the country music. She checked her casual, messy chignon with the touch of her hand, but it was useless. No super-hold hair putty or spray would withstand the rain. "I should warn you, I'm not good at winging it."

"Don't worry." Venus tilted her chin up and stepped off the curb. "I have it all under control."

"That is what's worrying me." Stephanie hurried after Venus. She was discovering that the boots were not that easy to walk in.

Venus looked over her shoulder and made a face. "Stephanie, you need to learn how to delegate."

"I need to learn the plan for tonight." She scurried to Venus's side. "What are we going to do? Shut down the electricity? Start a food fight?"

Venus patted Stephanie's shoulder. "Your duty is very simple. Keep Jack occupied for five minutes."

Her pulse skittered frantically at the idea. "I can't guarantee anything. He doesn't want to have anything to do with me."

"Yeah, he does." Venus cast a knowing look in Stephanie's direction. "I'm surprised he didn't jump you in the front yard."

"That's because he was too interested in running me out of town." She pressed her lips together in a straight line, anger flashing inside her. She was more furious about the ultimatum. When she told Venus about it, her friend acted like she had expected nothing less.

"Well, hold his interest for as long as possible." A trace of exasperation made it through Venus's voice. "Do what you can and do it now."

"Now?"

"He's coming right at you." Venus gave a dazzling smile and did her beauty-queen wave. "Hey, Jack."

Jack Logan stood in front of Venus and Stephanie. He stuffed his hands in his trouser pockets, drymouthed and nervous. The collar of his chambray shirt suddenly felt too tight.

He found it impossible to keep his eyes off of Stephanie. Probably because her upswept hairstyle annoyed him. The raindrops shone like diamonds against her dark hair, but the style was too formal, too different from when they first met. He wanted to pull the pins and watch the brown curls cascade gloriously down her neck.

The perfume had to go, too, now that he thought about it. The floral scent wasn't true to her personality. She should wear something hot and spicy with a hint of sweetness. Something that would hit him in the back of the throat and kick him in the groin before it gave him a buzz.

And the black dress . . . He'd settle for crushing the dark material in his hands until it tore under his taut fingertips. Where was the energy that had crackled from Stephanie? The wild colors that matched the attitude? The shiny boots were the only hint of that side of her personality.

Jack searched Stephanie's face, waiting for her to look at him. It was going to be a long wait. Her eyes were downcast. The carefully made-up face didn't expose a flush of anger or passion.

She looked so different from the first time they met. On that fateful night at the holding cell, Jack had felt a connection unlike any other. It was as if his soul had recognized its mate. But he also knew that this woman would be his paradise and his perdition.

Now, as he looked at her, knowing it was for the last time, he realized that Stephanie Monroe was much more. He would never look at the world the same way. Something inside him had shifted. He had changed because of her.

"Yoo-hoo." Venus's brash voice cut through his thoughts. "Earth to Jack."

"Sorry." Jack forced a smile and turned to Venus. He did a double take. "Nice hat."

Venus's smile widened. "Thank you. Oh!" She made a production of looking past him. "There's Old Man Schneider. That guy owes me money. Be right back."

Stephanie's head jerked up. She stepped forward to go with her friend, but it was too late. The crowd swallowed Venus before she could follow.

"Stephanie," Jack said in a rush before he lost the opportunity, "I'm sorry about this morning."

Her eyes widened with surprise. "You are?"

"I . . . lied to you." He rubbed the back of his neck with his hand. "I wasn't trying to get you out of town because of the river."

"Really?" The sarcasm was so heavy, her voice dropped. "You don't say?"

He felt his eyes narrow. "It's because of the citizens' complaints."

"I'm getting complaints?" She drew back, startled. "I didn't know that."

"Yeah, it tends to happen when you vandalize property and wear clothes that can cause whiplash."

"What makes you think I'm a vandal?" She looked up as the shower of rain started to fall harder.

"The point is," he said tightly as the muscle in his jaw started to twitch, "some very powerful people were insistent that I deal with the problem—and fast."

She held her palm out to test the steadiness of the rain. "When you say 'problem,' you mean me, don't you?"

"You and Venus," he clarified. "I have other priorities and I took the easy way out. I should have told those citizens that it would be handled in a timely manner. I could have discussed it with you."

He stumbled over his words as he felt someone standing next to him.

"Hey, Jack." She placed her hand on his arm.

He tensed. "Missy."

With one glance, he could tell Missy was on the prowl. The tight dress, heavier-than-usual makeup, and teased hair were signs. The fact that she didn't have her two friends around was the bigger clue.

The woman had set her sights on him earlier this year. He figured it had something to do with there not being a lot of men to choose from in their age bracket. The only guys who seemed to be left on her list were Croft and him.

"Are you going to dance with me tonight?" She leaned against his side, pressing close, and Jack wouldn't have been surprised if he found a streak of makeup on his shirt.

It was going to be tough extracting himself out of this one, but he didn't want to waste one second away from Stephanie Monroe.

"No, he's not," Stephanie replied for him, her voice firm. "He will be dancing with me. All night."

Jack didn't get a chance to comprehend those words or Stephanie's possessiveness. Missy jerked her head back and noticed Stephanie for the first time. Her lips formed into a sneer. "Aren't you Venus's friend?"

The woman's vehemence startled Jack. He gave a cautious look at Stephanie, who seemed to have taken the response in stride.

"Yes, I am." She gave a little wave. "Buh-bye."

Missy's mouth opened and closed. Her cheeks flushed angrily. She said something that Jack assumed was a "harumph," whirled around on the tips of her high heels, and stomped off.

"What was all that about?" Jack said, watching Missy's retreat. Her tight dress threatened to split with each angry step.

"Girl stuff," Stephanie replied, glaring at the back of Missy's head. He wouldn't have been surprised if the woman's blond hair combusted into flames right about now.

"There's nothing going on between Missy Keller and me," Jack felt it necessary to point out. "Never has been, never will."

"I wasn't even going to ask. Wait." Her head swerved back to Missy, then to him, and back to the blonde. "Her last name is *Keller*?"

Stephanie's heart thumped hard as the slivers of information started to connect. "Missy. Keller."

He glanced from the corner of his eye. "Yeah, that's what I said."

Keller. The name boomed into her head. Keller was the key to everything. But how did it fit?

Stephanie looked around the jubilee, trying to understand. The music blared in her ears, the scent of grease making her nauseous. She felt hot, then cold.

What did Venus have against the Kellers? It couldn't be anything like a battle between the Hatfields and the McCoys. Or could it?

Nah. Stephanie discarded the possibility. The two families were nowhere near neighbors. The Kellers lived in a mansion on top of the highest hill. The Gold trailer was down by the river.

The bad blood had to be from something else. Did Mary Gold used to work for the Kellers? Even if she had, did that have anything to do with Venus and Missy? It didn't make any sense why the younger generation would continue the fight.

She felt Jack's concerned gaze on her. Stephanie reached out and found his hand. She squeezed and held on tight. The sense of impending doom was suffocating, but she didn't know how to explain it. She didn't even know if her instinct was right, or if her mind needed a disaster to fixate on.

"What's wrong?" she heard him ask, but it was like his voice came from a long tunnel.

She was trying to remember. It must have been Thursday. She had asked Venus if the fight between Missy and her was about a guy. *Kind of.*

Kind of. It was a clue, but not much help. What did Venus talk about afterwards? Something about high school and how lucky Stephanie was to be invisible.

Guy. Invisible. Stephanie silently chanted the two words, feeling the time ticking away. *How about* guy *and* visible? She pondered that for about a second. Okay, she's got nothing.

Stephanie looked around the festival, staring at the men who were about her age. *Guy. Invisible.* The guys still looked alike, so she didn't know why she would think the answer would pop out in front of her.

The problem was, Stephanie thought as her gaze darted from one guy to the next, there were all kinds of guys in a teenage girl's life. There was the unattainable crush and then there was the guy you wished would get lost and stop following you around.

There was the boyfriend and the guy best friend who would explain how the boyfriend's psyche worked.

Guy. Invisible. There was also the annoying teenage guy neighbor and the overprotective father. The teachers, the coaches, the bosses. And then there were the brothers and his friends. The list was endless.

Visible. Guy. It didn't help matters that Venus showed no particular interest in a specific guy. She didn't ignore anyone, either.

In fact, it looked like she could care less about any man within the city of Mayfield. *Invisible. Guy.* So the guy must have moved or . . .

Stephanie gasped as the idea burst inside her. She got it! And all this time she thought it was over some stupid boyfriend. Just like Venus wanted her to think.

She felt Jack place his large hand against her spine. "Are you okay, Stephanie?"

"Who are Missy's parents? Where are they?" Her questions were rapid-fire, but she couldn't slow down. Her instincts were right-on, and she had to move fast. "They have to be at the jubilee."

"No, they died a while back." His forehead wrinkled with a frown. "There was this snowstorm—"

She puffed her cheeks out with frustration. She thought she had it. "Who raised Missy?"

He stared at her as if he was trying to catch up with her thoughts. "Her grandparents. You might have heard of them. Ronald and Freda Keller."

Stephanie smacked her palm against her forehead. "Of course! That *would* happen in a town where three generations would live on the same block."

"What's so strange about that? No, forget I asked."
He shook his head. "It doesn't matter anyway, because the Kellers all live in the same house. It's big
enough."

"That's right!" Stephanie tossed her hands up as
events started clicking together. "The brewery and
the statue."

Jack gave her a weird look.

"Don't you get it?" Stephanie grasped the front
of his shirt and pulled him closer. She bunched
the material into her fists. "The brewery and the
statue are both Keller."

"Uh-huh." He curled her against his side. "Let's
go find a place for you to sit down."

"Missy is"—she enunciated each word—"a Keller."

"That's what I said." He paused. "And I think I
said *that* twice."

"Never mind." It now made sense. Stephanie had
thought Venus's antics were random, but all this
time she was making a point. More like giving warnings. And tonight—"Oh, no!"

"What?" Jack's hold tightened. "Stephanie, what
is going on?"

"I'm not sure, but . . . quick!" She frantically
looked around the festival. "Point out Ronald Keller
to me."

Jack's eyes clouded with confusion. His mouth
opened and closed. "Okay," he finally said. "Come
with me." He grasped her elbow and escorted her
through the jubilee.

Too many people crowded the sidewalk and
Jack veered onto the wet grass. Stephanie lurched
as her heels sank into the saturated ground. She

felt like she was being tugged away and held back when she needed to run at supersonic speed.

"He's probably next to the stage," Jack said as he guided her toward the gazebo where they had once shared a stolen kiss. The small structure looked different with the lights and banners. It looked gaudy. Nothing like the clean simplicity she remembered.

"Yep," Jack said, breaking her reverie. "There he is, sitting in the gazebo. He's the guy in the middle."

She looked at the elderly gentleman Jack pointed out. *That* was Ronald Keller? The man was small and almost shrunken. The statue had exaggerated more than just his height. The man didn't have a commanding presence or vibrant aura. There was nothing significant about him.

Ronald Keller turned his head. Stephanie gasped as she stared at his profile. Her mouth sagged open in shock. That nose! She would recognize that distinctive nose anywhere. It didn't look anything like what she had seen on the statue, but it was *exactly* like Venus's.

Venus. She should be hunting for her friend. Stephanie scanned the area, looking for the lampshade. She was nowhere near the Kellers. "Where's Venus?"

"I don't know." Jack looked over the crowds. "I don't see her anywhere. Why?"

Okay, she didn't want to accuse Venus of something that might happen, but, on the other hand, Stephanie needed reinforcements to prevent trouble. "It's kind of hard to explain, but I—"

"Good evening, Mayfield!" Venus Gold's bold voice came through the crackling loudspeakers.

Stephanie glanced up at the speakers, wondering where the sound system was located. She was surprised by Venus's tactic. She had expected something brazen. In-your-face. Somewhere—

"There she is." Jack's voice was low and urgent as he nodded in front of him.

Stephanie drew her attention to where Jack indicated. *Somewhere in the spotlight.* She stared at the makeshift stage off to the side of the gazebo.

Her friend had commandeered the microphone from the lead singer and was in the middle of the stage. The lights danced along the electric blue dress. While Stephanie was relieved her friend had abandoned the party hat, she knew no one was going to care what Venus was wearing after tonight.

"This can't be good," Jack muttered. His stance was casual, but Stephanie could feel the tension emanating from his muscles.

"I'd like to take this moment and say congratulations to Ronald Keller," Venus said, strolling gracefully along the edge of the stage. She seemed to be in her element, having all eyes on her.

"Oh, no." Stephanie closed her eyes in protest. Dread hit her so hard she wanted to throw up.

"He's receiving the Humanitarian Award," Venus explained to the uneasy townspeople. "I didn't even know Mayfield had one."

"We have to stop her," Stephanie hissed. Jack nodded, grabbed her by the wrist, and they made their way to the stage. They zigzagged around the couples and families, who had stopped in their tracks.

"And what I would like to know," Venus continued, gesturing toward the gazebo with the grand sweep of her arm, "is how this man qualifies?"

Jack stumbled to a halt. "Oh, shit."

"After all," Venus's voice took on an edge, "what kind of a humanitarian would ignore his own flesh and blood?"

Stephanie felt the growing outrage of the audience. "We have to get her."

"No," Jack said. "That's going to cause more of a scene. I say we pull the plug."

"Good idea." They headed toward the side of the stage, and Stephanie hoped Jack knew where the electrical outlets were located.

"In fact," Venus continued, "what kind of Good Samaritan would intimidate a young, pregnant woman carrying his son's child?"

Stephanie reluctantly glanced at the gazebo. Ronald Keller's stony expression didn't convey much other than displeasure. The heightened color in Freda's face clearly advertised her anger. The older woman's narrowed eyes glittered with anger, and her mouth pinched into a straight, uncompromising line.

"What kind of man," Venus continued, refusing to heed the obvious signals, "what kind of *humanitarian*, I should say, won't acknowledge his granddaughter although she lives in the same town?"

Faster . . . faster . . . The words chanted inside Stephanie's head. She saw Deputy Cochran hurry behind the gazebo, heading for the stage. Stephanie could imagine Cockroach tackling Venus if given half a chance.

I'll never get there in time to stop her. Stephanie's

stomach churned as she considered the consequences.

"Now that I think about it," Venus playfully tapped her finger against her chin, "Ronald Keller might not possess the requirements to deserve this award."

Stephanie cringed at the bold comment. Her friend was going to get into so much trouble. They would be run out of town and the bon voyage party wasn't going to be pretty. Maybe they could sneak out when no one was looking.

"But I'll fix that," Venus said and gestured toward the man of honor. "Tonight I would like to publicly acknowledge Ronald Keller as my grandfather."

Stephanie and Jack made it to the side of the stage, but they were too late. She hunched her shoulders as the gasps of horror rippled through the jubilee. The shift of attention was almost tangible. Against her will, Stephanie's gaze followed. She slowly turned toward where Ronald Keller sat.

"Come on, everybody!" Venus said, clapping her hands loudly, with just a hint of sarcasm. "Let's give my grandpa a hand."

A smattering of weak, shocked applause faded into silence as Ronald Keller slowly rose from his seat. Freda stood up next to him, her chin wobbling with pride.

"Whoo-hoo!" Venus cheered into the mike. "All right, Grandma *and* Grandpa!"

Stephanie couldn't breathe as she watched the older man glare at Venus. Her breastbone ached as time seemed to stand still. It was quiet as everyone watched and waited.

It dawned on Stephanie that Venus hadn't exposed a family secret. From the look on the people's faces, it was common knowledge that Venus had Keller blood. A small-town secret, if there ever was an oxymoron.

It was also common knowledge that the topic was forbidden. That was why they gasped in shock. Venus broke the unwritten rule, and no one knew what to do. They looked at the elderly man for guidance.

Ronald Keller slowly turned his back on the stage and walked away. Just like in the past, he was going to keep silent on the subject. After all, Stephanie thought as her mouth twisted with derision, why break tradition?

"Or . . . maybe not," Venus said into the microphone as Freda followed her husband. The old cronies and their wives that had been sitting in the gazebo got up and left, one by one.

Stephanie saw a streak of blue on the stage and turned in time to see Deputy Cochran run across the stage. Venus tried to dodge the police officer, but she didn't move fast enough. "Good night, everyone!" Venus said as Cockroach tried to wrestle the microphone away. "Drive home safely!"

The citizens of Mayfield didn't respond, with the exception of a few furtive glances. The low hum of whispers grew into a loud buzz. The townspeople followed Ronald Keller's lead, left the stage area, and ignored Venus Gold.

Chapter 14

"Venus!" Stephanie grabbed her friend by the arm and hauled her away from Cockroach. She needed to get the information before Jack finished talking to his deputy. "Why didn't you tell me that this was all about the Kellers?"

Her friend sighed heavily. "You'd try to talk me out of it." She sat down on the stage, allowing her legs to dangle on the edge. Venus suddenly looked like a lost and defeated child.

"Are you kidding me?" Stephanie hurriedly sat down next to her. "Any guy who turns his back on family isn't worthy of an award. And he definitely deserves more than getting trashed with toilet paper."

"I didn't hear that," Jack said as he approached them. He sat down on the other side of Venus.

"Can you believe they were going to give him a humanitarian award?" Venus asked them in a raspy voice. She shook her head in disgust. "My mom struggled to survive and not once did he offer a hand. No, he tried to push us down. He made us suffer."

"I hope you don't take this the wrong way," Stephanie said, "but why did you guys hang around? Wouldn't it have been easier had you moved?"

"I think Mom was too naive." Venus made a face. "She believed that if the Kellers watched me grow up and got to know me, they would eventually love me."

"And what's not to love?" Stephanie wrapped her arm around Venus's hunched shoulders and gave her a tight hug. Stephanie wasn't much of a huggy-touchy-feely person, despite her years in L.A., but Venus's trampled spirits cracked through her reserve.

"After a while, I think we stayed out of defiance," Venus said, resting her head on Stephanie's shoulder. "At least, that's why I did. I headed for L.A. the day after I graduated from high school. Maybe Mom stayed because she didn't feel like starting over again. Or maybe she had nowhere else to go. I don't know."

"So how come your name is Gold?" Stephanie asked, trying to make sense of it all, and wishing she had figured it out sooner. "And why is your mom Mrs. Gold? Is that made up or something?"

"No, my mom was a teenage divorcée before she met my dad, which is one of the reasons why the Kellers didn't approve of her." Venus grabbed her lampshade party hat and held it in her lap. She fiddled with the fringe. "Missy's mom married my dad the year I was born. Missy has the family name, so she gets everything."

Stephanie couldn't imagine that everything the Kellers could offer was all that it was cracked up to be. She also couldn't imagine being ignored by your family while another—and probably undeserving—relative received all the attention and support.

"That's their loss, not yours."

Venus pulled away. "Stephanie, you're beginning to sound like my mom—and that's kind of freaking me out."

"Come on, let me take you home." Stephanie patted Venus's shoulder encouragingly.

"If it's okay with you, I want to be by myself." She took a deep breath and slowly exhaled. "And I need to tell my mom what happened without an audience."

"Gotcha." She understood perfectly. And, quite honestly, she didn't want to be anywhere near the trailer when the news hit.

"I'll drive you home, Stephanie," Jack offered.

"You know what?" Venus asked as she hopped off the stage. "Ronald Keller is still getting his award. Missy is still the favored child. Nothing I did changed a thing. Oh,"—she tapped the side of her head with her hand—"except lose my good name in L.A. and in Mayfield."

"Venus—"

"It's okay," Venus told Stephanie as she walked away. "Because for one moment, when I exposed Keller for what he was, it was worth it."

Stephanie drank the dregs of her coffee. The dark, rich brew didn't warm her up as well as Jack's body heat. She scooted closer and leaned against his arm. They silently watched the last of the jubilee crew get into their cars and pickup trucks.

"We should go, too," she said as she twirled Venus's bright red umbrella above her head. Jack was officially off the clock. And there was the small fact that the bench was beginning to feel cold and uncomfortable.

Jack reached for her empty coffee cup and pitched it into the nearby trash can. "In a minute." He sprawled his legs out, unconcerned that the steady rain sprinkled against his dark trousers.

Stephanie was just as reluctant to leave. The rain was relentless, but the air was crisp and clean. She tipped her umbrella back and lifted her face to the sky. The cool drops splattered against her warm skin.

Jack looked at his watch but didn't get up. "I guess you're going back to L.A. tomorrow."

"Yeah," she said with regret. "I have a huge mess waiting for me back at the office." Maybe that was why she didn't want to go.

"What did Venus mean that she lost her good name?" Jack asked.

"We had a big opportunity and blew it." The fact still hurt. Stephanie nestled closer to him and found a hint of the peace that she sought.

"You'll get another chance," he said with absolute confidence. "You guys make a good team."

His compliment made her feel guilty. "I wish I hadn't been so hard on her."

"I'm sure you weren't." Jack tenderly wiped a raindrop from her face. She closed her eyes, enjoying his gentle touch. "She's lucky to have you at her side."

"It goes both ways."

"But you don't give loyalty easily," Jack said as

his lips brushed her brow. "When you do, it's for life."

Wow, Stephanie thought, her last protective wall collapsing. He got it. He *got* me.

A knot of emotions formed in her throat and she cleared it away before leaning over to Jack. She brushed her lips with his. He tasted of coffee and substance. She deepened the kiss, slicking her tongue across his bottom lip.

Jack's chest rumbled with pleasure. He parted his firm lips, allowing Stephanie to dart in with her tongue. She greedily explored the mouth that had brought her so much satisfaction. She jabbed her tongue against his. As she expected, he refused to surrender.

His tongue dueled with hers. The thrusts and parries left her breathless. She pulled back and Jack reprised the sensual attack. Before she knew it, she was defending her own territory as he surged his tongue past her lips. Stephanie grasped the underside of his chin with her hand and tore her mouth away from his.

Panting for air, she looked into his face. Her heart beat a wild tattoo as lust fogged his brown eyes. She knew Jack desired her. Cared enough to protect her. But she wanted more. She wanted his love.

"What's wrong?"

No way would she tell him what was on her mind. She knew better than that. "Nothing," she whispered and kissed him again.

Her touch was softer and slower. She wanted to savor each moment because she knew this would be the last night she had with him. What they had was a wild weekend. It wasn't meant to last forever. It wasn't his fault she'd made the mistake of falling in love instead of keeping her emotions out of it.

Her fingers ran down his muscular chest. Deftly unbuttoning his shirt, Stephanie splayed her palms against his bronze, smooth skin. She burrowed her hands in his shirt, captivated by the warmth.

Jack returned her kisses, lazily working his way from one corner of her mouth to the other. He cupped his hands on her shoulders and slowly dragged down the wide neckline. She shivered as he revealed her to the night, inch by inch. The dress clung against the peaks of her breasts, ready to fall.

Stephanie ended the nibbling kisses and glanced around. Mayfield's streets were quiet. No one was outside, thanks to the constant rain. The streetlights barely cast a glow against the night. The jubilee was over and a lone car whizzed by, its tires spraying a fan of water.

She shouldn't be doing this. Stephanie licked her lips, swollen from kisses. Considering how her life was going at the moment, Cockroach would stumble across them and shine a big spotlight on her. Worse, Jack would be found out and have to deal with consequences when she left town. There were too many reasons for them to stop.

Jack pulled her dress down to her waist. Stephanie's nipples puckered from the cold air. He reverently cupped her breasts and she shuddered, arching back as he thumbed her beaded nipples.

All of the reasons to stop couldn't compare with the need shooting through her like a jagged branch of lightning. The stark need stamped on Jack's face made her want to peel the dress off and kick it aside.

"Wait," she said softly. Disappointment flitted across his eyes as she gathered the soft folds of her dress against her. Her umbrella slid down her grasp and bumped against her head. The sharp metal snagged her hair, but she ignored it as she rose from the bench.

Stephanie stood in front of Jack and gave him her umbrella. Cautious anticipation glowed from his eyes as she hiked up her dress. As her pale thighs were revealed for his eyes only, she raised her leg and curled it around his hip. She hooked her other leg and straddled him.

"Much better," she said, smiling at him. The red umbrella bumped their heads. It shielded their faces from the elements and cast a bold red hue on their skin.

Stephanie rocked her hips against him. Jack dropped the umbrella handle between them and wrapped his arms around her. His hands tangled underneath the fabric pooled at her waist. Raindrops speckled and ran down their legs.

Wickedness rolled through Stephanie like thunder. Her simple dress looked naughty crumpled around her waist. She felt bold and daring as her body was vulnerable to Jack.

She leaned against him and her sensitive breasts rasped against his shirt. Her bare bottom rubbed against his cock. The sensation was too addictive and she couldn't stop moving. She rotated her hips, hoping to find the ground to set her feet. Instead, the heels dangled inches above the sidewalk behind Jack.

Stephanie pressed kisses along Jack's jaw. His whiskers scratched against her lips. Her kisses became frantic as she slicked her tongue down his throat. She shivered and arched away as his fingertips grazed her naked back.

"Jack!" she exclaimed. He bent his head and nuzzled the valley of her breasts before latching onto the tight peak. She tensed as he laved his tongue, teasing her tight nipples even tighter until they stung.

Stephanie blindly tugged his shirt from his waistband. Her fingers bumped against the belt buckle. Jack grazed her nipple with the edge of his teeth, silently warning her to slow down.

She muffled a shriek as the bite roared through her veins. Her head lolled back as she struggled against the fiery sensations zinging through her. She felt her hair fall from its haphazard pile and swing against her cheeks and neck.

Grabbing the sides of his face, Stephanie roughly tilted his head toward her mouth. She kissed him, grinding her lips against his until their teeth bumped into each other and her lungs threatened to collapse.

She tore her mouth away and shoved her fingers into his hair. She clutched the silky strands as Jack fumbled for his belt. His hands brushed against the apex of her thighs, swollen and greedy for his touch.

The drag of his zipper sounded loud in her ears. Stephanie clutched harder at his hair, her tight knuckles scuffing against the metal bars of the umbrella. She moaned and squeezed her eyes shut as she felt his thick cock bob against her flesh.

Stephanie rose, determined to sink into him. Ready to fill the ache that invaded her. Jack's fingers tightened around her hips, his fingers bruising her skin.

"Not yet." His voice came out raspy as his hand dove in his pockets and retrieved a condom. His fingers shook as he tore the foil packet. Stephanie grabbed the condom and efficiently rolled it on his hard cock, enjoying Jack's hiss and strangled groan.

"Now?" she asked, her voice laden with impatience. She boldly met his hot gaze, allowing him to see every emotion swirling in her.

A wild gleam flashed in his deep brown eyes. "Now." He guided her onto him. She bore down, accepting his full length. Their gasps mingled as they relished the tight fit.

Jack paused, the lines on his face deepening as he tried to gain control over his body's rampant impulses. His fingertips dug into the soft curves of her bottom, not ready to steer her into a rhythm.

Stephanie exhaled a staggering sigh. He stretched and filled her. She felt him pulsing and twitching inside. His movements had a ripple effect as she felt the sensations intensify. She wiggled against him, trying to find a better position.

Jack growled in her ear. His hands held her firm so she couldn't move. "Wait."

"I can't," she confessed. Shivers traveled up her spine. She grabbed his shoulders and rocked her hips.

His fingers dug into her skin. "Stephanie—" Jack's voice was a mix of agony and awe. He leaned back to counteract the intense sensations.

Stephanie rode his cock, guided by what her body craved, and countered every move Jack made. She set a wild pace, desperate for relief. Desperate to get closer.

Her face bumped against his. Puffs of steam clung between their mouths as they gasped and groaned. The metal handle pressed against their chests as the red umbrella pitched onto their rolling shoulders.

"Stephanie—" His voice roughened with sharp desire. "I can't take much more of this."

Joy bubbled inside her and she smiled widely. "I don't want you to." She clenched the inner walls of her core, squeezing the last of his control.

Jack bucked against her. He tossed his head back and a moan ripped from his throat. The empty street echoed his release back to them. The sight of his climax spoke straight to Stephanie's soul. The moment was pure and beautiful, sending her over the edge with him.

Her spine arched as she came. She was defenseless when the white-hot energy forked through her, taking her last bit of strength with it. She slumped against Jack's shoulder and nestled her cheek against his sodden shirt.

She didn't move until her heart regained its natural beat. Her legs were slick with rain. She felt the cool breeze waft against her reddened skin. "Don't you think it's time you took me to bed?" she murmured against his neck.

Jack's chuckle rumbled against her ear. "With pleasure."

Chapter 15

Jack carried her into his shadowy bedroom, his eyes only on her. The rain hit the window in sheets. His heart thudded slowly as he slid her down the length of his body until the tip of her boots touched the floor.

He hesitated to kiss Stephanie. His fingers hovered above her slender waist. How could he say good-bye without making more promises?

He didn't know. All he knew was that he wanted each second to last an eternity. He wished this night would never end.

That wasn't possible. The only thing possible was giving Stephanie this night. Make her remember how good they were together and show how much he adored her.

His fingers caressed her back, drifting up and down in a random design. Jack fought for the self-control that steered him all these years, but for once, it was absent.

"Jack," Stephanie murmured.

He looked down at her, pressing his lips against her brown hair. He inhaled her fragrance as his mouth basked in her warmth. "Mm?"

"Kiss me."

He felt her urgency. The night was like sand in an hourglass, trickling too quickly and then they wouldn't have any time left. The desperation shimmered in the air along with the possibility that they wouldn't get that last kiss before the sun rose.

Jack tilted her face up with his bent knuckles. He lowered his head and brushed his mouth against hers. It was the first of their last kisses. Jack ruthlessly pushed the thought aside. All that mattered was saying good-bye to Stephanie the best way he knew how.

He deepened the kiss, meeting Stephanie's frenetic mouth with slow certainty. Desire thickened his blood. Her lips yielded beneath his as he surged his tongue into her mouth.

Cupping the back of her head with one hand, Jack arched her against him until they were joined at the mouth and hip. She was soft surrender against his hard aggression. When he finally tore his mouth from hers, Stephanie clung to him, fighting for her next breath.

Jack stared at her flushed face, fascinated by her beauty that became more glorious each time he looked at her. He kissed her eyebrows and brushed his lips over her closed eyelids before sloping down her cheeks. He slicked his mouth down her throat, reveling in her gasp as he nipped at her pulse point.

His pulse rapped a wild beat as he undressed her. Jack bent down and pressed his mouth against her moon-kissed skin. She tasted of heat and sweetness. The floral fragrance wasn't right for her, but he knew after tonight, he would always associate it with Stephanie.

He felt her stomach tighten under his mouth as her fingernails dug in his shoulders. He pushed the crushed dress down and made a slow, sensuous journey with the curl of his tongue and the edge of his teeth.

She grabbed for the buttons of his shirt. Jack placed his hands over hers and pulled her away. "Don't rush me," he ordered huskily as he nibbled his way along her collarbone.

He felt her swallow awkwardly. "But it's way past midnight."

"Trust me," Jack's mouth eclipsed the peak of her breast. Stephanie mewled in response, her body taut as she arched under him. Her fingers dove into his hair and pressed him closer.

Jack swallowed as his pulse roared in his ears. Okay, so maybe he wasn't as in control as he pretended to be. He wanted to touch her forever but he needed her *now*. He was going to have to compromise.

He latched onto her other breast as she clutched his hair. The tang of rain from her heated skin was a call to the wild.

He splayed his hand against the soft swells of her hips, and discovered that her gentle curves against his cock were a savage comfort. Jack captured her mouth with his and kissed her ferociously. Stephanie matched his ardor until he felt his knees buckle.

He rushed her to the low bed and they fell against the mattress. Jack nestled between her legs that dangled from the edge of the bed. She still wore her sleek thigh-high boots that seemed decadent against the sheets. The cotton bedding slithered underneath them, surrounding their bodies in a pool of ivory.

Jack slowly caressed her as his body tightened painfully. She reached for him, but he held her hands above her head. This night was about her.

He touched her with his hands and mouth, discovering the crevices and clefts that made her shriek or cry. Jack reached between her legs and found her clit. He caressed her until she went wild, bucking toward him, thrashing her head from side to side. "Jack!"

Stephanie's startled whisper nearly undid him. Jack reveled in the knowledge that he made her this wild. Only he could bring out the primitive side in her.

He kissed a trail down her body, his tongue laving against her sweat-slicked skin until he reached the silky cloud of hair and tasted her. Stephanie moaned, tangling her legs around his shoulders.

Her climax was swift and all-consuming. Her body arched and dipped as his mouth claimed her. The strokes of his tongue darted shorter and faster as she pulsed underneath him.

Jack skimmed his hands over her quivering muscles as he continued to taste her. Cupping her breasts with his palms, he plucked and rubbed her beaded nipples until she writhed and begged for release. A low groan escaped her lips as another climax stole her breath away.

Stephanie collapsed against the crumpled sheets. Jack could hear her gulping for air through her raw throat. His chest heaved for oxygen, but it was nothing like the thunderous roar of his heartbeats.

Jack reluctantly pulled back. He wanted to give her more pleasure until he was blinded by the sweeping stars of her orgasms. As one of her legs slipped off of his shoulder, he felt her exhaustion. Jack ignored the pain of his need and placed soothing kisses against her legs that quaked from the aftershocks.

He lowered his head against her stomach and felt her womb twitch. Jack wondered if he had the strength to leave her embrace when the sun came up. He was afraid he didn't.

A bluish tinge bled through the night sky. Soon dawn would break and Stephanie would have to leave. The fact punched at Stephanie like a fist, the sting that resided in her heart searing through her muscles. She winced and immediately forced her eyes open. She refused to rest although exhaustion pulled at her heavy eyelids.

Time was already pulling them away. Jack's beeper went off early in the morning. It was now stowed away in a drawer of the bedside table. He had disconnected the phone right after that.

Those actions meant more than the hushed, sexy words he had been whispering in her ears all night. She felt cherished. Important. It was like she was the only thing in his world. She didn't know how to react.

Stephanie did know that she couldn't waste a second of his undivided attention. Every moment counted. She watched Jack, rubbing the tip of her thumb against his firm mouth. She noted his grave expression as he captured a rope of her hair and wrapped it around his finger.

Stephanie burrowed into his embrace, shivering as his shirt scratched her sensitive nipples. She felt decadent and wicked lying naked next to a fully clothed man, but she didn't like having his body hidden from her. She needed his skin pressed against her skin, his heat curling around her, making her feel protected and cherished.

She rose to her knees and straddled his powerful thighs. Her boots were long gone, thrown in a corner of the room. Stephanie silently tugged at his sleeves. Jack unraveled his hand from her hair and took off his shirt in one fluid movement.

Stephanie stared at his bronze chest dusted with whorls of dark hair. She felt like she knew his body intimately. Knew how his muscles rippled under his skin, and how they bunched when she grazed her nails across his flat, brown nipples.

And this was the last chance she had with him. One night, one weekend was not nearly enough, Stephanie thought as a ray from the sun punctured the darkness. Time was racing across the sky and all she could do was stare at Jack and wish for more.

Stephanie nuzzled her head into his neck and inhaled his scent that drove her wild. Her mind was frozen. Her needs were growing. The tips of her breasts grew heavy and the sensations floated deep in her pelvis. She bumped her head against Jack's cheek and pressed quick kisses along his jaw and lips.

This time Jack didn't try to slow her down. His

silent agreement that they didn't have much time
spurred her on. She pushed him into the jumbled
pile of pillows and cupped his face with her hands
before she devoured him with a surprising fierce-
ness.

His jaw, covered with whiskers, rasped against
her cheek as his trousers scratched her soft, swollen
flesh.

Stephanie's hand trembled as she pressed her
palm over his heart. The steady beat rippled into
her pulse. As the sunrays flared past the horizon,
Stephanie looked into his dark eyes. "I love you,
Jack," she whispered before she kissed him hard.

Jack greedily kissed her back. He grasped the
sheets strewn on the bed and pulled them against
her waist, pressing her infinitely closer to him.

She pressed her lips against his throat and chest
as the light boldly drenched the sky. Stephanie
paused and looked into Jack's eyes. The night was
over. Their time was up.

Without hesitation, Jack suddenly flipped the
sheets over them.

Yes, Stephanie thought wildly, her fingers spear-
ing across his flat stomach. Ignore the sunrise. Act
like it doesn't exist.

She pushed his trousers down his legs and he
kicked them into the tangle of sheets. They held
each other chest to breast, hip to hip. Her heart-
felt moan reverberated in their hiding place. Jack
rolled her over onto her back, the wrinkled sheets
a billowing cocoon that collapsed on top of them.

Her hungry kisses flitted hurriedly across his skin.
She whispered urgent, incoherent fragments as she
clutched onto his shoulders and back, unwilling,

unable to let go. He parted her legs and she opened for him willingly, even though she knew it was a signal for the end.

Jack slid into her. She gripped him, clinging to the irresistible sensation that she was now complete. She wanted to hold on forever.

With every move, Jack created a coil of delicious tension. It threatened and teased her toward an intense release. Stephanie craved the bursting shower of stars as much as she needed time to stand still.

Jack paused and looked deep into her eyes. Her breath hitched in her chest as she couldn't move under his mesmerizing gaze. Stephanie let out a sob as her climax hit. The sheets fell away, exposing her to the harsh sun as sparks of liquid heat exploded underneath her skin and rushed through her body.

Jack's release set off another intense firestorm through her. He groaned with agony and pleasure before collapsing on his forearms that bracketed her face. He tenderly gathered her in his arms and held her close. Jack whispered tender words until she was unable to hold her eyes open any longer.

Stephanie discovered it was impossible to tiptoe while wearing thigh-high boots. After a prolonged good-bye kiss in Jack's car, she snuck into the Golds' trailer and thought she could make it into the living room without disrupting anyone's sleep.

She jumped as the lights went on. Venus lay on the couch, wide awake. It looked like she had struggled with her sheets and pillow and lost the battle.

"And where have you been?" Venus covered her

eyes with her hands. "Oh, my God. Now *I'm* sounding like my mother."

Stephanie winced. "Sorry. I didn't know you would be waiting up for me."

"I wasn't." She flipped her hair out of her eyes. "I just couldn't sleep. And then the phone rang before you came in."

"How'd it go with your mom?" Stephanie sat down on the couch and started removing her boots.

"It went okay." Venus scooted up into a sitting position, her sequined nightie twinkling under the tableside lamp. "Better than I expected."

"Glad to hear it." She wrestled off one of the boots.

Venus tilted her head and studied Stephanie. "You did it, didn't you?"

"Did . . . ?" She grunted as she pulled off the other boot.

"Jack."

Stephanie couldn't stop her smile. "Yeah, I did."

Venus's mouth dropped open. "No way."

"Way. It was amazing." She felt her smile grow larger. "Absolutely amazing."

"That good?" Venus sounded intrigued.

"Better than good. He made me feel . . ."

"Wild?" Venus supplied the word.

Stephanie stopped and gave Venus a quick glance. "Are you sure you haven't been with Jack?"

"I'm sure."

"I feel like I finally fit in my skin, you know? That when I wear these outfits"—she pulled at her black dress—"I'm not playing dress-up in my mom's clothes."

"Please!" She held up her hand. "Your older, cool sister's clothes."

"Anyway, I want to say thanks." Stephanie got up and set the boots in the corner of the room. "I wouldn't have had the guts to do this without your encouragement."

"So . . . no regrets?" Venus asked.

"None."

"Good." Venus seemed relieved. "Maybe you'll get another chance with Jack."

Stephanie walked to the suitcase, shaking her head. She didn't want to wish for things she couldn't have. "That's impossible."

"Why?"

"Because we're leaving today." She became aware of the heavy silence. Stephanie quickly straightened and looked at her friend with suspicion. "We are, aren't we?"

"Uh, yeah . . ." Venus scratched her head. "About that."

"No!" She quickly lowered her voice in order not to wake up Venus's mother. "No way are you backing out now. You promised!"

Venus winced. "I know I did."

Stephanie jabbed her finger in Venus's direction. "We are leaving today."

"We can't." She gnawed on her bottom lip.

"Even if I have to drag you out of here." Stephanie pointed at the door, the anger tightening each move.

"You can't."

Don't tempt me. "We had a deal. I gave you the time you needed," Stephanie reminded her.

Venus pressed her hand against her chest. "This isn't about me."

"Then what is it about?" She couldn't imagine what Venus was thinking. The woman should be sneaking out of town instead of trying to stay. "Is this about the Kellers? Your mom? Am I getting close?"

"Not even." She jabbed her thumb behind her. "It's about the bridge."

"What?" Stephanie's whirling, chaotic thoughts screeched to a stop. "What bridge?"

"The O'Leary Bridge."

Stephanie stared at her friend with incomprehension. "What's so great about this bridge?"

Venus made a face. "Not much, but—"

"Don't tell me." Stephanie rubbed her fingers against her aching head. "It's where you lost your virginity."

"Which time?" Venus asked.

"And you want to graffiti it because, oh, I don't know,"—she plucked the first idea that came to her head— "Keller's grandfather's . . . foundry took part in building it?"

"No, but it wouldn't surprise me."

Stephanie splayed her hands out to the sides with exasperation. "Then what?"

Venus hesitated. "It's covered in water."

"Keller's grandfather's foundry?"

"No, the bridge," Venus answered impatiently. "The river level has reached the O'Leary Bridge. No one can cross it safely."

"Uh-huh." Venus looked at her expectantly, but Stephanie didn't understand what was going on. "What does this have to do with us?"

"The bridge was our way out of Mayfield," Venus said, hunching her shoulders. "We're stuck here."

Chapter 16

"Stuck?" Stephanie's pulse tripped and skittered to a stop at the news. She shoved her hands in her hair. "Stuck!"

"Yeah." Venus squinted.

"We can't be!" Her fingers curled into her hair, her scalp tingling. "What do you mean, *stuck*?"

"The—"

"What kind of place is Mayfield? A one-bridge town?" Her heart pounded so fast that it hurt. Stephanie dropped her hands to her sides and started pacing. "There has to be another way out. We'll just go a different route. Even if it means doubling back."

"You can't do that. Every direction out of town is affected by the flood. All the roads and bridges are damaged, washed out, or under water."

Stephanie leaned against the wall, doing her best not to slide down and collapse. "How can that be? We're not on an island."

"When you live in a river town, you're surrounded

by connecting waterways," Venus explained. "There are bunches of streams and creeks around here."

"We can take a boat," Stephanie suggested as hope bloomed in her chest.

Venus shook her head. "No one in their right mind is going to navigate a boat through this stuff."

Stephanie dazedly rocked her head from side to side. "I can't believe this is happening to me."

"Why are you worried?" Venus grabbed her pillow and held it tight against her chest. "I'm the one everyone in town hates."

"You don't understand." Stephanie pushed off the wall and started to pace again. "Jack and I—" She stopped, not sure if she wanted to confess everything. "I mean, we . . . Well, really, I—" She stomped her foot. "Argh!"

"Okay." Venus watched her from over the corner of her pillow. "I didn't get a thing out of that."

Stephanie squeezed her eyes shut as if she could block it from her mind. No such luck. "I told Jack that I loved him," she announced in a wail.

Telling him how she felt was a very honest and pure moment. It was supposed to be the perfect ending to an affair to remember. Of course, Mother Nature had to screw everything up!

Stephanie sighed deeply and felt the heavy silence permeating the room. She looked out of the corner of her eye. Venus stared at her like she had lost her mind.

"Were you drunk?"

"No." Stephanie's shoulders dipped and she shuffled her way to the couch, each step screaming with defeat.

"Hmm." Her friend pondered the situation. "Were you doing *it* at the time?"

"I might have been," Stephanie answered carefully. She wasn't willing to give too much information on the matter.

"Then you're in the clear." Venus dismissed Stephanie's concern with a flick of her wrist. "Never believe anything said during sex. Guys follow that cardinal rule all the time."

"But I meant it." Stephanie flopped down on the couch, grimacing as a spring prodded her in the back. "And I think he knows that."

"Did he say it right back at you?"

"He didn't say a thing." And maybe that was what bothered her. She felt vulnerable. Stupid. Trust her to make what was supposed to be a carefree, wild weekend into a life-altering experience.

"Oh, that sucks." Venus mulled it over before smacking her hand against Stephanie's arm. "Why did you have to go ruin good sex with telling him something like that?"

"How did you know it was good?" she asked, rubbing the sore spot above her elbow.

"Easy." Venus wagged her eyebrows. "I can see it on your face."

Her hand stilled against her arm. "You can not."

"Can, too," Venus said in a singsong tone. "Is that what made you say it?"

"I don't know what possessed me to do such a thing." Stephanie slumped forward and put her elbows on her knees. "I felt like I would regret *not* saying it. I wanted him to know. I wanted him to understand how much he meant to me."

"But that is so unlike you. There was no"—she snapped her fingers, trying to remember—"what's the phrase you're always blathering on about?"

Stephanie scoffed at the word. "I do not blather."

"Return on investment." Venus tapped her forehead. "That's it! Why tell him you love him if you were planning to leave the next day?"

"I wasn't thinking that far." Which was so weird for her. She always had long-term, short-term, and contingency plans. At least she used to until she hit Mayfield's city limits. "I was going with my gut instinct."

"That's what I always do." Venus snuggled deeper into the lumpy couch.

"A lot of good that did us both," Stephanie pointed out. Acting on impulse was like a crazy roller-coaster ride. Fun and breathtaking while it lasted, but now she felt disoriented and sick to her stomach.

Venus tucked the pillow under her chin and stared at the wall in front of her. "At least you get to see Jack again."

"You don't get it." Stephanie rested her head on the back of the couch. "If he sees me again, it's going to be boring old Stephanie Monroe. The woman who has to-do lists coming out of her ears and worries all the time. Definitely not the wild woman who had sex with him outdoors or—" She winced, belatedly realizing she'd said too much.

Venus swerved her head. "You didn't. Where?"

"It was supposed to be my final impression." Stephanie felt the blush creeping up her neck and did her best not to make eye contact. "The one that was going to make him wake up in the middle of the night, thinking of me. The one that would—"

"Make him get hard at the sound of your name?"

Stephanie turned and glared at her friend. "I was thinking of something a little bit more romantic."

Venus puckered her lips and thought about it. "Ruin him for all other women?"

"Exactly." Stephanie settled back into the couch and stared at the ceiling. "And now it's all messed up."

"Where outdoors, exactly?"

Stephanie rolled her eyes. "I'm not telling you."

"Aw, come on," Venus pleaded. "You know that I would tell you."

"Oh, now there's an incentive to share. How about if you tell me what to do about Jack, instead?"

"Simple, my exhibitionist friend," Venus replied in an all-knowing drawl. "You hide out here with me."

"Good plan." She stared at the ceiling for a minute. "Remind me again. Why are we hiding?"

"Hello?" Venus flashed an incredulous look. "The Keller Jubilee? I made my big announcement in front of everyone. Any of this ring a bell?"

"Right." Acid scorched her stomach at the memory. The town might feel the same way and ready to forget. "That'll blow over once there's something else to talk about. The flood should be the big news today."

Venus snorted. "Think again."

She was probably right. The townspeople might want to focus on something other than the flood.

"So we'll wait here," Stephanie decided. "And we can do our office work in the kitchen."

"Fine. Let's hope the power doesn't go out again."

Stephanie closed her eyes in weak defense. Call her spoiled, but she needed her electricity. She was not made to rough it. She was not *Little House on the Prairie* material. "How long do you think it'll take before the O'Leary Bridge will be safe to cross?"

"I don't know."

"Can you give me a roundabout figure?" Stephanie asked as she gritted her back teeth. She wished she had the answers right at her fingertips. Obviously another sign of how much she was spoiled.

"Mmm . . . nope," Venus answered. "I don't think Mayfield has been flooded before."

"Really?" Stephanie sat up straight. "Never?"

"Never. We deal with tornado season every year. And there's the occasional earthquake."

"Wow, this place is paradise, isn't it?"

"And, of course, there's at least one blizzard every five years," Venus added. "But no floods. I just hope we don't lose everything."

Warning prickled at the back of Stephanie's neck. "What are you talking about?"

"There's a chance—an itsy, bitsy chance, really— that Mayfield will get wiped out."

Stephanie gasped. "What?"

"And the flood could crush our homes, sweep the ground out from under our feet, and let us rot in our watery graves."

She stared at Venus in silent horror.

"More or less," her friend added.

"Oh, my God!" Stephanie bolted from the couch,

her knees wobbly with panic. "Why didn't you tell me? How can you be calm about this?"

"It's not going to happen," Venus said with supreme confidence.

Stephanie gawked at her friend. There were times when Venus's optimism drove her insane. This definitely ranked as one of the top three moments. "Aren't we living next to one of those streams?"

"Yeah, near one." Venus made a face. "Not *on* it."

Stephanie ran to a window and looked out. She didn't see a body of water from where she stood, but she knew it was there. Waiting . . . Ready to pounce.

"We're all going to die," Stephanie announced in a strangled whisper.

"No, we're not. Look on the bright side."

"Bright side?" Stephanie's voice went up an octave and she waved her hands around. "What bright side? There are no sides to this kind of situation! It's all bad."

"But don't you see? You are finally in a natural disaster. Now you can use all that information you've been storing."

Stephanie clenched her jaw until she thought it would shatter. "Venus, do me a favor. Shut up and show me where the emergency supplies kit is kept."

"Emergency supplies kit?" she asked, as if Stephanie spoke in a foreign language.

"Okay." Stephanie shrugged and walked out of the room. "It's official. We're all going to die."

Jack stormed out of the mayor's office, the panic clawing at him. Everywhere he turned, no one could help him. No one wanted to take responsibility, Jack thought as he cast a glare at Dean's door.

What was he going to do? Everyone was asking for help. Everyone demanded answers. And he didn't know what the hell he was doing. He was in way over his head and he prayed he wasn't going to take everyone down with him.

Jack saw a flash of color from the corner of his eye. He turned, his ribs tightening when he saw Stephanie standing by the entrance. Guided by instinct and a deep-seated need, he found himself walking to her.

Stephanie shook water off the red umbrella. Rain glistened from her windswept brown hair to the bright pink raincoat dotted with glitter. He had previously seen her wear the wraparound black shirt and frayed denim skirt. Her bare legs were impossibly long and he remembered exactly how they felt wrapped around him.

Stephanie looked up as she closed the umbrella. "Jack!" She looked around as if she might have walked into the wrong building. "What are you doing here?"

The desire flickering to life in her eyes made him want to press her against the wall, cover her body with his, and claim her in the most elemental way.

"I had a meeting with the mayor." Jack kept a safe distance from her. "Why are you here?"

"I heard the library had a computer I could use." She looked around the city hall building. "Which room is it?"

"It's in the basement. I'll show you where it's at."

He grabbed her hand, and felt the spark between them from the simple touch. He wasn't going to act on it. He truly wasn't. No matter how much he wanted to. Clenching his back teeth, Jack took her to the door that would lead them to the library.

He guided her into the silent stairwell, the door slamming behind them. Stephanie tugged insistently at his hand. Jack stopped on the landing and turned around.

"What's wrong?" she asked, her eyes narrowing with concern.

"Nothing." Jack felt his nostrils flare as he reined in his emotions. He reached up and caressed her heated cheek with the brush of his knuckle. It was like a balm to his dark mood. "Everything is under control."

Her eyebrow arched up. "You can tell me."

"Like I said, everything is under control." He surrendered to the urge that had been prickling at him and delved his hand into her hair. Her heat coiled his skin and lured him deeper into the thick mass of waves.

"I know how to keep a secret," she said earnestly as she placed her palm on his chest. His heart thudded from her touch.

He dragged his hand down through the tangled hair until he cupped the base of her head. "Okay, here's the deal. I've been ordered to start evacuating Mayfield."

Her eyes widened. She stepped back against the wall. "No way."

"Just the areas that are in the most danger," he quickly assured her. He leaned into her until their foreheads touched and her softness cradled him. He pressed his hand against the wall behind her. The umbrella dangled from her loose grasp.

The tip of her tongue swiped her lush bottom lip. "How are you going to get people out of town?" she asked in a whisper. "More importantly, how can I get in on the deal?"

A smile tugged on his mouth. "You can't. These citizens aren't leaving. They're relocating within Mayfield. We want to prevent any fatalities."

"Then what's the problem?"

"A lot of the old-timers refuse to evacuate, and I can't make them," Jack explained, his gaze on her wide mouth. "They think they're safe because a flood has never taken their homes before."

"Oh," she said dazedly. "They have a point."

His mouth was a kiss away from the lips that could soothe his mind and bring his body to ecstasy. Their hot, ragged breathing mingled and suspended in the air.

"But it's more than that," Jack revealed. "I can't evacuate everyone. I don't have the resources."

"Meaning manpower?" Stephanie's eyelashes wafted closed. A swift emotion stung his eyes at the open trust and passion on her upturned face. Jack brushed a kiss on each feathery crescent moon. His stubbled jaw rasped her skin like sand against silk.

What had she asked? Manpower. No, lack of manpower. Right. Got it. "Among other things. Our designated building for evacuations can't hold everyone. What if I evacuate a group that doesn't really need evacuating and I don't have room for the ones who really need it?"

"I see what you're saying."

He longed to crush her against him until they melded into one. He wanted to shield her from danger with his body. Hold her proudly by his side and never let her drift away.

His muscles shuddered with slipping control as his mouth pressed against her high, slanted cheekbone before dipping down to her jaw. Her scent intoxicated him and recklessness surged through his blood. Stephanie nestled her cheek against his and he heard the shallow breath lodge in her throat as he kissed a trail closer to her lips.

Jack reached the corner of her mouth. His lips grazed hers. The touch tingled and he tried to remember why he shouldn't be doing this.

Stephanie turned her face away a fraction. Jack's mouth barely clung to hers. With a frustrated groan, he pressed her closer.

"Jack," she whispered fiercely as her eyes opened with alarm. "We can't do this. Not here. Not now."

That warning was like ice to his veins. His chest rose and fell as he reined in his runaway needs. With great reluctance, Jack drew away. "Sorry."

What was he doing? He couldn't be distracted. Not now. It didn't matter that her touch comforted him. Inspired him. He had to focus one hundred percent on the job.

Stephanie stepped away from the wall. "You know," she said casually as she raked her fingers through her tangled hair, "this reminds me of a documentary I saw on TV last year."

"What? Oh, you mean the flood." Stephanie seemed to watch everything from news programs to music videos. He couldn't believe it. The woman of his dreams was a TV addict.

She grasped the metal banister and slowly went down the steps with shaky legs, the only sign that she was still affected by his touch. "There were these computer geeks who could create these maps on water drainage."

"Was that the official job description?" He followed her down the stairs, wishing he could wrap his arm around her waist and hold her against him. But he didn't trust himself.

"Geeks. Geologists. Geographers. Same difference. It was something that started with a 'g'." Her voice echoed in the stairwell. "Anyway, there was this flood and these guys could pinpoint exactly which properties were the most crucial to evacuate. They were able to evacuate a few neighborhoods within a matter of hours."

He paused on the step. The fear inside him faded as his mind whirled with possibilities. "Really?"

"Yep."

"So what happened?" Jack hurried after her, each step he took echoing in the stairwell. "Any fatalities?"

Stephanie shrugged. "I'm not sure. I don't remember. I might have turned the channel in the middle."

Jack stared at her. She had turned the channel. This could be the answer to his problem and she had turned the channel. "Why are you telling me this?"

"All I'm saying is," Stephanie raised her hand in her defense, "you should call the nearest big city.

See if there's someone in their local government who's a geologist or geographer."

"Or computer geek."

"Funny." Her eyes narrowed. "See if the guy has this computer technology. If he does, then you can find out who to evacuate. That means less time and fewer resources are used."

Hope galloped through him. Jack wanted to get right on it. "And this was a true story?"

"It was a documentary. Has to be true."

"It's worth a try," he muttered to himself.

She stopped at the foot of the stairs and looked at him. "Jack, don't worry about making the wrong decision. You want to protect everyone, and in my book, that's the best guidance. I have absolute faith in you."

"Don't say that." He didn't want to fail and have her see it. He didn't want to fall short of her expectations.

"I wouldn't say it if I didn't mean it." Stephanie stopped and looked down. Jack couldn't tell if she had something more she wanted to say, or if she was trying not to say something more.

Stephanie cleared her throat. "But I do have a suggestion," she continued in a brisk, businesslike manner. "Give these townspeople something to do. A job. A committee. Something. Anything. They're already driving me crazy."

Jack nodded in agreement. "Nothing makes you feel as helpless as watching nature take over."

"If you want to get any news or message across, I say start with Mrs. Vicks." Stephanie rolled her eyes. "She treats gossiping like it's her vocation. But if you want to get some volunteers, go with Mr. Knox."

Jack tilted his head and studied Stephanie. How did she see all that from being in Mayfield for just a few days? "Sounds like you've got everyone pegged. I guess it comes from all that small-town living."

"Shh!" She pressed her fingers against his mouth and looked around in case anyone heard. The sensations he had been trying to bank roared through him from her touch.

Jack cupped his hand over hers. "Yeah, yeah. I know nothing." He brushed his lips against her palm. "I can keep a secret, too."

Stephanie grabbed the driver's door and opened it wide. The rain pounded hard against her raincoat and the interior of the car door. The gloomy weather triggered the streetlights, but it was only late afternoon. "Get out of the car, Venus."

"No way." Venus folded her arms across her chest and refused to budge. "I can wait for you here."

Stephanie reached over, unsnapped the seat belt, and removed the keys from the ignition. "I have way too much stuff to buy and I can't carry it by myself. Now, come on!" She grabbed her friend's arm and yanked hard.

Venus went flying out of the car, her feet splashing in the puddles on the road. Her white denim jeans were immediately drenched from the knee down. She squawked as the rain plastered her red hair against her skull. Stephanie slammed the door behind her and locked the car with a press of the key chain.

"I can't believe you're making me walk around

in public!" Venus complained as she hurriedly put on her hood.

"People are going to talk no matter what," Stephanie yelled over the downpour. "So you might as well get it over with. Anyway, the sooner you get it over with, the easier it will be. Trust me on this."

"Oh, yeah, you're the expert. You've given people so much to talk about." Venus hopped over a series of puddles and jumped onto the curb, her heels making tiny, almost cartoonish footprints on the pavement.

"Let's get a move on, here." Stephanie tucked her head down and made a straight line for the store. "We need to get supplies before Mr. Knox runs out."

"Stephanie, don't judge Mayfield by your own standards. No one is going to think of this stuff until it's too late."

"Don't count on it." Stephanie swung the door open and the overhead bell clanged, announcing their arrival. Stephanie looked at the front counter and saw the storekeeper busy with another customer. He glanced up.

"Hey, Mr. Knox," Stephanie said.

The older man greeted her with a smile. "Afternoon, Stephanie." He looked over her shoulder and his smile dimmed. "Venus," he said flatly.

She felt a tension sweep through the store. All the activity out front and in the aisles went still. The customer, a young woman with a toddler on her hip, turned around and stared at them. Even the kid seemed to glower at them while sucking ferociously on his pacifier.

Stephanie ignored the change in the atmosphere. She didn't look to see what Venus was doing, but she hoped it included a sweet smile and not the middle finger. She wrestled with grocery carts, each move more awkward under so many stares. Stephanie finally extracted one from the tangled nest and headed down the first aisle.

"It's like that time when the tornado touched down," Venus continued in a low voice, trailing behind Stephanie. "No one had emergency supplies, even though there had been tornado warnings all that summer."

"Please, one natural disaster at a time." Stephanie grabbed the printout list of emergency supplies she'd gotten from the library.

"You wouldn't believe how many people were driving *through* the tornado because they forgot batteries."

"You're exaggerating." She kept walking, scanning the items on the shelves.

"You wanna bet? You know those hicks you see on the TV news after a tornado? The ones that are all 'It done blowed off my roof'? That's Mayfield."

"Stop it." Stephanie clucked her tongue and turned the corner. She came to a sudden stop when she saw Cockroach blocking her way. "Hey, Deputy Cochran."

His nose twitched and he rolled his shoulders back. "Afternoon, Ms. Monroe. Ms. Gold."

Dread hit the pit of Stephanie's stomach when she realized Cockroach showed no signs of getting out of the way. Instead, he braced his legs apart and glared at Venus.

"Any news on the flood?" Stephanie asked brightly, determined to steer the conversation before the guy confronted Venus. "I'm sure you have all the latest."

"Yes, of course I do." He puffed out his chest and placed his hands on his hips. "There's talk that the Corps of Engineers will break the levee south of here."

"On purpose? Why would they do that?" Stephanie asked. That information didn't sound right, but Cockroach would be the kind of guy who took pride in knowing everything.

"That will make the floodwaters flow back into the river channel," Cockroach informed her with a touch of arrogance. He looked down his nose at her, which was quite an achievement since she was taller.

"You don't say?" Stephanie murmured.

Stephanie gave a start as the radio on Cockroach's shoulder blared into life. She couldn't decipher the garbled voice interspersed with static.

"If you will excuse me?" Cockroach tipped the brim of his hat. "Duty calls."

Stephanie bestowed a smile on him. "Of course. I understand. See you later, Deputy." She didn't relax until he was out of her sight.

"What are you doing?" Venus hissed in her ear.

"Nothing." Stephanie fought with the stubborn wheel on the cart and maneuvered it into the skinny aisle.

"You're talking to everybody and saying hey," Venus pointed out. "What's up with that?"

Stephanie shrugged off the complaint. "Just being polite."

"You initiated a conversation with Cockroach.

Complimenting him?" Venus shuddered. "That goes way beyond being polite."

"I was finding out the news." Stephanie looked down and studied her list. She wondered if Mr. Knox carried duct tape in this tiny store.

Venus reached over and placed her hand on the list. "In case you have forgotten, we're trying not to bring attention to ourselves."

Stephanie looked up at her friend. "I thought it would bring attention to ourselves if we didn't say hi."

"Okay, okay." Venus backed off. "I see what you're saying. But you don't have to be all neighborly about it."

"I'm not," Stephanie replied, wondering if that was a lie. She found herself falling into a rhythm. It was familiar and comfortable. It felt natural, and that worried her.

"Next you'll be stocking up on Mayfield's finest," Venus said, motioning at the display from Keller's brewery.

Stephanie puckered her mouth as she remembered the tart flavor. "Not a chance."

Chapter 17

"Venus?" Stephanie called out as she hurried into the Golds' trailer the next afternoon. The muggy air made her T-shirt and denim shorts cling to her skin. The rain had stopped, but the clouds were still gray. She predicted another thunderstorm on the way. Either that, or Mayfield reeked of rain. "Hey, Venus? Oh, sorry!"

She skidded to a halt when she saw her friend on the phone. Venus held up her hand, motioning for her to wait.

Notes and wadded-up paper cluttered the kitchen table. Guilt flashed through Stephanie. It was technically a workday. She should be on the phones drumming up business for Venus & Stephanie.

But the flood seemed to have skewed her priorities. Everything else could wait today as she helped out. Stephanie didn't know why she felt this way. It could be because she wanted to help Jack, but she had a sense the reason was bigger than that.

"What's up?" Venus asked as she hung up the phone.

"Do you guys have a shovel and can I borrow it? I looked around back, but I didn't see any tools."

"Shovel?" Venus looked taken aback by the question as she walked back to the table. Stephanie realized that someone who dressed as a sex kitten—and a glittery, sequined one at that—probably didn't remember what garden tools looked like, let alone where they were located.

"I thought about buying one at the hardware store," Stephanie said. "But there's always the chance that someone else might need it more."

"Why would you need a shovel? Is this part of that emergency supplies kit?"

"Actually, it is, but that's not why I'm asking." Stephanie jerked her thumb in the direction of town. "I was talking to Mrs. Lang and—"

"You were what?" Venus whirled around and gripped the edges of the table. "Being polite to that old bat?"

"Well, yeah, but guess what? It turns out there's a reason why she's so grumpy." Stephanie leaned forward and lowered her voice. "Did you know that she suffered from—"

"Time out!" Venus made a "T" with her hands. "What are you doing talking to her?"

"I saw her at the hardware store. She was getting things for her emergency supplies kit. So you see, I'm not the only one," Stephanie teased.

Venus stared at her like she was an alien from outer space. "You talked to her while you were in line?"

"Yeah." Okay, that did seem odd. Back in L.A.,

she kept to herself. She didn't see the need to talk to people in line or strike up conversations in the elevator. She did it out of self-protection, and quite possibly out of self-absorption. There was also the good chance that she would get stuck talking to a weirdo.

But here in Mayfield, the rules changed. Not only could she spot weirdos a mile away, but she could identify their quirks and work with them. Around here, she wanted to know the gossip and the news. She was willing to come out of her protective shell.

"This is so unlike you." Venus kept staring at her. "Are you coming down with something?"

"No, I'm not." Stephanie leaned against the doorway. "Anyway, that doesn't matter. Now, where do you keep your shovel?"

"You do remember that Mrs. Lang hates us, right? She's probably making up stuff about you and talking behind your back."

Stephanie shrugged. "I'm not worried."

"I don't believe you were talking to Mrs. Lang." Venus sank into her chair. "My friend—the only one who is on my side in this damn town—was gossiping with Mrs. Lang."

"Oh, grow up!" Stephanie rolled her eyes. "The gossip wasn't anything bad. It turns out that Old Man Schneider's home is too close to some stream and he's going to get flooded out. So a bunch of us—"

"Us?" Venus arched her eyebrow.

"Are going to sandbag his yard," Stephanie finished, ignoring Venus's response. "You wanna come?"

Venus snorted. "Hell, no."

"Think of it as a party," Stephanie suggested.

"And I'm the piñata."

"Everyone is going to be too busy to think about you. Come on, Venus." Stephanie pushed off the wall and walked toward her friend. "You like Old Man Schneider."

"Yeah, so what?" Venus scooped up some papers and tapped them into an organized pile. "I'm not going anywhere near those guys."

"But—"

"In case you haven't noticed," Venus interrupted, her voice sounding like a low, angry hiss, "I'm working. Which is what you should be doing."

"This is more important right now." And that was such a surprise to hear herself say that. Work had always been her top priority. Nothing would ever stand in the way of creating her own cosmetic line. She didn't know what was happening to her, but her priorities were shifting.

Venus made a face. "How can you say that? You don't even know the old man."

"It doesn't matter. He needs help and I'm giving it to him." Stephanie turned and headed out of the room. She stopped at the sound of Venus's voice.

"You know, we're living next to the same stream."

Stephanie shivered. "Don't remind me."

"Our luck might not hold," Venus continued. "If you think anyone will help us, you are so wrong."

Jack yawned widely as he drove down to check on Old Man Schneider. He couldn't remember a time when he had felt so tired. When everything was back to normal, Jack swore he would take a week off and sleep the entire time.

But at least he tackled one major problem and could breathe a little easier. Even now, his chest didn't squeeze tight. He could feel the flood and the trouble it caused rushing to the end, but it wasn't coming fast enough for his taste.

Jack turned at the entrance of Schneider's small farm. He paused when he saw cars parked at every angle on both sides of the long driveway. He found a spot to park and headed toward the house.

"Little Jack!" Old Man Schneider waved to him from the shady wraparound porch. The elderly gentleman wore a bright yellow slicker and matching hat, although he was sitting on his rocker, shielded from the insistent rain.

"Mr. Schneider," Jack greeted as he climbed up the porch steps. He didn't even rile up at the hated nickname. He was more tired than he thought. "I didn't know you were having company."

"I didn't, either, until a bunch of them showed up. Even the stranger." He pointed to the far end of his property by the stream.

"Stranger?" Jack paused, wiping the rain off of him. He looked where Schneider pointed and saw Stephanie.

Her brown hair was slicked back from the rain and her red glitter raincoat hung loosely from her slim shoulders as she accepted a sandbag from Mr. Knox. Stephanie suddenly smiled.

His breath hitched in his throat. He felt like one of those sandbags hit him in the stomach. Jack fought to remain upright as his knees felt like caving in.

He didn't know what was going on. He'd seen her smile before. Anticipated it and dreamed about it. It made him stop in his tracks, but he'd never felt like this.

"Mighty fine woman you have there, Little Jack." Old Man Schneider's voice sounded very far away.

Jack couldn't look away from Stephanie. Her jeans, with all the fancy embroidery and fake diamonds, were caked with mud. Her face was shiny from the rain and she didn't wear a scrap of makeup, but she was the most beautiful woman to him. And the most unattainable one.

"She's not my woman," Jack said hoarsely.

He felt Schneider's eyes on him. "Then you best make her yours."

Jack shook his head. "I'm a small-town boy. Stephanie Monroe is a city girl."

"Her? A city girl?" Schneider looked at Stephanie. "No, she ain't."

The old man was losing it. His floppy yellow rain hat was obviously too tight. And Jack knew better than to wish for it. But as he watched Stephanie, he noticed a few nuances he had missed.

She didn't stand out, but she was by no means invisible. He didn't know what it was that made him think she fit in. It wasn't like she was winning over the town. Far from it, if the gossip he'd heard since the jubilee was anything to go by.

He didn't like the gossip being spread about Stephanie, and he'd let it be known. On more than one occasion, the messenger had stuttered into silence at his icy glare. But Stephanie's bad reputation didn't make any difference to him. He knew the truth. Jack felt the satisfaction seeping through his bones. Stephanie Monroe had a wild streak, but only with him.

"Now that I think about it," Old Man Schneider said, his rocker slowing down, "that stranger has been working nonstop. You better bring her in from the rain."

Jack slid a sideways glance. "*I* better?"

"Yep, you better. I don't think she's going to listen to anyone else."

Old Man Schneider was a pathetic matchmaker. Jack was tempted to call him on it. Instead he found himself crossing the muddy field, intent on bringing Stephanie in from the rain.

"Stephanie!" he called out as he drew close.

"Hey, Jack." Her smile nearly undid him. "What are you doing here?"

"I came by to see if everything's okay." He nodded to the other townspeople in the assembly line.

"We're fine." She studied him and Jack wondered what she saw. The deep worry lines? The sprout of new gray hair? Yeah, he was a keeper, all right.

"In fact," Stephanie said as she raised her arms above her head and stretched before pulling off her sodden work gloves. "I'm about ready to take my break."

"Uh-huh. Okay." He had a feeling his exhaustion might have helped her make the decision. There was that gleam in her eye as if she was going to take care of him, whether he liked it or not. And, strangely enough, he was going to let her.

"By the way," he said as they trudged through the mud to Old Man Schneider's house. "I took your advice."

"What advice?" Her face suddenly lit up. "Oh, you mean about the documentary?"

Jack nodded, hunching his shoulders against the rain. "We found a GIS specialist."

Stephanie held up her hand. "You've already lost me."

"Geographic Information Systems specialist. Or so Mackey tells me. The specialist works for a government agency. He was able to produce a digital map that would show me exactly which houses and properties were in immediate danger."

Stephanie climbed the porch steps, trailing mud behind her. "So you're going to start evacuating?"

He gave a nod of acknowledgement to Old Man Schneider, who looked very smug. "Done."

She jerked her head back and looked straight in his eyes. "No kidding?"

"No kidding." He sat down on the porch swing.

"Heh." She sat down next to him, her leg pressing against his. "And my mom says all that television rotted my brain. I'll be sure to tell her about this."

Jack was comforted by her warmth and her softness. At the same time he wanted to provide his heat and protection to her. She might want to take care of him, but he wanted to take care of her, too. He could get used to that arrangement.

"If you don't need any extra help, I should be on my way." Jack didn't make a move. Sitting down was probably a mistake. He could imagine falling asleep in the next couple of seconds.

"Where to next?" She laid her head against him.

Okay, he was definitely not moving. It felt too good having Stephanie curled against him. "I'm going to head back to the station."

"The station? Oh, no," Stephanie complained. "Not yet. I don't want to take my break all by myself."

Jack looked down at Stephanie and knew he couldn't fight it anymore. He had fallen in love with the wrong kind of girl. She wasn't from Mayfield and she wasn't someone he'd known all his life. But she was perfect for him.

Jack sighed as he accepted the inevitable. He loved her, and she loved him back. As far as he was concerned, all was right with the world. Jack relaxed against Stephanie and closed his eyes.

Night had fallen and the crew of volunteers had left, tired and satisfied with a job well done. Old Man Schneider went to stay at a friend's house on higher ground, leaving Stephanie and Jack behind, sitting on his porch swing.

Stephanie looked out at the sandbag wall with a critical eye. It wasn't as strong or as large as she expected. It seemed insignificant for the task it had to accomplish.

She rested her head back on Jack's chest and he curled his arm around her shoulders. It was just the two of them suspended, floating in the air, looking out at the world. "Do you have to go back to L.A.?" Jack's soft voice pierced the silence.

Stephanie's sigh echoed in the yard. "Yes."

"I want you to visit Mayfield. As often as you can."

Stephanie nodded. Her eyes stung from the unshed tears. She'd seen this coming. She thought that since she'd said good-bye before, it should have been easier, not harder.

But she had been lying to herself. Because this time she wanted more. She wanted Jack, and she wanted him forever.

Jack's hand curled under her chin. His gentle touch sent a shudder through her. "Promise me that you'll come back as soon as possible," he requested softly.

She took a deep breath. She had to get this over with. She wasn't going to prolong the agony. "What for?" she asked, turning to him.

"For this." He cradled the back of her head with his large hands and covered her mouth with his. He surged his tongue past her lips and Stephanie immediately surrendered as the heat formed deep inside her and streaked through her limbs, leaving her clutching Jack's shoulders.

The kiss lacked sophistication and refinement. It was raw. Earthy. The rough touch was what her senses craved, but she knew she had to put a stop to it before she lost herself completely.

Stephanie pulled away, but her mouth clung to his. "I'm not coming back." She said against him, her voice husky. "This relationship isn't going to work because we want different things. We should end it now rather than let it go on."

"I want it to last." Jack held her close, the heat of his body tantalizing. "I love you, Stephanie," he said softly. "We should be together."

Stephanie blinked. "Together?" Her heart fluttered with a dream she hadn't allowed herself to wish for.

"Yes." Love and desire shone from his brown eyes. "Let's get married."

Her mouth fell open. "Married?" Wow. She hadn't been expecting that. It was impulsive, it was crazy, and she was incredibly tempted to cast aside her lists of pros and cons and say yes.

There were too many reasons why she couldn't be his wife, but she had difficulty recalling them. Stephanie's mind whirled until she felt dizzy. "Where would we live?"

"Here," Jack said matter-of-factly. "In Mayfield."

Ah. Stephanie felt like she had been tossed down onto the ground with a bump. She knew there had to be a catch. She exhaled wearily.

She knew she couldn't go back to small-town living. She wasn't going to wind up like her mom and sisters—women who allowed their environment to shape their dreams instead of the other way around.

"I can't," she said, ready to bolt from the swing. Stephanie had to get away from him before she changed her mind. She craved him like a drug and was desperate to be with him. She cherished Jack and what they had, but she would have to give up her goals and dreams if she wanted to continue having a relationship with him.

Jack captured her fingers. "You said you love me," he reminded her.

"I know I did." She couldn't deny him when he was so close. She had to be strong. For her, for him. For the both of them. It was the only way. She scooted away from him. "But that doesn't change a thing."

"Did you say those words in the heat of the moment?" He hooked his leg over hers, effectively trapping her. "Or are you changing your mind?" His demanding tone indicated that she'd awakened the angry beast inside him.

"Of course not!" She felt caged. Contained. But the fragmented memories of the past week smashed through. "It's just that . . ." The old hurt bled inside her. "I don't belong here."

"You're wrong." He bent his head and kissed her fingertips. "You belong here, with me."

"I want to be with you," she said. It was hard to think, let alone argue, when Jack's mouth was traveling down her jawline. Her skin tingled from his touch as her pulse leapt erratically. Stephanie cleared her throat, trying to remember what she had to say. "But I'm just not Mayfield material and . . . I don't want to be."

Jack slowly pulled away. He dropped her hands and removed his leg from hers as hostility clearly marked his face. "Why did you tell me that you loved me when you weren't willing to fight for it?"

"That's not true! You're asking me to give up everything I worked for." She hated the way her voice shook. "How about you drop everything and move to L.A.?"

"I can't." Jack's jaw twitched. "My life is here. I'm needed here. This is where I belong."

"And I belong in L.A."

Jack slowly rose from the swing. Disappointment deepened the lines around his mouth. "Then I guess that's that."

"Now look who's not willing to fight for us." Bitterness burned inside her. "You decided you don't belong in L.A. and you won't even visit the place."

"Like you said," Jack said as he strode off the porch and into the rain. "What for?"

"Told you so."

Stephanie ignored Venus's muttering. "Less complaining and more bagging." She grabbed a burlap bag of sand and stacked it onto a shallow wall.

There was no way they could get the wall done in time, Stephanie realized. They would have to work faster. She reached up and wiped the hair from her eyes. Her work gloves were wet and stained reddish brown from the sand.

Stephanie didn't think she had enough strength to get through the rest of the day. Their electricity had gone out early in the morning. The stream had risen enough that it would reach the Golds' property by tomorrow. The only good thing about the day was that the rain had stopped.

"This is so unfair!" Venus stabbed her shovel into the mud. "All this work you put into sandbagging other people's homes and when it's our time, does anyone come rushing to help? No!"

"I didn't sandbag their homes to gain points," Stephanie quietly pointed out. "I did it because they needed help."

"Selfish, greedy bastards."

Stephanie wouldn't go that far. The townspeople helped their own, except for those who broke the rules. It was the law of the land, following the way they survived generations ago.

In other words, the citizens of Mayfield were backward and unfair hicks. Not that she was bitter or anything, Stephanie thought with a self-deprecating grin. Even if she wanted to waste her energy by changing their ways, she couldn't do it overnight.

But, if she was going to be completely truthful with herself, she would admit that it hurt a lot that no one came to their assistance. For a couple of days Stephanie felt like she was a part of something bigger than her very narrow life. Today was a rude wake-up call.

Stephanie put her hands on her back and arched her spine. She cringed as she heard something crack. Forget her decision to hire a personal trainer. What she needed to find was a good massage therapist.

"How much do you want to bet that the Kellers had the entire town helping them out?" Venus grumbled as she fiercely shoved sand into an empty burlap bag.

"Their mansion is on the highest hill," Stephanie reminded her. "The water won't reach them."

"But if they wanted help, they would get it," Venus decided, her voice growing louder. "No questions asked. And did you see any member of that family volunteering? Nope, I don't think so!"

"I haven't seen them since your little announcement," Stephanie grunted as she hoisted another bag.

"That's because the rain would melt them."

"I don't understand what's going on," Mary Gold said, pushing the wheelbarrow of sand. "I thought breaking the levee south of us would take care of the water level."

"Who knows when it's supposed to take effect?" Venus said. "I guess it takes time moving thousands of gallons of water."

They fell into a weary silence as they kept bagging and building the wall. Stephanie tried to ward off the gloominess. It was tough not noticing the difference when she had helped the others around Mayfield.

She thought she had been part of the camaraderie, but she was wrong. A sense of community was something she had been missing, and she thought she had found it. She forgot that people act differently during emergency situations.

She allowed herself to believe she was one of them. What a fool she had been! The townspeople tolerated her while she did something for them. Venus had warned her of this outcome, but Stephanie hadn't listened. She refused to believe Mayfield was like every rotten small town she had lived in.

Stephanie straightened her aching back when she heard the sound of a car engine. She turned to see Jack's car pulling up in the driveway. Her breath shriveled up in her lungs as the car wheels crunched against the gravel.

"I'll deal with this," she said as she pulled off her work gloves.

Venus looked over her shoulder and glared. "Tell him he's not welcome unless he plans to work."

She would do no such thing. It would be best if he kept his distance. By the time Stephanie reached Jack, she found him grabbing more sandbags from his car. "Thought you could use some help," he said by way of a greeting.

"We're fine, thank you." She bestowed her most polite smile upon him while her gaze traveled up and down his body, memorizing every detail.

"With just three of you?" he asked in disbelief. "No, you're not. You'll be up all night, and you still won't be finished in time."

"It'll give us something to do." Her cheeks ached from the fake, toothy smile.

He met her gaze head-on and gave a sharp nod. "I see. Well, okay. If that's what you want. I guess I should call off the others."

"The others?" She looked at the driveway entrance and saw several cars turning in.

"Why didn't you call me and ask for help?" Jack asked, standing beside her. "I found out from Mackey that you came around the station requesting sandbags."

"I didn't see the point." In reality, she was afraid her requests would be rebuffed. She didn't think Jack would have said no, but what if he had? What if her rejection made her dead last on his list of priorities? She didn't think she could have handled the disappointment.

"Stephanie, remember this." He cupped her cheek with his hand. The tender touch nearly undid her. "If you call me, I'm there. Always."

She closed her eyes, unable to break away, knowing it would be for the last time. "That's your job."

His fingers tensed under her face. "This isn't about my job. It's about you and me." She heard the edge in his tone. "And I mean it. I'm here for you."

Here. As in Mayfield. "Got it." She pulled away as a car parked inches away from her.

Croft jumped out from the driver's side. "Let's get this party started," he announced, walking around to the trunk and unlocking it.

Stephanie was surprised to see the bartender. He might be Jack's friend, but she knew he didn't think too fondly of her. "Isn't the tavern open?"

"Nope." He pulled out a shovel from the car trunk. "Not until this place is sandbagged."

In all the times she moved apartments around L.A., not once had her friends offered to help. Yet here was a guy who had closed up his bar to lend a hand, and he didn't even like her!

"Thanks," she said, her voice breaking. Croft hurried away as if the show of emotion freaked him out.

Stephanie looked at Jack. "I mean it. Really."

"Like I said, I'm here for you. Always."

Chapter 18

Venus Gold set the phone down with careful precision. There was something about the way she did it that caused Stephanie to glance up from her paperwork. She cautiously watched her friend, wondering if her nerves were going to survive the news flash.

It had already been a tense couple of days before the water level started to go down. Stephanie did her best not to look at the water bumping up against their sandbags, or think about how the trailer home didn't really have any foundation . . .

Venus braced her legs apart, arched back, and let out a rebel yell. "Whoo-hoo!"

"Oh, God." Stephanie tossed her pen aside and flattened her hands against her ears. "I can't stand morning people."

"The O'Leary Bridge is open!" Venus yelled at the top of her lungs. She punched her fists into the air. "Watch out, world! I'm leaving Mayfield like a bat out of hell!"

Stephanie slowly dropped her hands. Did she hear right? The bridge was open? "We can leave?" she said in a daze. "We can leave right now if we wanted to?"

"We *are* leaving. Pronto." Venus did a karate kick. "Yee-ha!"

Stephanie smiled weakly. She was ready to leave, but she couldn't garner as much enthusiasm. She didn't understand why. She'd been desperate to leave since she got here.

Okay, maybe not *desperate*, and not the whole time she was in town. When she wasn't trying to cause mischief or battling nature, she had found her wild side, thanks to Jack Logan.

Jack. Stephanie gnawed on her bottom lip and looked out the window. Would she see him before she left?

"Pack your bags." Venus started doing something that was a cross between the cha-cha and the rumba around the kitchen table. "And let's blow this joint."

"I don't have any bags," she reminded Venus. The loss was actually freeing at the moment. She could get up and go right now. Nothing was holding her back. Well, she looked at the window again, almost nothing.

"Even better!" Venus declared. She spread her arms out wide and whirled around like a demonic ice skater. "I can't wait to get out of this place."

"Me, too." She rose from her seat and followed Venus into the living room, her path blocked as her friend did some bizarre bunny hop. No way was she going to join in.

"Are you sure your mom's going to be okay without us?" Stephanie asked. Okay, Mary Gold was a grown woman. And Jack promised he would look after her.

"Yeah, she'll be fine." Venus didn't seem to be worried. "She's been through worse."

"That's true. I guess all those tornadoes and earthquakes prepared her for emergencies." Although there hadn't been any disaster kit, Stephanie remembered. Maybe Mrs. Gold used up all the supplies before they got here?

"Hey, what was it that you called Mayfield?" Venus asked as she gathered the clothes she had thrown on the floor the night before. "Oh, I remember now. The armpit of civilization."

Stephanie winced as Venus hooted with laughter. She should never have shot off her big mouth like that. "That was before I got to know the place," she explained as they pulled the luggage out from the corner of the room. "And the people."

Venus unzipped one of the suitcases. "Now it would be more like the asshole of civilization, huh?"

"Not at all!" Stephanie bristled and froze. What was she doing? Mayfield wasn't her town. They made that quite clear. She didn't need to defend its honor. She would be the last person given that duty.

As for the people, some of them didn't improve after repeat meetings, like Cockroach. Others, she only needed one encounter to last her a lifetime. Freda Keller and her husband went under that heading.

She'd like the chance to say good-bye to Old Man Schneider. While they had been sandbagging, she had listened about what life was like when he had been growing up. She had felt a connection, both with the elderly gentleman and with Mayfield after learning its history.

And then there was Croft . . . Stephanie slammed on the brakes of her wayward thoughts. She was doing it again.

She was getting too sentimental. She was placing too much importance on chance encounters and stolen moments. These people didn't care if she left. They probably didn't even remember who she was while she was still in town.

"Stephanie?" Venus's voice disrupted her wandering thoughts. "Are you okay?"

"Who, me?" She turned her attention to Venus and watched her toss clothes into her suitcases. She refrained from grabbing the tortured scraps of fabric out of her friend's hands and folding them neatly. "Oh, yeah. I'm fine. I'm tired, that's all."

"You've been working out in the rain too much," Venus said. She balled up a shirt and stuffed it into a suitcase that was already overflowing. "I hope you don't catch anything."

"It's unlikely." Unless there was something like the Mayfield Malaise that could only be contracted by drinking that swamp sludge. Knowing her luck, she would be the first textbook case.

Venus stopped what she was doing and gave Stephanie an odd look. "You sure you're okay? I thought you'd be dancing on the ceiling right about now."

"I'm sure." Stephanie gave a smile and touched the side of her head. "I'm trying to figure out my to-do list. There's so much stuff we have to do when we get back to Los Angeles."

"Los Angeles!" Venus squealed with excitement. "That is music to my ears!"

"Mine, too." *Or it will be, once I'm out of town and on the road.*

"On Wednesday morning at 10:30 A.M.," Deputy Cochran read out in a monotone voice, "a citizen complaint was made at the station about Stephanie Monroe's see-through blouse, citing indecent exposure. Sheriff Logan is handling the investigation."

How much longer was this blotter going to take? Jack propped his hand against his chin. Ever since Stephanie hit town, the police record had doubled in size.

"On Wednesday afternoon at 3:00 P.M., a citizen complaint was made by telephone about Stephanie Monroe's denim miniskirt, citing indecent exposure. Sheriff Logan is handling the investigation."

Jack frowned. He liked that miniskirt on Stephanie. It showed off her long, bare legs.

"On Wednesday evening at 9:00 P.M., a citizen complaint was made to an officer on duty about Stephanie Monroe's appearance, citing indecent exposure. Sheriff Logan is handling the investigation."

Jack couldn't remember what Stephanie had been wearing on Wednesday night. Which outfit would have caused a complaint on her overall appearance? Was it that skintight yellow dress? Probably. He knew his blood pressure went up a few notches when he saw it.

It took a few moments for him to realize that Cochran had stopped talking. "Is that all for this week?" Jack asked hopefully. At the deputy's nod, Jack breathed a sigh of relief. "Okay." He stood up from his chair, desperately needing to stand and get out of his office. "Let's send it off to the newspaper editor."

Jack followed Cochran out of his office and paused at the threshold. The police station was deathly quiet. He looked around, the silence scraping at his nerves.

This was what he had been striving for all these weeks, Jack reminded himself. The inactivity was a change from the past couple of weeks. The clean-up from the flood was difficult and time-consuming work, but once it was done, life would get back to normal.

And that sounded incredibly boring all of a sudden. His duties would be less about protecting and more about keeping the peace. His days would be filled with giving out speeding tickets rather than receiving citizen complaints on Stephanie Monroe.

Stephanie. He glanced over in the direction of the holding cell. That woman was nothing but a nuisance, just like her friend. Yet, he found himself on more than one occasion waiting to see what she was going to do next. Mayfield wasn't going to be the same without her special brand of trouble.

What was he thinking? Jack frowned and rubbed his forehead. He wanted peaceful, and Stephanie Monroe didn't fall in that category.

From the first moment he laid eyes on her, he'd been a mess. Distracted, impulsive, and craving her.

The wild, bad boy that he had erased from all existence had roared back full force.

If that wasn't inconvenient enough, he had fallen in love. Not just with anyone, but with a good girl with a bad girl's body. A city girl with small-town sensibilities. It was no wonder he felt punch-drunk.

He guessed that's what love did to a guy. Jack thought he had been in love before, but it was nothing like how he felt with Stephanie.

But he had to go ruin it all with his marriage proposal. His one and only marriage proposal had been rejected. Jack closed his eyes, feeling battered and bruised.

Yeah, he messed up. He shouldn't have been so impulsive. He should have wooed her, but he felt time slipping away and he didn't want her to go back to California. He knew that once she went back, he wouldn't be able to compete with what that lifestyle had to offer.

It was bad timing all around, Jack decided. Stephanie didn't get to see Mayfield for what it truly is. She probably thought it was a magnet for natural disasters. But even if she had been around when the town celebrated the holidays, she wouldn't have given it a chance. It wasn't where she wanted to be.

Jack's sigh rattled around his chest. There was no use wishing for what he couldn't have. He had to move on.

What he really needed was to get out of this station. That's all. Jack headed toward the front desk. He'd been working and worrying nonstop. He needed to take a vacation the first chance he got or he would be risking burnout.

Jack looked over the high counter of the front

desk and saw Officer Mackey. The guy just opened his mouth wide and took off the end of a foot-long sub. The wrinkles on the policeman's forehead deepened with every chew.

"Hey, Mackey," Jack said, watching with amazement. The sandwich was piled high with toppings, but the guy didn't even drop a crumb.

"They're packing up in the car right now," Mackey said, his voice muffled.

"Who is?"

The officer rotated the chunk of sandwich to one side of his mouth. "Venus and Stephanie."

Something inside of Jack froze. They were leaving. Stephanie was leaving without saying good-bye. He hadn't expected that.

"How do you know this?" Jack asked.

"Switchboard." Mackey said around the tip of his straw before he slurped down a third of his soda.

"I'll be back." Jack felt the heaviness weighing on his chest. He stepped away from the front desk and turned. "I'm going to lunch."

"Hey, Sheriff?"

Jack paused in midstep. Sheriff? Mackey never called him that before. No one did. When the name Sheriff Logan was being used, everyone knew that it was Big Jack being discussed.

When Jack first won the position, he had naively assumed that it would be a matter of time before people addressed him as Sheriff. Then he had started to believe that he had to earn the title in their eyes.

After a while, he gave up. The only person who

ever called him Sheriff was Stephanie. Not always in the most respectful tone, Jack thought with a smile.

Jack looked over his shoulder. "Yeah, Mackey?"

"Can you bring me back something?" the officer asked as he took another big bite. "A bag of chips, maybe?"

"Sure, no problem."

He strolled over to Croft's Tavern, wondering what caused the title change. Was it because Mackey always heard Stephanie use it? Or did it have something to do with the way he proved himself while dealing with the worst of the flood? It could have been a little of both.

"Hey, Jack," Croft said as Jack stepped into the shadowy tavern. "What are you doing here? Venus and Stephanie are leaving."

Jack scowled at his friend. "Yeah, I heard." He walked to the bar and sat down.

Croft grabbed a tall glass and gave Jack a look from the corner of his eye. "Why aren't you at the Golds'?"

Because I'll just be in the way and Stephanie will run me over on her way out of town. "I already said my good-bye."

"So it's like that, huh?" Croft said as he filled the glass with ice.

"Pretty much." He didn't like it, but he knew better than to fight it. He was already down and out. No use getting his teeth kicked in while he was at it.

Croft shook his head as he filled the glass with soda. "Why aren't you stopping her?"

"What do you expect me to do?" Jack splayed his arms out wide. "Set up a road blockade?"

"Sure." He slid the drink to Jack. "She might find that romantic."

"No, she won't." He gripped the glass with tight fingers and stared into the murky drink. "Because she doesn't want to be here."

"Bummer." Croft rested his elbows on the counter.

"How can you say that?" Jack asked. "You didn't want her here in the first place. You thought I should hook up with Danielle. You even set up something."

"True, but that was before I saw Stephanie with you. It was like having the old Jack Logan back."

Jack heard the squealing tires outside. He turned his head and looked out of the pitted glass just in time to see Venus's car racing past. His breath hitched in his throat as his chest squeezed tight. He forced himself to look away. "It doesn't matter anymore."

Stephanie craned her head to see Croft's Tavern one last time, but it whizzed right by. It was probably for the best, she decided as she settled back in her seat.

She couldn't believe they were already on their way. After days and days of waiting, it seemed almost surreal that they were heading out of town. She hadn't realized how small Mayfield was until she was zipping through the downtown area in less than ten minutes.

Stephanie glanced down at her yellow halter

top, periwinkle jeans, and Lucite heels. She was finally in her own clothes. But they didn't seem to survive the ordeal. The halter top didn't seem as bright and cheerful. The jeans looked pale and dingy. There must have been something in the water, because everything lost its sparkle and shine.

Venus screeched to a stop at the stoplight and Stephanie winced as she jerked forward before slamming her head back against the seat. She silently double-checked the strength of her seat belt and looked around.

The streets and sidewalks were still covered with puddles. The drains at the corners chugged down the little streams of water. Droplets clung to the trees and flowers. Everything was peaceful after the storm.

Venus rolled down the windows, letting in the warm summer breeze. Stephanie saw Mr. Knox standing at the door of his store, waving at them. A warm glow filled her.

Stephanie smiled and waved back. Venus responded by cranking up the music from her car radio. The high-pitched guitar riffs and bawdy lyrics blistered the quiet day.

The light turned green and Venus hit the gas. The wheels skidded against the wet pavement. Stephanie closed her eyes tight as the car lurched forward.

"You know, you might want to slow down," Stephanie said, holding on to the seat belt stretched across her chest. "We don't want a speeding ticket."

Her friend let off the gas and glanced at the rearview mirror. "You're right. I don't think I could cope with any more delays."

City Hall was suddenly on her left. Stephanie watched it pass by in a blur. To her, the dull and respectable building represented a stolen moment with Jack. Her skin tingled as she remembered his touch, his mouth just a kiss away from hers.

That was the problem with a small town, Stephanie decided as she looked away. She probably visited every store and building. Met over half of the citizens. Now every inch of the community gave her a memory.

"Good-bye, Mayfield!" Venus cried out. She reached over to Stephanie's open window and flipped up her middle finger.

Stephanie grabbed her by the wrist. "Why don't you wait until we cross the city line before you do that?" She placed Venus's hand back on the steering wheel.

"Aw, come on," Venus pouted. "We should do something. One big send-off, you know?"

"No way." Stephanie was turning in her bad-girl badge. She wasn't cut out for making trouble. She thought she was getting an ulcer during her one and only prank. "I think we already left enough of an impression."

"Not even," Venus snorted.

Which Stephanie thought was depressing.

Venus stomped on the brakes and Stephanie grabbed for the dashboard. "Jesus! How many stop signs does this Main Street have now?"

"Wow," Stephanie drawled as she slowly settled back into her seat. "You are in quite a rush for someone who dragged her weekender into *several weeks.*"

"Yeah, well." Venus gave a chagrined look. "The

trip down memory lane turned into a nightmare. I am willing to admit that coming back was a waste of time."

"It was not."

"Yeah, it was." Venus sighed. "The Kellers and their friends will act like nothing happened. The others will follow their example. Pretty soon, everyone will forget."

Stephanie couldn't believe it. She wasn't able to make a difference. She wasn't even able to leave a mark on a small town. So much for being a wild and wicked woman.

She looked out her window and saw the downtown park. Stephanie straightened in her seat. "Venus . . . when did you have the time to do that?"

"Do what?" Venus slowed down and looked at where Stephanie was pointing.

The bronze statue of Ronald Keller stood proudly in the middle of the park. A platinum blond wig sat on his head, the high ponytail flapping in the breeze. The black bustier fit snugly against the statue, creating unnatural curves. The metal-tipped bra shone in the sunlight.

"Madonna?" Stephanie guessed. "I'm going to say, during her Blond Ambition years."

Venus's forehead wrinkled. "I didn't do that." She clucked her tongue at Stephanie's look of disbelief. "I didn't. I swear."

"I didn't, either."

A smile slowly appeared on Venus's mouth. "Well, jailbird, I do believe we started a tradition."

"Don't call me jailbird."

Venus pressed firmly down on the gas pedal. "Would you prefer exhibitionist?"

Stephanie's jaw clenched as she held back her temper. It was going to be a long way back to L.A.

"Let's make a pact," she suggested, holding out her hand. "Whatever happens in Mayfield—"

Venus shook her hand. "Stays in Mayfield."

Chapter 19

"I can't believe we found the perfect jacket for Carla's interview!" Venus said into her tiny cell phone as she and Stephanie walked to the exit of the department store. "And at twenty percent off!"

Stephanie struggled to keep up with Venus's brisk walk. And she wasn't the one talking on the phone or maneuvering through the elegantly dressed crowd. Nor was she the one wearing a tight black rubber dress that was supposed to make walking difficult.

Somehow Venus's outfit fit right in with the heiress-and-hip-hop crowd that frequented the exclusive shopping center. Stephanie's ice blue sheath screamed expensive and was perfect for the California summer. Her strappy heels were from a designer who was going to be touted in all the fashion magazines next month.

But it didn't matter. She felt out of step. Awkward. Dowdy.

Stephanie cringed at the thought. She should

have known better than to volunteer for this shopping expedition. It was putting her in a bad mood. She blamed her rare acquiescence on temporary insanity. She only wished she had suffered from it a little longer so she wouldn't have been lucid while shopping.

While Venus seemed to get an afterglow, Stephanie found shopping with her friend similar to preparing for an Olympic event. Not that she had any experience with that, but she had watched the games on TV since she could remember. From what she gathered, the training required strength, fortitude, and a single-mindedness that would be considered unhealthy in normal life.

They hurried past the cosmetics counter and Stephanie automatically glanced at the new shades and products. For some reason, she didn't slow down and take a look. She must be more depressed than she thought!

Stephanie remembered a time when she was a hick teenager fresh from the farmland and in awe of this ritzy store. She had pressed her nose against the glass, and her hands left streaks. She could have stayed there, salivating over the makeup, but the snobby saleslady shooed her away.

After being dismissed on more than one occasion and ignored by the haughty salesclerks who wore their smocks like officers in the military, the kernel of a dream formed and grew. Ten years ago she made the decision that her cosmetics line would never be seen here, even if the company begged. Oh, she'd let them beg, long and hard. And then she'd shoo *them* away.

She was going to take the razzle-dazzle of L.A.,

package it up, and sell it out of every pharmacy and discount store. Her goal was more than just making bazillion dollars and seeing her ideas succeed. She wanted to make glitz accessible to women who didn't have a glamorous life.

So how did she drift away from that goal? Stephanie frowned as the question crept into her mind. She didn't drift away. Not really. Her current role at Venus & Stephanie was laying the foundation for her dream.

Although it seemed like it was taking too long to lay the foundation. Was she doing something wrong? Maybe she hadn't taken the right path. Had she taken a detour and just not known it?

Stephanie wondered about that as she passed the men's cologne section. The customers were all the same. Pretty boys or ultra-muscular. Their perfectly groomed hair didn't make her fingers tingle with the need to muss. She didn't have the urge to caress their unlined, tanned skin.

Those guys didn't do a thing for her. She wasn't sure where the problem lay. Were they too pretty, too perfect?

She walked by one of the guys as he sprayed cologne on the tester stick. Stephanie stumbled as the scent hit her. It smelled like a tropical rainstorm. Fragmented images blurred past her, all of them of Jack.

Jack Logan. A sigh stuttered in her lungs, the ache lingering. Everything reminded her of him.

It didn't seem like it would ever end. If she saw a police car racing past her, she'd think of Jack. A red umbrella was on sale in the accessories department, and she had immediately thought of Jack

Logan. Even the low timbre of her upstairs neighbor's voice—which she could hear all too clearly when she was trying to sleep—made her remember Jack.

She had to get over the sheriff. She would draw up a 12-step program and start immediately. Then again, it might be too late.

Obviously she went about ending the relationship the wrong way. She went cold turkey when she should have allowed the relationship to end naturally. It would have fizzled out, which most long-distance romances do.

Maybe she should go about it from a different angle. Rather than avoidance, she should call him. She'd listen to his sexy voice and go all gooey. That was an important hurdle to cross before she could realize they wanted different things. After a couple of phone calls, she'd remember why she made this choice. Perfect!

Stephanie took a quick peek at Venus, who was still reliving her great buy, step by tedious step. Stephanie retrieved her phone from her purse and flipped it open. She stared at the tiny screen. She didn't have Jack's number.

How could that be? How could she not have the phone number of the most important person in her life? She had her mom's number. There was the phone number for her manicurist. And her favorite Indian take-away restaurant. It was essential to have chicken *tikka masala* a push-button away. Where was Jack's phone number?

Oh, right. Stephanie flipped her phone closed. She didn't write it down. On purpose. What was the thought process in that?

Stephanie knew she would have this moment of weakness and she prepared for it. She rolled her eyes in self-disgust. Good for her. Great anticipation. She could really kick herself right about now.

"Who are you calling?" Venus asked as she ended her call and they exited the building.

"No one." Stephanie dropped her phone back into her purse. "Just checking messages."

They walked over to the valet station and Stephanie immediately put on her sunglasses. The sun scorched the pavement and blinded her. It seemed brighter than usual, but that was probably because she had spent all that time in the rain. Although it had only been a month since she left Mayfield.

As they waited for the valet to bring their car around, Venus tilted her head back and smiled. "Stephanie." She extended her arm, barring Stephanie from moving. "Inhale."

She watched Venus inhale. What was it with all her breathing exercises? Stephanie took a hesitant sniff and made a face. "Gross! Why did you make me do that?"

"Don't you love that smell?" Venus asked as their car pulled up alongside the curb.

She wrinkled her nose. "It's called smog."

"No, it's the smell of Los Angeles. God, how I missed it." She smiled brilliantly as she tipped the valet.

"Venus, it's not like you had to do a tour of duty," Stephanie said as she got in on the passenger side. "You were gone for what? A month, tops?"

"It felt like more than that."

"That's your birthplace that you're talking about." Stephanie buckled up.

"That doesn't make it sacred." Venus said as she gunned the engine.

Stephanie was beginning to think that it should. She had been born in a small town that she had neither revisited nor could find on the map. She wished she had a connection with the place. Maybe she wouldn't feel as lost as she did now.

"Oh! I forgot to tell you!" Venus stomped on the brakes twice. The woman always used the pedals like punctuation marks when she talked. "Guess what? We have another award ceremony gig!"

"No kidding?" That was the best news she'd had in a while. "Who is it?"

"Amanda . . ." Venus snapped her fingers. "Okay, the name escapes me, but it's Amanda something."

"Terrific," Stephanie drawled, her eyelids at half-mast. "We're off to a great start."

"I'll have to look it up again." Venus stomped on the gas pedal. "It's some Internet celebrity. One of the most downloadable women."

"Internet?" Stephanie wrinkled her nose. It wasn't like she had anything against the medium. She used it constantly. But the Internet wasn't their niche. "What's so glam about that? Wait a second, is this ceremony going to be held online?"

"Don't know, don't care." She hit the brakes as a zippy sports car cut in front of them. "It's a job, it's a ceremony, and this woman is determined to make a splash."

Venus had a point. It was their job and they needed to show what they were capable of doing. "So you need to put together one of your wildest outfits," Stephanie suggested.

"With your most extreme makeover," Venus added.

Extreme. Stephanie's flagging spirits took a hit. She'd been doing a lot of extreme makeovers lately. Not gorgeous. Not stylish. Extreme. She hoped it was a fad. A very, very brief fad.

"Okay, we need to get back to the office and figure out our schedule."

"But the Internet." Stephanie sighed, unable to contain her disappointment. "That's not really our focus."

Venus shrugged off the comment. "I bet that's what everyone said when TV was invented."

"That's not the point."

"And just think," Venus interrupted, her eyes gleaming with enthusiasm. "We'll be the leaders of that area before all the other stylists wake up and realize that's where the money is at."

"Yeah, but—" Stephanie knew she was being a media snob. She shouldn't turn her nose up at a good-paying client and the wave of the future.

Venus stomped on the brakes. Stephanie pitched forward before slamming back against the headrest. Her hair flopped in her face.

"Oh, this traffic!" Stephanie yelled, shoving her hands in her hair. "I can't stand it!"

"It's not that bad. Rush hour hasn't started yet."

"You're right. You're right." Stephanie pressed her sunglasses firmly on the bridge of her nose. She would act calm and rational while she figured out what was wrong with her. The noise, the traffic, the men—everything rubbed her the wrong way.

She probably caught a parasite from all that

floodwater. It was time to call a doctor. Or an herbalist. At this point, she'd make an appointment with an exorcist. Whatever it took to get her head on straight before she threw away everything she had worked for.

He should have followed her to L.A.

Jack looked up from his computer and stared out the window. It was raining, again. He was sick of rain. He bet it was hot and sunny where Stephanie was.

No doubt she wasn't thinking about whether she should have stayed in Mayfield. What had he been thinking, asking her to leave California? L.A. had more to offer a vibrant, ambitious woman.

All Jack had to offer in Mayfield was himself. That had been a no-brainer of a decision. He was surprised it took Stephanie more than thirty seconds to give her answer.

Jack slowly shook his head in self-disgust, rubbing his face with his hands. He definitely should have followed her to Los Angeles.

But he wasn't going to prolong the inevitable. They would never have worked out. He belonged here in Mayfield. He had lived outside the city limits when he attended college and the police academy. After a few years in the bigger cities, he knew it wasn't for him.

Jack propped his head against his fist and watched the raindrops hit the window. Those times away from Mayfield weren't bad. It just wasn't home. Then again, he didn't give those other cities a chance because he knew he was going back home.

"Hey, Sheriff?" Deputy Cochran peeked inside. "Do you have time to go over the police blotter?"

Jack glanced up at the ceiling. *Kick me while I'm down, why don't you?* He wished he had a good excuse to avoid the weekly ritual. "Sure, come on in."

Cochran sat down in front of the sheriff's desk. He held out his clipboard, and Jack tensed. The deputy cleared his throat, and Jack silently willed Mackey to intervene with an urgent call.

"On Friday evening at 6:00 P.M.," Cochran began, "an officer detained Missy Keller for a license violation. The suspect was issued a warning and released."

Hmm, Jack thought. The blotter would be more interesting if Stephanie was still around. Sure, it would also be a hell of a lot longer, but it made the task more bearable as he remembered the outfits she wore.

"On Friday evening at 7:45 P.M.," Cochran read aloud, "an officer responded to the report of someone skateboarding on the ramps in the downtown park. Officer made contact with two individuals. One skateboard was impounded."

Jack wanted to know why Big Jack started this practice of going over the blotter. He knew his father had been something of a control freak—it was something they had locked horns about numerous times—but this ritual was a waste of time.

"On Saturday morning at 8:10 A.M., an officer detained Lisa Farber for a license violation. The suspect was issued a summons and released."

Did other police departments waste their time like this? He had never thought to ask. Jack followed the same schedule that his father did unquestioningly.

"On Saturday morning at 9:00 A.M., an officer received a report that a bicycle bell had been stolen. An investigation has been initiated."

Why couldn't he get out of this task? What was stopping him? What could be the worst thing if he didn't do it?

"On Saturday morning at—"

"Cochran!" Jack interrupted, more urgently than he had intended.

The deputy looked over his clipboard. "Yes?"

"I've been thinking . . ." Jack hesitated, and he didn't know why. Were the traditions that ingrained in him? Was he concerned that if he made a change, it would have a ripple effect he wouldn't be able to control?

"Sheriff?" Cochran prompted.

Jack slowly lowered his palms on his desktop. He wanted to sound firm. Act like he knew what he was doing. "We need to make some changes around here."

"Changes?" Cochran looked at him as if he had said a filthy word. "Like what?"

"I think you should be solely responsible for the police blotter." Jack saw how Cochran perked up, giving him the incentive to continue. "You no longer need my authorization before sending it to the newspaper. Unless you don't feel ready for it."

"No—I mean, yes." Wesley Cochran stopped and started over. "I'm ready for it. Absolutely."

"Are you sure?" Jack teased, keeping his expression serious. "The job requires a person of your . . . attention for detail."

Cochran bolted from his chair. "I won't let you down, Sheriff."

"Good. Then I'll leave you to it." *And I hope I never have to go through that blotter ritual again as long as I live.*

He watched Cochran back out of the door, overflowing with gratitude. Well, he was glad he made someone's day. If only he could do that for himself.

Jack stared at his computer screen, the document a jumble of words and numbers. How many changes would he need to make before he could be happy?

Could he be fulfilled living in a big city like Los Angeles? He didn't think so. But he could do it if it meant being with Stephanie.

He remembered how it felt having her in his bed, her long hair streaming over the pillow. Her face flushed with satisfaction that he gave her. Her eyes shining with love.

Love. He loved her and wanted to spend his life with her. He wanted them to create a life together, no matter where they were.

He wanted it enough to give up his job, his town, risk everything, and follow her to L.A. Because Los Angeles had one thing he couldn't live without. It had Stephanie. The love of his life.

What was keeping him back? Duty and tradition. He didn't have family here since his dad died. He had a circle of close friends. But none of those friends could substitute for Stephanie or how he felt about her.

Okay, he knew what he had to do. Jack shot up from his seat. He was going after her.

Wait. Jack sat down, second-guessing his impulse. He couldn't just drop everything and head west. That bordered on stalker behavior. He hadn't spoken with her since she left Mayfield.

Maybe he should call first. Jack reached for the phone and stopped. He rolled his eyes. Nah, too wussy.

He should fly to L.A. and call her from there. Jack smiled as the idea took hold. Yeah, he decided, rubbing his hands with anticipation. That would prove he was willing to do whatever it takes.

He turned to his computer, exited his program, and went online. He would buy the earliest plane ticket, tell everyone he was on vacation—

A timid knock on the door interrupted his train of thought. Jack looked over his shoulder and saw the front desk officer at the door. "What's up?"

"We've got some thunderstorms that caused damage on the north side."

His gut instinct went on full alert. Mackey didn't get up from his seat for something like that. Dread pricked at the back of his neck. "Anything else?"

"Well, we've got some flash flood warnings," Mackey said, ticking off the list with his fingers. "Heavy rain is coming, and there's a chance the river might flood again." Mackey paused and counted his fingers. "Yeah, that's about it."

"Fuck!" Jack growled out, startling Mackey. "Sorry," he immediately apologized to the front desk officer. "I'll be right there."

Once Mackey closed the door behind him, Jack returned his attention to the computer and clicked out of the program. It was like nature was out to

get him. He would go after Stephanie, but his duty
came first.

Two weeks later, Stephanie was reorganizing
her professional makeup kit. The cleaning job was
tedious as she washed all of the brushes, culled
through her trays of powders and creams, giving
everything a good wipe-down. Whenever she felt
like her life was a mess, she cleaned out her makeup kit. The kit was sparkling these days.

"Stephanie," Venus said over her shoulder. "You're
driving me crazy."

She paused from wiping the drawer with her
damp cloth. "I'm driving *you* crazy?"

"Yes," Venus said emphatically. "Certifiably, round-
the-bend, going-cuckoo insane."

Stephanie looked up. "How is that possible?"

"You've been moping around for weeks," her
friend pointed out. "And it's time you snapped out
of it."

"Really?" And here she had knocked herself out
trying to keep an upbeat attitude. Show a professional, focused image. A lot of good that did her.
Stephanie leaned back in her chair and calmly
looked at her friend. "What do you suggest I do?"

"How should I know?" Venus tossed her hands
in the air. "I have no idea why you've been all depressed and cranky. You never were this way until
we left Mayfield."

Bingo. Stephanie returned to her task of wiping
out the trays. As she dug into the corners, she felt
Venus's intense gaze on her.

"So that's it," Venus said softly as it finally dawned on her. "You're missing Jack. Missing him *real* bad."

Sure, rub it in, why don't you? "I'll get over him," Stephanie said matter-of-factly.

"Why would you want to?" Venus sat on the edge of the desk next to Stephanie. "He's employed, he's single, and he's hot for you."

Is that all? Stephanie frowned as she considered Venus's list of virtues. Her friend forgot that Jack Logan was an incredibly patient and gentle man, but could be tough and brave when he needed to be. His sense of humor matched hers and, while she didn't agree with his devotion to Mayfield, she admired it. And she also wanted to add that Jack was a creative and generous lover.

Argh! Stephanie dug harder at the brown speck in the corner. Venus's pep talk wasn't helping! "What of it?" Stephanie replied in a growl.

"Are you kidding me?" From the corner of her eye, Stephanie could see Venus doing a scissors kick with her legs. "Do you realize how hard it is to find just one of those qualities in a man?"

"Yes." Stephanie put the damp cloth to the side. "I'm quite aware of it, thank you very much."

"So, you fell in love with your weekend fling." Venus gave an exaggerated shrug of her shoulders. "These things have been known to happen."

Well, she was glad to know she wasn't the only stupid woman on the planet. "And what do you do?"

"You stretch that weekend to last days. Weeks. Mo—"

"I can't do that." Stephanie grabbed her pot.

and sticks of lip gloss and started to organize her drawer by color. "That's not going to work."

"Why not? Oooh." Venus clucked her tongue. "I get it. Jack doesn't want that kind of commitment."

Stephanie kept her head down as she sorted the various shades of red. "Jack wants me to move to Mayfield."

"What?" Venus vaulted from the table. Her body shimmered with outrage. "Is he stupid?"

"Apparently."

"Mayfield?" Venus spat out the word. "Mayfield!"

Stephanie put down the pots and watched her friend pacing the small workroom in their office suite.

"What a decision!" Venus said, her voice reaching a higher decibel. "Los Angeles on one hand, Mayfield on the other. Oh, gee." She raised and lowered the palms of her hands. "Which one should I choose?"

"I'm not going anywhere."

"I should say not!" Venus planted her fists on her hips. "I mean, what would you *do* in Mayfield?"

Stephanie grabbed her bunch of lipstick liners. "Exactly."

"There's no demand for makeup artists."

"True." Stephanie wasn't about to point out that she wasn't going to be a makeup artist until retirement age. Instead she lined up the slim pencils like soldiers. If only her emotions could be so orderly.

"You'll turn into one of them," Venus predicted.

"Turn into?" Stephanie looked up and raised an eyebrow. "Is that anything like the Stepford Wives?"

"Worse." Venus bent down and stared into Stephanie's eyes. "Did you see those Mayfield wives? Not exactly enviable."

"You don't need to argue your case," Stephanie said. "I'm not going to Mayfield."

"Good." She folded her arms across her chest. "You wouldn't like it there, anyway."

Stephanie frowned. It was more complicated than that. There were some things she liked, other things she could do without. Much like everywhere she had lived.

"I wouldn't like what I would become if I lived there," Stephanie clarified for her friend.

Venus tilted her head. "And what's that?"

"A woman with big, glamorous dreams stuck in a small farm town." Stephanie went back to organizing her makeup kit, her movements brisk and determined. "It happened to my mom, and it happened to my sisters. It won't ever happen to me."

"Uh, wait a second." Venus held her hands out as if she was stopping traffic. "You were from a small town? No way. You're lying."

"Believe me," Stephanie said as she filled the drawers and bins at rapid speed. "I wouldn't make something like that up. I know all about small-town living, and I know it's not for me. I'm staying right here in Mayfield."

Venus paused. "You mean Los Angeles."

"That's what I said." Stephanie slammed the kit closed and flipped the metal locks shut. "Los Angeles."

Chapter 20

"Jack Logan!" Mrs. Freda Keller barged into the sheriff's office as Jack was looking at times and departure dates for L.A. flights on his computer.

He clenched his teeth and reined in his frustration. He wasn't going to be delayed anymore. All of the bridges were in use or under reconstruction. The bigger waterways nearby were open for commercial river traffic.

Jack knew he could follow his heart to California in good conscience. Nothing was holding him back. He didn't regret doing his duty, but he needed to find Stephanie before it was too late.

"Jack!" Freda barked out, disrupting his thoughts.

"Good morning, Mrs. Keller." Jack rose from his chair and gestured for the older woman to take a seat. "I didn't hear you knock."

Freda didn't take him up on his offer. "Did you know that my husband's statue is dressed like a hippie?"

"No, I didn't know that." He'd have to drop by

the downtown park on his lunch hour and take a look. He couldn't imagine Ronald Keller with long hair.

"These costumes have to stop," Freda commanded. She thumped the point of her umbrella on the floor.

Jack stared at her. Did she realize that he and his officers had worked double-overtime during the flood cleanup? The top priority was getting Mayfield back on its feet while maintaining order and the peace.

"Every time I go to the park,"—Freda continued, her voice ringing in the small room—"the statue has been desecrated."

Desecrated? The woman had to be kidding. It was difficult, but Jack managed to keep a blank expression. He could imagine Stephanie's reaction if she saw Freda in full fury. Her eyebrow would be sky-high as she stared the older woman down.

Or would she be raising her eyebrows at him? What would Stephanie think if she saw him right now? She wouldn't understand why he was putting up with it, which was certain. Come to think of it, he didn't know why he tolerated Freda Keller's behavior.

The realization hit him hard. Memories—some hazy, others crystal clear—bumped against each other and overlapped. Jack had been following his father's lead again. Without realizing it. Without question.

Big Jack had always given Freda top priority. It must have been important for the first Sheriff Logan to grant favors to the richest—and therefore most powerful—woman in Mayfield. The current Sheriff Logan didn't feel the same way. It was time to break another tradition.

Jack sat back down in his chair. He grabbed his notepad and a pen. "Have any of the costumes harmed the property?"

Freda paused. He didn't know if she was thinking about his question, or if she was surprised that he was treating her complaint as if it was going to be fed through the system without any special treatment.

"No," she finally answered.

"Was there any graffiti on the premises?" he asked, in his most professional voice.

"No," Freda responded irritably. "That's not the point, Jack."

He looked up at her. "Any trash or broken glass?"

She glared at his hand as he set his pen down. "They are dressing up the statue. They are showing disrespect! What are you going to do about it?"

"Nothing." He tossed the notepad back onto his desk.

Freda stilled. "I beg your pardon?" Icy hauteur clung to each word.

Jack leaned back in his chair. "Unless there's destruction to public property or a violation of the law, I'm not doing anything."

"Is that right?" Freda asked. Her mouth twisted with anger. "Big Jack would have done something."

He gave a nod. "Yes, he probably would. But you are dealing with me now. Take a seat, Mrs. Keller." Jack motioned at the chair again. "I'll fill you in on the changes I've been making."

*   *   *

"No! This is all wrong!" Amanda whirled away from the three-sided mirror. "I don't like this! In fact, I hate it. You'll have to start all over again."

Stephanie bit her tongue as she watched the Internet celebrity, and all of her mirror images, have another temper tantrum. She leaned against the doorway of the walk-in closet as the other women calmed Amanda down.

"She needs something that's going to make people talk," Amanda's assistant explained. Stephanie couldn't remember the nondescript woman's name. She didn't think it was mentioned. She probably didn't have one.

Venus hurriedly assured their client. "Amanda, you look fantastic. This ensemble with—"

"No!" Amanda tossed back her mane of blond hair. "I want something that will really make people talk. Create a buzz. Like Liz Hurley's Versace dress. Or J. Lo's green dress she wore to the Grammys. I need something that's going to get me on the news!"

"This dress will do exactly that," Venus said. "The photographers will have all eyes on you, waiting to see if your dress will fall, or if you'll pop out. You won't, of course," Venus quickly added, "because we'll have taped your breasts to the dress."

"No! No! No!" Amanda stomped her foot. "This dress isn't shocking. It doesn't cause mouths to drop. I want something that would make Joan Rivers go mute."

Could it have lost its shock value because everyone with Internet access has seen everything the dress will be hiding, Stephanie thought. Not that she was being judgmental. Much.

She studied the barely-there dress that clung to the star's enhanced curves. The way Amanda went on about it, the dress was appropriate for church when, in fact, it wasn't something you would even wear to a Hollywood wedding, unless you had a vendetta against the bride. And Stephanie could guarantee that the outfit would have gotten the Internet star locked up for life in Mayfield.

Could it be that after dealing with so many revealing dresses, nothing can shock anymore? Stephanie considered the problem. After all, where was the elegance she grew up watching on TV? Sure, there had been some revealing designs, but the outfits were meant to create an image and establish an aura. The dress never was center stage.

"Let's flaunt something that hasn't been done before," Amanda continued to rant. "Give me something that will get censored. Give me something that will show off my ass!"

"You could go naked," Stephanie muttered. She chewed off a hangnail before she realized that everyone had gone silent and turned to stare at her. Damn, did she say that too loud?

"Well, maybe not *naked*, naked," Venus added, her eyes lighting up as the possibilities took hold. "But what if we give the illusion of nudity? Or, better yet, maybe something where you are as good as naked."

"What do you mean?" Amanda's assistant asked cautiously.

"I'm thinking . . ." Venus paused as she studied Amanda's figure. "A lot of body paint, a tiny thong, and a few pasties. What do you think?"

Are you crazy? Stephanie opened her mouth but nothing came out. *Don't you guys realize that I was kidding? You know, sarcasm?*

Amanda looked in the mirror and visualized what Venus had suggested. She flashed a smile that Stephanie knew cost more than her car. "Perfect."

Stephanie froze. Of course that woman would love the idea. Even the assistant seemed to like it. Or maybe she was just paid to agree. The only person who was dead-set against it was her. She had to wonder if she was the only one with common sense, or if she was one step behind everyone else.

"Excuse me," Stephanie said as she stepped outside the closet. She knew she had to get up and leave before she offended the client. Not that her presence would be missed, although Venus gave her a curious look.

Stephanie headed out of the bedroom and didn't stop until she made it to the hallway. She stood beside the grand window overlooking the swimming pool and counted to ten. She didn't feel any calmer and went for twenty.

Stephanie was at three hundred and ninety-four when she came to a few conclusions. First, her math skills still sucked, and second, she wasn't a step behind the rest. She was marching to a different drummer.

But was it a better drummer, Stephanie wondered as she saw Venus in the window's reflection. "Where's Amanda?" she asked without turning around.

"On a phone call." Venus rolled her eyes. They had been constantly interrupted all afternoon by phone calls. "What's going on?"

Stephanie turned and faced Venus. "Body paint? What possessed you to think of body paint?"

"Okay, so we'll have to call in a makeup artist who specializes in that." She put her hand on Stephanie's shoulder. "I'm sorry."

"That's not a problem." She didn't care if she worked on their top project. "I wouldn't want to spend that much time working on Amanda."

"Hey, those are some of the most downloadable features that you would get to see up close and personal."

"The less time I'm around Amanda, the better." The Internet celebrity was already a not-worth-the-effort diva in her mind. "Naked." She shook her head.

"Yeah, that was an inspired idea." Venus punched her lightly on the shoulder. "Good going. For a minute there, I felt like we were going to lose the assignment."

Stephanie's bottom jaw shifted to one side. "I was being sarcastic at the time."

"Oh." Venus blinked. "Really? You should try sarcasm more often. God knows what we'll come up with."

She didn't want her look to be based on cynicism or irreverence. That wasn't what she was about. "Don't you think it's too extreme?"

"It's edgy," Venus decided, as if that was all that mattered to her. "And that's what's going to get Amanda in all the important magazines like *People* and *US Weekly*."

"If that's what it takes to get press, I'm not sure I'm in the right industry." Stephanie turned back to face the window. "I don't want to be a makeup artist trying to dance along the edge of propriety."

"That's the game now. It's all about pushing the envelope," Venus said matter-of-factly. "I'm up for it. I've been doing it all my life. Don't worry, Stephanie, I'll mentor you. Before you know it, edgy will be your second nature."

"No, thanks," Stephanie said quietly. "It's not what I signed up for. None of this is."

Venus jerked her head back. "None—? What are you saying?" Her voice raised a notch.

"I'm not really sure."

"It sounds like you're ready to throw it all away."

"No!" Stephanie shushed her friend and looked around. "I've put too much work into Venus & Stephanie. I'm not going to throw it away. All I'm wishing for is a return of glitz and glamour."

Venus made a face. "It's going to be a long wait. Unless there's something like Edgy Glamour. Extreme Glamour. Hmmm . . ."

Stephanie sighed. That was what she was afraid of. "And it's going to be a longer wait until my cosmetic line becomes a reality."

What the hell was happening to her? Six months ago she felt like she had the world in the palm of her hand. She was making things happen. She was living the way she never dared to dream.

But now, every day was a struggle. It was like she looked over her shoulder and saw all the things she had sacrificed. And then she looked ahead and saw how far she had yet to go. The journey hadn't bothered her before, but then she hadn't realized what was missing.

"You know," Venus said hesitantly, "maybe it's time we went through a reorganization."

Stephanie frowned. "What?" She was surprised that Venus knew the word. "What are you talking about?"

"Let's hire more makeup artists," she suggested. "Let's find a business partner who can deal with the administration side of Venus & Stephanie."

"Are you trying to push me out?" Stephanie whispered fiercely. "Because I don't want to go edgy? Because of creative differences? Let me just say right here and now that we're partners and there is no way you are buying me out. Ever. Got that?"

"I know, I know." Venus held up her hand, stopping Stephanie. "Hear me out. The whole reason we partnered up was so I could be the stylist to the stars and you could have a springboard for your cosmetic line."

She gave a sharp nod. "Yeah."

"I love what I do." Venus flattened her hand against her chest. "I'm influencing fashion and taking it to the extreme."

"You certainly do."

"I'm living my dream." Her face radiated with the satisfaction she got from her job.

Stephanie ignored the stab of envy. "Lucky you."

"And you're still waiting to do what you love."

It was true, unfortunately, but there wasn't much she could do about that. The wait will have been worthwhile when she finally achieved her dream. Her mom always said good things happened to those who wait. Okay, maybe that was a bad example. Mom was still waiting to win big in the lottery.

"I'm still waiting for a perfectly good reason," Stephanie explained. "Like the fact that I'm not ready to go big yet."

"Yes, you are."

"No, really. I'm not. We're not." She could try and give Venus all the reasons, but that would take too long and be way too depressing.

"Yes, really," Venus lobbed back at her. "You are. We are."

If this was her friend's debate tactic, they would be at it all day. Stephanie decided to touch on one irrefutable fact. "Venus & Stephanie isn't a household name. We need to be famous if we want the line to survive the competition."

Venus shrugged. "We may never be famous."

The idea was like a punch in the stomach. Stephanie was surprised she wasn't sucking in air. How could Venus be so blasé about it? They had to create name recognition. If they didn't become well known, then her dream would never have a fighting chance.

"I can't abandon this dream." It was something she clung to during her worst jobs, and while living in the most disgusting apartments. It was what kept her going when nothing else went as planned.

"Don't give up." Venus cupped her hands on Stephanie's shoulders. "I'm not saying that. I'm saying, stop taking baby steps and go for it."

"Go for it," Stephanie repeated dully. "Just . . . go for it. As in now?"

Venus nodded. "Right now."

"I can't do that!" Her friend was talking crazy. She was oversimplifying a complex situation. Stephanie knew she couldn't throw caution to the wind.

"Give me one good reason. Not excuses," Venus challenged. "Reasons."

"We don't have enough capital." Stephanie zinged the reason right back at her.

"Get creative," her friend suggested. "Do without. Some of our best ideas were born out of necessity."

"I'm not prepared." Stephanie felt the panic forming deep in her belly.

"Bull." Venus gave her a disbelieving look. "You have plans coming out the wazoo."

"You don't understand." She held her hands against her stomach. "Those plans are designed to take effect years from now."

"So speed up your calendar. Look how well that worked for you the last time." Venus wagged her eyebrows.

Jack. Stephanie closed her eyes, but it was too late. She could recall every detail of his face. She remembered how good it felt being in his arms. How perfect it felt being with him. "A lot of good that did me."

"Wrong attitude." Venus clucked her tongue. "You are so unbelievably negative, Stephanie. Think of all you *almost* missed out on."

"The angst? The tears? The insomnia?"

"No." Venus shifted her jaw to one side as she reined in her patience. "I'm talking about how you felt before you left him."

Stephanie leaned her head against the cool windowpane. She'd tried not to think about it because she didn't feel strong enough to fight the emotions that came with the memories. She tried to forget that when she was with Jack, she had the time of her life.

She missed Jack Logan and missed what they had together. There were days like today when she thought, *I gave up Jack for this?* Those moments were occurring more frequently than she cared to admit.

"You know, maybe you're right," Stephanie admitted, raising her head.

"I usually am."

She ignored Venus's statement. "Maybe my day-to-day activities with the company are drawing to a close. It's time to make Venus & Stephanie support my dream."

Venus put her hands on her hips. "Now you're talking."

"I need to stop getting caught up in the details of the business." Stephanie stepped away from the window as hope buoyed her. "I have to stop going through the moves. Start working on my dream today."

Venus gave a sharp nod of approval. "Damn right."

"Even if it means taking risks . . ." She walked down the hallway, new ideas and big plans swirling around her head. "Getting out of my comfort zone . . ."

"You're on a roll," Venus called out to her.

"Even if I'm scared." She stumbled to a halt as she said the words out loud. Suddenly, her fears of failure didn't hold much power. "No, scratch that. I have to work on my dream because I'm scared. I have to work past that and not let it hold me back."

"There's no holding you back now, Stephanie," her friend said with a wide smile.

"I'm going to do this." Pure, wicked energy

raced through her veins. So this is what it felt like to be bold. To be truly brazen. Wow. This could be addictive. "Oh, my God. I'm really going to do this. Even if I don't have all the capital. Or the name."

"Don't let those details get in your way."

"Even if it means leaving Los Angeles." She headed for the stairs, determined not to squander any more time away from her dream.

"You—what?" Venus stuttered. "Uh, pull back a minute here. Stephanie? Yo, Stephanie? That wasn't what I meant!"

Chapter 21

"You can't leave!" Dean confronted Jack Logan on the steps outside the police station. "As mayor, I have the right to refuse your request. Consider this a decision from the executive branch of Mayfield."

"I'm taking my vacation," Jack announced, sidestepping the mayor. He would refrain from telling Dean what he could do with that executive decision. "It starts next week."

The mayor spluttered. "But . . . but . . ."

"Deputy Cochran will be in charge during my absence." He felt uncomfortable about that, but that was how the system worked. He wouldn't change the rules based on a personality clash.

Anyway, Jack reasoned as he walked down the steps, he was going to be gone for a week. Cochran couldn't cause that much damage in seven days. At least, nothing that couldn't be fixed.

"Cockroach is in charge?" Dean asked, his pale complexion turning a sickly shade of white. Everyone knew that the deputy and the mayor were mortal enemies since kindergarten. Jack was sure he'd hear all about the next installment of their petty war when he returned.

"I'll be back," Jack promised as he strode to his police car. He wasn't going to abandon his duty, but he had to take a chance and go to Los Angeles. He had already put it off too long.

"What about the river?" Dean called out to him.

"It won't rise again." The experts said so, and Jack had faith in their predictions. He glanced up at the sky. There were clouds, but no hint of rain.

"—and the Kellers—"

Jack leveled the mayor with a steely glare. "They are your concern. Not mine."

"Sheriff, we need you here. You can't leave," Dean pleaded. "Not now."

"Already bought my plane ticket." Sure, he could change the dates, Jack thought as he opened the car door. But he wouldn't.

"You can go in the winter," Dean suggested, trying to sound authoritative. "We need you here."

"I know." He rested his arms against the top of the car door. "And I've been here when it mattered. I took care of everything when Mayfield needed i the most."

"Now, wait a minute." Dean pushed his bottom lip out with indignation. "I wouldn't say *everything*."

"I would, and so would most of Mayfield. Asl anyone. They saw how you hid out in your hilltop home while almost everyone else joined in to figh the flood. That will look really good come re-election time."

"I had an ear infection!" Dean pointed to hi left ear. "I was dizzy! I was on antibiotics."

"Tell it to your constituents," Jack said as he got into the car.

Dean held his arms out and looked beseechingly at the cloudy sky. "Why is it no one believes me?"

Jack didn't want to get into it. "I'm taking a vacation and Mayfield is going to have to do without me." *And they might have to get used to it.* But he wouldn't say that out loud. Yet.

"What am I supposed to do while you're gone?" Dean almost wailed.

"Oh, I don't know." Jack swung the door shut. "Take charge?"

Welcome to Mayfield. Population 13,000.

Stephanie clenched the steering wheel as she read the sign. She couldn't believe she was doing this. She handed over the reins of Venus & Stephanie to their new business manager and was going after her dream. She hoped she was doing the right thing.

Maybe she wasn't ready to go after her lifelong dream. Stephanie gnawed on her bottom lip until she tasted the metallic tang of blood. She might not recognize and take full advantage of every opportunity. She wasn't experienced enough to predict every problem.

Her knuckles whitened as panic flashed through her. She should turn back right now. Before it's too late. Return to L.A. and . . .

No, she couldn't do that. Stephanie decelerated and squeezed her eyes shut. She'd moved out of her apartment. All of her worldly belongings—

and there were pathetically few—were in storage. And if she even tried to return, Venus would kick her butt.

God, there were times when she really hated being so organized. Stephanie let out a growl and tapped the gas pedal with her foot. She'd managed to organize herself right out of Los Angeles.

It was going to be okay. Stephanie started taking short, choppy breaths that were supposed to calm her down but only seemed to make her lightheaded. Terrific. She didn't have a paper bag in the car the one time she started to hyperventilate. Figures.

No, she wasn't going to hyperventilate. Because everything would turn out fine. She would make it work.

The first step of her plan was finding Sheriff Jack Logan. Her stomach fluttered with nerves. She hadn't seen him in almost three months. She hadn't called to let him know she was arriving. The flutters started to twist painfully. That was one element of her strategy that she should have planned better.

What if he didn't remember her? She hadn't considered that possibility. Stephanie's mouth went dry at the thought. Oh, please let Jack remember.

What if he had moved on? The idea made her sick to her stomach. What if he had moved on with that—what was her name? Danielle. Yeah, that was it. The sweet-looking, small-town girl who would make the perfect sheriff's wife.

If that was the case, then Stephanie was not responsible for her actions. She would do whatever was necessary to get her man, achieve her goals, and live her dream life.

Yep, she was the new and improved Stephanie Monroe. She could be impulsive and wild when it counted. She wasn't going to be ladylike when it came to getting what she wanted. She—

Could get pulled over for a speeding ticket. She glanced at the flashing lights in her rearview mirror. No. Way. No freaking way. Her insurance agent was going to just love her after this year.

Stephanie tried to remember the steps involved in getting a ticket. She had never been pulled over before. She always followed the speed limit.

Venus had always thought Stephanie had been lying about her perfect driving record. Stephanie didn't think it was all that difficult to achieve. That was, until she visited Mayfield. This was her punishment for bragging.

Stephanie saw what she assumed was Schwartztrauber Creek, aka the puddle, up ahead. She pulled to the side of the road, several feet away from a small bridge. That bridge had to be new. There was no possible way she could have missed it, even during a rainstorm at night.

She rolled down her window, turned off the ignition, and pulled out the key. She looked in the mirror, wondering which officer it was. She really, really hoped it was Jack, but that was unlikely. A sheriff probably had more important things to do.

She grabbed her purse, her keys dangling in her hands, wondering if all of this was an omen. Or if history was going to repeat itself. Just don't let the officer be Cockroach. That was all she was asking.

Stephanie took a quick glance at her outfit. The white T-shirt, faded jeans, and old sneakers should be fine. No indecent exposure as far as she could tell.

The clothes were comfortable to travel in, but it wasn't a did-you-miss-me outfit. The plan was to change and dress up before she saw Jack. She hoped she wasn't gong to be pulled into the station with bed head and no lipstick.

Stephanie took a peek at the side mirror and saw the officer's legs as he approached the car. The dark blue trousers didn't tell her anything about the man's identity. She looked in her purse and grabbed her wallet.

Oh, please, don't let it be Cockroach. She was due for one thing to go her way. Let it be Mackey. She could sweet-talk him into anything.

She flipped open her wallet. Where was her proof of insurance? True, she never had the opportunity to show it before, but it had to be around here somewhere. She had paid big money to keep her coverage and, damn it, she was going to flash her card at everyone she could.

She started flipping through her cards, the anxiety welling inside her, when the policeman stood at the door. "Hello, Officer," she greeted in a chirpy tone.

"Stephanie."

She swerved her head. "Jack?"

Jack stared at Stephanie, taking in everything She looked better than he remembered. Everything about her, from the rich brown hair to the wide, full mouth was bolder. Vibrant. It was like his memor had been a pale, faded picture compared to the real thing.

"What are you doing here?" Jack asked hoarsely. His voice was low and careful, but his senses were alive and wild. Ready to break free.

"I . . ." She swiped her tongue across her lips. "I came to see you."

His heart started to pound hard, the blood roaring in his ears. Those words affected him more than they should. Jack opened the door and reached for Stephanie. His hand touched hers and the wild heat zipped through his veins.

Jack helped her out of the car and shut the door behind her. He wrapped his arms around her and held her close. A deep sigh staggered out of his lungs when she clung to his shoulders.

There were dark moments and lonely nights when he thought he would never get this chance again. He wasn't going to screw it up now. He knew all too well what it was like to be without her. "I missed you," he said rawly.

He knew his confession startled Stephanie. He felt her body jerk with surprise. "You did?"

"Hell, yes." Her disbelief bothered him. He pulled back slightly and looked down at her dazed expression. "How can you ask?"

"Well, I . . ."

His fingers flexed against her spine. "I was coming to see you."

"You were coming to L.A.?" She tilted her head back and studied him, searching for verification. "Los Angeles?"

"No, Louisiana." He felt the corners of his mouth slant up. "Of course Los Angeles."

Stephanie slowly shook her head. "No, you weren't."

"I was," he insisted. "Next week, I swear." He'd drag her back to his office and show her the plane ticket if he had to.

Her forehead wrinkled with a frown. "You said you would never visit."

"I didn't say *never.*"

"It doesn't matter anymore." She tilted her mouth up and brushed her lips against his. "I left L.A. and I'm here now. For good."

She left. For good. Stephanie's words shattered through his mind, pinging like shards of glass. Cutting deep until he felt the guilt oozing from him. Stephanie left her home. She gave up her dream for him.

Jack stilled against Stephanie as his mind whirled. He should be thrilled. Elated. He should be on his knees in front of her and showing how unworthy he was of her sacrifice and her love.

But he didn't want Stephanie to give up her dream. He never wanted that to happen. He didn't want to get in the way of what she worked hard to achieve.

He couldn't let her do that. He had to be strong. Strong enough for the both of them.

"Stephanie," he said against her soft lips. "You have to go back."

Her mind didn't register his words at first. Then it slammed against her and she reeled at the impact. She wanted to curl up. She felt like she was shrinking inside. "Go. Back."

"Yeah." His arms fell away from her, and she suddenly felt cold. Vulnerable. "I'm not going to let you stay here."

Not let her? What did he mean by that? She slumped against her car door. The car keys in her hand bit against her flesh. Her legs felt a bit shaky. She couldn't be here? Where would she go? "I can't."

"You have to." Jack took a step away. Stephanie dazedly watched him hold his arms behind his back. It was almost as if he didn't want to touch her.

"You won't be happy here," he said grimly. "I didn't believe you at first, but I see that now."

He didn't want her in Mayfield. Her body went numb, for which she was thankful. She didn't think she would have been able to withstand the pain.

She couldn't believe it. Only when she rearranged her life and moved halfway across the country, then Jack decided that he didn't want her. If that wasn't just like a man.

Stephanie stared at the street, unable to look at Jack. When was she going to learn? Every time she threw caution to the wind, it always blew up in her face.

"You said you didn't want to be Mayfield material," Jack reminded her. His brisk, almost flat, tone scraped at her nerves. "Why should I force you into being something that you don't want to be?"

"Why were you coming to L.A.?" Stephanie asked, struggling not to scream or cry. "Isn't that the same thing? Weren't you going to try and show me that you can thrive in the big city?"

"Yes, but that's different."

She glared at him. His harsh face held no expression. "How so?" she asked icily.

The muscles in his jaw bunched. "I can make it work."

Stephanie's lips parted open. And she couldn't? Is that what he thought of her? She had been stuck in a strange town with no resources and no way out. She made it work, and she could do it again. "Is that right?"

"Whenever I put my mind to something—" Jack trailed off and winced. "Okay, that didn't come out right."

He didn't think she could put her mind to it? She stepped away from the car and placed her hands on her hips. She'd show him. She'd prove it right now. "You don't think I can survive Mayfield?"

Jack held up his hand. "I didn't say that."

"I lived through a flood and I endured power outages," she reminded him, the anger crackling through her.

"Yes, I know."

"I took sides in the battle between Venus and the Kellers and survived!" Stephanie marched to the back of her car. "Oh, and let's not forget my warm welcome to Mayfield."

"I'll never forget it," he said gently.

Stephanie placed her hands on the trunk of her car and started to push. It didn't budge. This was harder than it looked. Had she put on the emergency brakes? "I should have hired that personal trainer."

"Uh . . ." He gave her a strange look. "Why?"

"Because." She pushed as hard as she could. "I." She bent her elbows at a ninety-degree angle, and pushed again. "Really. Don't. Have." Her body was suddenly diagonal to the street. "Any. Upper. Body. Strength."

His eyes widened as he approached her. "What are you doing?"

"How is it that I can land up in a creek when I don't want to?" Stephanie asked, blowing her hair out of her eyes. "But when I try to push my car down a hill, it won't budge?"

His head swerved back and forth. "Are you crazy?"

"Possibly." Stephanie decided her lower body strength had to be better. She sat on the edge of the trunk and pushed, her heels skidding against the pavement.

Jack stared at her, his mouth dropping open.

"I'm staying in Mayfield," Stephanie said, bumping her hips against the trunk, but the car wouldn't move. "And if you try to drag me across the city line, I'll be kicking and screaming the whole time."

"Stephanie." He grabbed her wrists and pulled her away from the car. "We don't have to live here."

"Can you think of a better place?" Stephanie asked. "I can't."

"But what about Venus & Stephanie?" His hands drifted to her waist.

"We're expanding. Our offices are now in Los Angeles and Mayfield. Headquarters are still in L.A., so I'll have to travel back and forth from time to time."

"What are you going to do here?" Jack asked, curling his arm around her waist and pulling her against him.

"I'm starting my cosmetic line now." She darted the tip of her tongue against her lips. Saying those words out loud always made her nervous. "I'm not going to wait for the perfect time or the perfect opportunity."

"Why not?" She felt his gaze drawn to her mouth.

"I don't work that way anymore," she said with a hint of pride. "I'll make any day the perfect time. I'll make any situation the perfect opportunity."

"Sounds like a great plan." He dipped his head to kiss her. "What's our first item on the list?"

She turned her head slightly to the side. Did she hear that correctly? "Our?"

"Stephanie," Jack said as he cupped her face with his hands. "I'm with you all the way. I'm going to make sure you get everything you wish for."

She stared at him. She had been wrong to worry. This guy wasn't going to keep her from her goals. He was going to protect her dreams and make sure they came true.

Stephanie closed her eyes and gave in to the sudden, wild impulse. She tossed her car keys above her head, pitching them as far as she could.

She opened her eyes, but didn't look back. It didn't matter where her keys landed. She wasn't going to go look for them.

"You . . ." Jack pulled his stunned gaze from over her shoulder and stared at her. "You just threw your keys in the creek."

"Then one of my wishes came true," Stephanie said with a wide smile. "I guess I'm stuck in Mayfield for a while. I could be here for the next, oh, I don't know, forty or fifty years."

"Guess so." He curled her against his side and guided her to the police car. "You'd better come down to the station with me."

"The station?" She was thinking more in terms of his house. Specifically his bed. "Why?"

"Reckless endangerment." He gave one final look at the creek and shook his head. "That's going to require some time in the holding cell."

"What?" Her voice echoed in the quiet.

"It's okay, Stephanie." His eyes held a wild, mischievous gleam. "I'll keep you company."

Here's a bonus peek at
Susanna Carr's
EX, WHY, AND ME
coming in July 2006 from Brava . . .

It was difficult going all the way with a guy when you're required to wear a tiara, but Michelle Nelson managed it. Barely.

She just never thought it would occur in the middle of the night behind the pinsetters at Pins & Pints, Carbon Hill's bowling alley and the only source of entertainment one could have standing up.

Michelle shifted, her knees aching against the hard, cold floor. The alley was closed, the lanes silent, but she was bumping up against ancient, oily machinery. The location hadn't been her first choice for her first time with her first love.

It didn't seem to hold the right ambiance for Ryan Slater, either. "Let's go back to my place," he suggested in a husky tone that made her skin tingle.

She glanced down at him, but the shadows made it difficult to read his expression. Michelle felt exposed as she straddled him, the weak overhead lights almost reaching her. Her evening dress from the J.C. Penney catalog bunched up against her thighs, the pink polyester rubbing her bare, flushed skin.

"No," she whispered, her heart pounding in her ears. She pressed her hands against his shoulders, pulling at his T-shirt with desperate fingers. "I can't wait that long."

It had to be now. She was leaving for Europe in the morning. Her bags were packed, she'd said good-bye to her friends, but there was this one last thing to do.

It had taken her all summer to get Ryan Slater. She could have pursued another local guy in a lot less time, but she wanted Ryan and no one else would do. It had been that way ever since she could remember, so at least twenty years. Unfortunately, all the prettier, bolder girls wanted him, too.

No matter what she had done in the past, it wasn't enough to compete for Ryan's attention. He'd never seemed to have noticed her. Not even when she'd wore the tiara and the Miss Horseradish sash for the past year. And God knew those were hard to miss.

He noticed her now. Had stared at her in awe. Or maybe he was staring at her tiara, which had a tendency to catch the light and blind people. That was probably it, but she couldn't do anything about it now. The crown was pinned and shellacked to her updo.

The glittery distraction would serve her well, Michelle decided as she glided the condom onto Ryan. She didn't want him to feel her hands fumble and shake. Rolling the latex down was not as easy as her best friend Vanessa had led her to believe.

The tip of Ryan's cock nudged against Michelle's flesh. The intimate contact made her feel hot. Tight. She grasped him at the base and lowered down.

Michelle jerked, startled, when Ryan clamped his fingers against her bare hips. "We'll take it slow," he said roughly, almost as if he said it through clenched teeth.

Her heart raced as he guided her. White heat crackled just under her skin when he gently filled her.

She closed her eyes, her breath hitching, as she relished every sensation. Michelle had been expecting pain. Nothing major, but something unpleasant. Nothing like the delicious heavy ache that flooded her muscles.

Michelle rocked against him, smiling as the pleasure heated her blood with a shower of sparks. She flexed her hips *Ooh* . . . She swayed the other way. *Mmm* . . .

"Michelle, slow down," Ryan said hoarsely, his fingers tightening, sinking into her hips.

She wanted his hands elsewhere. Everywhere. Cupping her breasts. No, squeezing them. Pinching her nipples until she begged him to take them into his mouth.

She wanted him to thrust. Grind. Drive into her.

Maybe that wasn't possible in this position. But she didn't want to change sides. Here she felt alive. Bold. Free. She was wild. Sexy. Powerful.

She moved against Ryan, each move fierce and unchecked. Her world centered where they joined. He bucked against her, his move shallow and hesitant.

Michelle countered with a deep roll of her hips,

but his cock didn't stretch or fill her to the hilt. She frowned and wiggled.

"Not like that." Ryan said, his voice bouncing off the machines. He tensed. "Damn."

He lay motionless underneath her. No thrusting, no rocking. Nothing. *This was it?* Michelle thought. *You have got to be kidding me!*

She felt his cock softening, drooping—

Michelle froze. *Oh, no* . . .

—As it slipped out.

I killed it.